TROPICAL SHORTS

Short Stories Set in Brazil

True Fiction Publishing
3454 Binyon
Ft. Worth, TX 76133

ISBN 1-57502-042-4

Edited by
Lee Carver, Sandy Hutson, and Pamela Yorston

Cover by Quinn Carver,
free-lance graphic artist

Printed in the U.S.A. by Morris Publishing
3212 E. Hwy 30
Kearney, NE 68847
800-650-7888

Contents

Introduction

Brazil is a fascinating country of startling contrasts that include great violence and enormous kindness, unsurpassed physical beauty and tremendous ugliness, obscene wealth and shocking poverty, cramped cities and uninhabited rural and swamp areas. Marching to its own beat, Brazil is forever slightly out of step with its neighbors; it is the only South American country where several races have successfully met and mixed over the centuries, where Catholicism and the old Yoruba spirit gods co-exist peacefully, and where Portuguese is spoken.

The goal of this book is to show the many facets of the country as experienced by a wide spectrum of English speaking writers living in Brazil. In this endeavor, the editors have relied heavily on readers Heather Liddle, Casey McCann, Marilyn Mangels, Mary Miller, John Murray and Thomas Pleiman, all of whom generously committed time and effort to assist in the success of the anthology. The editors are deeply grateful.

There is a distinctive rhythm to the language, music and very lifestyle in Brazil, a cadence that surrounds and enfolds everyone, creeping in and furtively taking root. Only after leaving Brazil and experiencing *saudade*, or a nostalgic longing for the country, is one aware that the spell has been cast. Readers of this collection will be exposed to the country's successes and failings, laughter and tears, cupidity and generosity and it is hoped that, after the final pages, these readers will also experience *saudade*.

D.B. FINEGAN, a former special education teacher in the United States and Australia, has lived in São Paulo with her husband Richard since 1976. She was previously published in the *São Paulo Sunday News* and the short story anthology, Brazil Brazilonia.

A Fine Christian Woman

by D.B. Finegan

The broad, black face stared back at her belligerantly. She tried a smile, hoping to ease the tension around the eyes. Oh Lord, she sighed. Luiza, her youngest, was right. Her teeth did look like big white Chicklets.

While Juracy stood frowning at her reflection in the mottled, old mirror, her husband Zé came into the bedroom. He watched her for a long moment, then came up quietly behind her and gave her a squeeze. With dismay, she noticed that his arms could no longer reach all the way around her waist.

"You are one fine-looking woman," he said, pulling her against him. "One very, fine, big woman," and buried his face in the nape of her neck.

"Silly man," she tsked, shrugging him away. Zé knew she was pleased with his compliment in spite of her brusqueness.

"Leave me alone now, I have to get this dress exactly right."

"Looks exactly right to me," he said over his shoulder as he changed into a clean shirt. "I have to leave anyway. I've got a job over in Granja Julieta." He ran a stiff brush through his wiry black hair and smoothed a neatly trimmed mustache. As he inspected himself in the mirror, Juracy watched him with pride and more than a little love. He was still a good-looking man, even now in his fifties, she thought. Small, neat as a pin, Zé Pinheiro was a good man, a kind husband and generous father. Juracy counted her blessings daily, not allowing herself to become smug or complacent, even when some neighbor woman self-righteously pointed out how lucky she was. She too thought she was lucky.

"You won't be gone long, will you?" she asked. "Flavio is bringing the Combi here at seven o'clock to pick us up."

"I'll be back in plenty of time woman, you just get this fine dress of yours exactly right." As he left, he gave her a quick kiss on the cheek, and picked up his bag of tools.

Turning back to the mirror, she once again stared critically at her reflection. The floor-length white lace dress, with its layers and tiers, reminded her of a fancy wedding cake. She adjusted the top to bare her shoulders, pleased with the look of the wide band of heavy lace that fell from the bodice to her elbows, flowing gracefully when she raised her arms. The soft white fabric and her glossy black skin made a nice contrast. The head-dress was wound like a turban and fit snugly; she tucked a few stray wisps of hair up inside. If Juracy had been a vain or self-centered woman she would have acknowledged that she looked quite regal. As it was, she decided that the dress was finally all right.

Tonight she would dance in the Spiritist ceremony for her patron saint the Goddess Iemanja. And tomorrow, being a good Christian woman, she would attend early morning mass at the Catholic church three blocks away. If anyone had thought to question Juracy about a possible contradiction within her religious beliefs, she would have been astounded: the two were one and the same to her. She was a God-fearing woman and Spiritist, enough said.

****

Juracy wrapped her dress and headpiece in a clean sheet and placed it carefully on top of the coolers at the back of the van that held the soft drinks. She didn't want it getting crushed. Now she was all ready and sat proudly in the front seat between Zé and Flavio, anxious to leave. Her hands were folded in her lap to keep them still. The van could comfortably hold another six passengers, but it looked as if at least eight were going to crowd on board.

At last the door was slid shut and Flavio was about to pull away when a small commotion at the curb caught his eye and made him hesitate.

A slim, attractive woman tottering on a pair of ridiculous high-heeled ankle strap shoes pushed past the onlookers and banged on the side of the van.

"Did you forget I was coming?" she demanded. Hiking her tight red dress to an indecent height, she wrenched open the door, and climbed in behind Juracy. She brought with her the provocative aroma of a warm female body mingled with a flowery cologne. The other passengers grumbled good-naturedly and shifted around to make room for Flavio's aunt, Tatiana.

A sharp red fingernail poked Juracy's shoulder from behind. "I hope you didn't plan to leave without me, Dona Juracy?"

Tatiana's use of the formal "Dona" was meant to be sarcastic. She believed that Juracy gave herself "airs" and thought herself superior. There was no love lost between the two women, but Juracy was too much of a lady to say what she really thought of the tarty Tatiana da Silva.

"No, I thought that you had simply changed your mind."

Tatiana wriggled back into the seat, making herself comfortable. "Change my mind? Why I wouldn't dream of missing the Saturday night services, especially when you will be dancing." She fanned herself with a scrap of paper she found lying on the seat. "Pass me a *soda limonada* Zé, I'm dry as dust."

The sun was setting when the Combi pulled up to the simple cinderblock house that served as the Spiritist church. Red dust puffed around their feet as the passengers got out and started to unload the van. A gust of cooler air rose from the surrounding hills, promising relief from the day's intense heat. Zé held out his hand to help Juracy down. As she walked to the rear to get her dress, she overheard Tatiana speaking to her husband.

"Well Zé, you must be proud that your wife was chosen to dance tonight."

Juracy strained, but couldn't hear Zé's response. As she folded the heavy dress over her arms, she saw Ze and Tatiana walking toward the church. Tatiana, her arm linked in his, was leaning close to him and whispering something into his ear. The light from the open doorway illuminated her husband's face, and Juracy could see that he was smiling happily, looking ready to burst into laughter.

"You better be careful of that one. She's got mischief in her heart."

The voice, coming out of the darkness startled Juracy. Alair, one of her neighbors, had been taking her time getting out of the van and had witnessed the whole scene.

"Perhaps Exu is the one you want to light candles for tonight; not Iemanja." The arthritic old woman arranged her shawl against the cool breeze and hobbled on swollen feet toward the church. As she made her way up the cement steps, she spoke once more, quietly, but distinctly, "For some things the Goddess isn't the one you want."

Later that night, a large woman, her dark clothing blending with the shadows, silently made her way toward a crossroad beyond the village square. There were no streetlights on these simple Brazilian roads, so she passed unseen by all but the most vigilant. Juracy's house had been quiet and dark when she stole out onto the street. Zé and the children were sound asleep, as were most of her neighbors.

The ceremony that evening had been lively, the spirits had been in abundance and many participants had experienced a spiritual possession. Juracy felt that she too would have been entered if only her concentration hadn't been disturbed by the sight of Tatiana clinging possessively to her husband. These unpleasant pictures and upsetting thoughts scurried around in her head and she quickened her pace. The entire evening had been spoiled for her.

Arriving at the crossing, she set the straw basket she was carrying in the road and knelt beside it. Her skirt billowed around her, getting covered in dust, but she was oblivious to everything except the task at hand. She placed a large square of red satin, fringed with shiny black thread, on the ground. In the dark it was difficult to see the white embroidered symbols in its center, but she could feel the raised outline of stitches against her palms as she smoothed the creases. She readied two white candles, tying them together with first a red, then a black ribbon. A bottle of *cachaça*, the local sugarcane alcohol, and several thick black cigars were set close to the cloth. To call up Exu of the closed paths was a risky business and Juracy would never dream of doing such a thing for anything less important than the love of her Zé. She intended to "close" Tatiana's path and make her life as disagreeable as possible.

The night seemed to grow darker, denser, drawing in on itself as she bent her head and started the intonations to the demon, Exu.

****

Sunday morning was overcast and cooler. Clouds were building over the hills in the distance. It looked as if the long, hot, dry spell was coming to an end. It was a relief to walk to Mass in fresh air that smelled of rain. Zé and Juracy walked along, each in thoughtful silence. They knelt as they entered the church, then slid unobtrusively into their usual places.

Head bowed in prayer, Juracy heard a rustle of clothing and smelled a familiar floral scent, as someone slipped into the pew beside her. She opened her eyes a slit, and tried to sneak a look at the new arrival. Tatiana's lace shawl obscured her face as she knelt and bowed her head in prayer. A moment later she rose and took her seat.

"Juracy, I must speak with you." She spoke quietly, but there was an undeniable edge of urgency in her tone.

"Why?" Juracy asked. It sounded like an innocent question even to her, but she kept her eyes fixed straight ahead, not wanting to meet the woman's gaze.

"I'm afraid that there's been a misunderstanding between us." Tatiana paused uncertainly, then added quickly, "I feel that I must try to clear it up, explain......."

"A misunderstanding, Tatiana?" Juracy felt a guilty little thrill, realizing that she, for once, held the upper hand. "I don't believe so," she continued. "I think I understand you very well." Her eyes flicked to her right to see if Zé was paying any attention to the conversation. She was relieved to see that his chin was resting peacefully on his chest and his eyes were closed.

Tatiana tucked her long, full skirt around her, but instead of sliding back and settling comfortably into her seat, she remained rigidly perched on the edge of the pew.

"I know you went to the crossroads last night." As she spoke she pushed the shawl away with annoyance and turned awkwardly in her seat to face Juracy.

"How do you know that?" Juracy scanned the woman's smooth, unblemished face for any sign of change. I guess suppurating sores were too much to ask, she thought with a pang of disappointment. To her credit, this gave way almost immediately to a flood of relief that she hadn't actually done anything harmful after all. At least nothing that she could see.

"How do I know?....... How do I know?" Tatiana's voice had risen an octave, and even though she was still whispering, Juracy could hear the shrill ring of mounting hysteria. "I know because......." her voice cracked, and she drew a shuddery breath to compose herself.

Juracy unconsciously slid closer to Zé, feeling suddenly very uneasy about where this conversation was heading.

"I know because I have grown.............. a tail." This last came out of Tatiana's round little mouth as a thin wail that wavered in the air above them for a long moment, then abruptly plunged into a deep sob.

"A tail?" repeated Juracy, too stunned at the moment to even feel sorry for the wretched woman next to her.

As if on cue one side of Tatiana's skirt rose a few inches, quivered there for a moment, then flopped back onto the seat of the pew with a soft thud.

"Imagine that," Juracy whispered, not even trying to disguise her awe and amazement. Staring with barefaced, wide-eyed curiosity at Tatiana's posterior, she was hoping for another sign of the tail.

"What kind of tail did you grow? Is it a dog's kind of bushy tail, or is it more like a demon's tail, you know, sort of thin and leathery?" Juracy could barely suppress the temptation to peek under the skirt and get a first hand look at this wonder.

"That's none of your business," snapped Tatiana, and drew her skirt tighter around her legs. "But what is your business, Madam," she continued, "is how you're going to get rid of it."

"Get rid of it?" Juracy asked softly. The tinge of regret that had drifted into Juracy's voice caused Tatiana to lash out in a fury.

"Of course, you great ninny." The desperate woman had drawn so close that Juracy could feel her hot breath on her skin.

"Get rid of it," was hissed viciously into Juracy's startled face.

"Yes, well that could be a problem," Juracy was trying to sound reasonable, not wanting to excite the hysterical woman further.

"I mean, I really don't know how I actually did it." In all fairness, she supposed that she would soon have to start worrying about this predicament, but right now all she could think about was what an incredible thing had happened. And, if she admitted it to herself, what a rather wonderful, incredible thing.

"Well, you had better figure it out. And soon," Tatiana added ominously, then continued quickly. "I'll meet you at the crossroads tonight, and you better be able to undo this........this mess." With that, she rose clumsily and flounced down the aisle. When she reached the front, she turned carefully around and eased herself backwards through the double doors of the church.

Juracy watched in bemused fascination as Tatiana strode off down the road, muttering firey curses and batting angrily at something that twitched and swayed persistently beneath her skirt.

For the Love of Matthew

by D.B. Finegan

Rosiedalva shifted uncomfortably in the chair. She would have been much happier standing in the kitchen instead of sitting here in this stranger's fancy living room. Hard to believe that three years had passed, and here she was right where she had left off. Not one step of progress. The thought depressed her so, she pushed it from her mind and turned her attention to the lady across the room. The American woman's voice droned in quite passable Portuguese but Rosiedalva listened with only the polite outside part of her mind. The intonation rose and fell as the do's and don'ts of the house cleaning job were listed and explained. It was made clear to Rosiedalva that the position was for a period of two years, at which time the family would no doubt be transferred out of Brazil.

"It's said 'Hosiedalva', ma'am," she interrupted. "Not 'Rosiedalva'." At least she could have her name said right, she thought.

There was no resentment or defiance in her voice or attitude. Those were luxuries she could no longer afford. She still had her pride, and her dignity would return when she was once again employed.

"Well, Hosiedalva," the woman finished a little breathlessly. "I guess that's just about it. Do you have any questions?"

"No, Senhora Parker." The family's name was difficult for her to pronounce, but she would make a point of mastering it quickly.

"Please call me Alexis, after all you're going to be part of our family for the next two years."

Good Lord, "Alexis". That was even worse. Why can't these people have normal names? she wondered. But she made sure her face displayed only a polite smile for her new employer to see.

****

The days went by in a mindless haze of floor polishing and window washing. Rosiedalva kept mostly to herself, choosing not to participate in the joking, back fence gossip between the other maids and the rest of the household staff. It was a decent job, and she would do her best, but she did not want to get involved. It was not her intention to spend the rest of her working life as a cleaning woman in someone else's house.

Two years here, and not a minute more, she had vowed to herself when she took the job. After much meticulous figuring Rosiedalva had decided that in two more years, with careful saving, she would have enough to see her over any rough patches. She realized that, for a time, she might have only her savings to live on until she got established in her new career.

Her ambition was to be a manicurist, and she wanted to work in a place like the small beauty shop she saw each morning from the window of her bus. Looking down at it with its cheery lights shining out into the gray morning, it seemed like a rosy little haven. Sometimes, when the bus paused in traffic, she had been able to get a glimpse inside. The women working there always seemed to be laughing. Rosiedalva longed to wear one of the shop's pretty pink smocks and find things to laugh about first thing in the morning.

Not a sophisticated woman, she understood little of the economic changes and upheavals that had taken place in her country in the last few years. What she did know, was that her financial woes were not due solely to her own bad luck.

****

Tuesday was bedsheet changing day. Dona Alexis had a rigid schedule typed out for each member of the staff to follow. Everyone knew what they were supposed to do and where they were supposed to be, each day of the week. These efficiently prepared lists enabled the Dona of the Casa to attend her bridge games, take her tennis lessons and enjoy her various luncheons and teas knowing that, at home, everything was running like clockwork.

The master suite bed was a huge, king-size affair that always gave Rosiedalva problems. It seemed that no sooner had she one corner of the fitted bottom sheet in place, than the opposite corner would magically spring off the mattress.

While grunting and silently cursing the bedsheet, she gradually became aware of a pair of bright blue eyes watching her from behind the closet door that stood slightly ajar.

Four-year-old Matthew Parker stared at the heavyset black woman bending over his parents' bed. Her huffing and puffing had piqued his curiosity, drawing him from his hiding place in his mother's closet.

"Who are you?" he asked with the straight- forwardness that only young children have.

"I'm the cleaning woman," she answered flatly. The fact that she had never seen this little boy did not surprise Rosiedalva, since she came and left during the hours that he was in school. She knew him only by the toys and clothes she tidied in his room every Monday, Wednesday and Friday. What did surprise her was that he was so young. She had expected an older child. He seemed much too little to be attending school all day. Foreigners are different, she mused, confirming her opinion that she would never fully understand them and then dismissed the thought as none of her concern.

"Who are you?" She felt that it was only polite to show the same amount of interest in his identity as he had shown in hers.

"Matthew Thomas Parker," he replied with grave formality.

"Well, Matthew Thomas Parker, what are you doing in your mother's closet?" Even as she asked him the question, she silently reprimanded herself. Now why did I start this? Just mind your own business, woman.

"Waiting," he answered simply, as if that one word explained everything.

"I see. In that case, help me with this bedsheet, while you're waiting."

For the rest of the day, Matthew followed Rosiedalva around the house as she did her chores, helping whenever he could. The two of them didn't speak much. They didn't seem to need to talk. Both were content to simply be in each other's company. That evening, when Dona Alexis came home, tired from her day's outing, nothing was said about Matthew having stayed home from school. The other household staff hadn't taken much notice of Rosiedalva's silent little helper, and she had decided that it wasn't her place to inform the lady of the house as to the whereabouts of her child.

****

Weeks stretched into months, and the months rolled slowly, yet relentlessly by. One day, toward the end of April, it occurred to Rosiedalva that her two years with the Parkers were very nearly at an end. She had done well, carefully saving as much as she could from her salary. The dream of working in that small salon had carried her along on the most tedious, tiring days. That, and her quiet friendship with young Matthew Thomas Parker.

After that one day, Matthew had never again played hookie from school. That is not to say that he and Rosiedalva did not see much of one another. It seemed that he would have frequent bouts of fever and coughing that would keep him home for a couple of days each month. Rosiedalva also found that it became more and more difficult for her to finish her chores by four p.m. and frequently found herself staying until five or even six o'clock. It was in these ways that she and Matthew found the opportunity to be together and gradually become friends. Their favorite times would be spent with him helping with her work, or when she could steal a moment to sit in the chair beside his sickbed while he rested.

****

The first week of June is traditionally one of excitement and change within the foreign community. This is the time of year when transfers to other overseas assignments are made public. Families prepare to leave. They sell off all their unwanted household goods, and buy too many last minute souvenirs. Rosiedalva was waiting for Dona Alexis to announce the date of their departure.

When the day finally arrived, Rosiedalva could feel it in the air much the same way you can sense the coming of a storm. Dona Alexis was to have lunch that day with Mr. Parker, which was an unusual event in itself. That, along with arriving home at two in the afternoon, fully four hours earlier than normal, signified that something was definitely about to happen.

Rosiedalva could hear the Dona of the Casa calling from downstairs. She gathered her cleaning cloths and made her way down to the kitchen, where she saw that the rest of the staff had already gathered and was listening attentively.

"So you see," she concluded, "this is the best possible news for all of us." Mrs. Parker was giving the group a dazzling smile as she finished her announcement.

"Oh, Hosiedalva, I was telling the others our good news." She paused dramatically. "Mr. Parker has received a promotion in his job and we are going to stay here in Brazil. Isn't that wonderful?" she asked, not actually expecting an answer.

"And of course we want all of you continue working here," she added benevolently to the group.

"You will stay with us won't you, Hosiedalva?"

Rosiedalva was completely unaware that everyone's eyes had, as if by a common signal, turned toward her as Mrs. Alexis Parker waited expectantly for an answer to the question. She was conscious only of one pair of eyes looking at her, the bright blue ones watching her from where he stood in the dimly lit back hallway.

"You will stay won't you?" the American woman pressed.

Rosiedalva stared steadily over Mrs. Parker's shoulder into Matthew's worried little face.

With an inward sigh, she mentally hung the pink smock back on its peg for just a little longer. "Yes, Senhora Parker," she answered in a firm voice, "I'll be pleased to stay."

The Ladies' Luncheon Club

by D.B. Finegan

Caught up in her own thoughts, Fiona Gilroy bumped her wheeled *feira* cart along the residential streets toward the street market. She couldn't help once again marveling at her recent good fortune. Only three months had passed since her arrival in Brazil and already she had been invited to join the prestigious Ladies' Luncheon Club of São Paulo. She'd be hobnobbing with the best, the wives of the most influential men in the ex-patriot community. It was a pleasant thought, but also a bit intimidating. Leonard, her husband, was understandably proud.

By 9 a.m. the *feira* was in full swing, seething with people bargaining and jostling for position in front of different stands. Competition amongst the vendors was fierce. They hawked their wares vigorously, calling and singing to passing potential customers. Carving off slices of melon or mango, several tried to lure "the lady of the house" to come over and take a taste.

Fiona mentally reviewed her menu for tomorrow's luncheon. She wandered past the various stalls heaped with fresh fruit and vegetables. There was still so much to do, so many things to buy, and she was as yet unfamiliar with a lot of the produce available in Brazil. Everything is so green in this country, she thought, feeling a little desperate.

As a new member to the Club, she hadn't been expected to act as hostess for the next luncheon, but she had delighted the other members by graciously volunteering to do the honors. This morning, as she hesitantly picked up a huge avocado then put it down again in exasperation, she regretted her grandiose gesture. Tense and nervous, she wanted everything to be perfect.

It must be something light, yet satisfying, different, original, with "eye-appeal", her mother was fond of saying. Cold broccoli soup to start, she'd decided, followed by a crab and shrimp quiche that she had made before with good results. A simple, elegant salad using some of the more unusual greens with an olive oil/balsamic vinegar dressing would complete the main course. Leonard always said she was a tasty, but not fancy, cook, so Fiona knew better than to try anything too complicated or *avant garde*.

"Stick with what you know, dear," he had advised as he left for the office that morning.

Fine, but what I know isn't very interesting, she thought as she eyed the fresh greens, wondering which ones to choose. At least I can make the salad a bit more exotic. Brazil, land of plenty, at least for herbs and lettuce.

****

The day of the luncheon dawned bright and clear. A soft breeze blew the insects away and rustled the tall palms along the garden walls. Not a single cloud marred the deep blue of the spring sky and the air was scented with the first gardenias of the year. Fiona had set up the tables and chairs outside on the veranda. She had worried all week about seating twenty-five women, indoors, if it rained.

The ladies arrived in billows of expensive cologne and silky prints. They chattered happily, oohing and aahing over the house, garden and Fiona's elegant table settings. Pitchers of white Sangria and trays of canapês were passed by maids in black uniforms. Conversations were lively and full of compliments for Fiona. A gracious hostess, she passed amongst her guests watching with pleasure as the women discreetly, almost covertly, admired the delicate crystal, the fine linens and the heavy family silver. Everything was going to be fine, she thought with relief, and allowed herself to bask in their praise.

****

Four hours later Fiona flopped into a chair and put her stockinged feet up on the coffee table with a contented sigh. It had been a perfect afternoon, she thought happily. The doorbell jarred her out of her pleasant reverie, and she got up reluctantly to answer the door.

Her friend Katherine was standing beside her car at the curb outside their front gate.

"Sorry to bother you with the luncheon and all," she called from the street, "but I wanted to drop this American Society stuff off and I was in the neighborhood."

Fiona clicked the small gate open and waited at the front door as Katherine came up the walk.

"How'd it go today?" Katherine asked.

"It was fine. No, actually it was great," she laughed. "They loved everything right down to the lemon souffle."

"Well then, congratulations. You're in the big time now, kiddo."

Fiona took the papers Katherine had brought and put them on her catch-all table in the television room.

"Come on in. Do you have time for a glass of wine? I'm sure there's an open bottle left in the 'frig unless one of the maids finished it off."

Katherine dropped her purse onto the sofa and followed Fiona into the kitchen.

"Sure, I've got plenty of time, plus I want to hear all the gory details." She leaned against the kitchen counter while Fiona poured them both a glass of white wine.

A maid was drying the last of the silverware, laying it carefully on a linen dishtowel to dry completely before being packed away.

Katherine peered into the remains of a large wooden salad bowl and picked out a piece of something green and leafy. She held it up, frowned slightly, sniffed at it daintily, smiled and popped it into her mouth.

"Feeling a bit bound up lately?" she asked. Her eyes were wide and innocently round with the question, but a smile twitched at the corners of her mouth.

"Of course not. What kind of question is that?" Fiona was tired, so the retort came out a bit sharply.

"Well, I just wondered since you put *erva doce* in the salad." She reached into the bowl once more, plucked out another piece and held up the feathery green herb for Fiona to see. "You know, fennel." They both turned and looked up in surprise as the maid tittered, quickly covered her mouth with her hand and fled the room in embarrassment.

Fiona, nonplussed, turned back to Katherine. "I put it in because it looked so pretty, such a nice dark green," she said defensively. "What's wrong with it anyway?"

"There's nothing wrong with it." Katherine paused, enjoying the moment, and then continued. "It's just that the leaves are frequently used as a laxative, an herbal remedy," she started to laugh but stopped when she saw the horrified expression on Fiona's face.

"A laxative? Oh my God." Fiona whispered faintly. "Are you sure ?"

"Um hum. It's slow acting, but very effective." Katherine peered into the salad bowl and poked amongst the greens to have another look. "How much did you put in here anyway?"

****

When the phone rang the next morning, Fiona felt her already low spirits drop a degree further. On the fifth ring, she reluctantly picked up the receiver.

"Fiona!"

It was not difficult to recognize the clipped, nasal voice of The Ladies' Luncheon Club's president, Sylvia Bagnussian. "Sylvia here," the woman boomed. "I must congratulate you on a delightful afternoon. Splendid luncheon, simply wonderful, all enjoyed it immensely."

Fiona sat in stunned silence on the other end of the line, listening to the president's strident voice.

"...... so light, and healthy. I told Edgar this morning, that this is the way we should always eat, make a habit of it," Sylvia continued.

"Frankly, I woke up this morning feeling quite a new woman." After a silence of several heartbeats Sylvia asked, "Fiona, are you there, dear?"

Finally able to breathe, she blurted out a hasty, "Yes, of course. Thank you. I'm so pleased." Relief flooded through her as well as a sharp, urgent call of nature, the second one that morning.

"Must run, Fiona, a busy day ahead. Now don't forget to share those recipes. I know I speak for everyone."

TOM MURPHY was born in 1951 in Paterson, New Jersey. A red-brick industrial city, Paterson boasts a surprising literary heritage. Poets Allen Ginzberg and William Carlos Williams hailed from Paterson. Novelist Jack Kerouac once lived there.

Murphy obtained a B.A. in political science from Georgetown University in Washington, D.C. in 1973. He moved to Brazil in 1977 and has worked as a professional journalist ever since. He is married and has two children.

Death in Paradise

by Tom Murphy

Dear Oscar:

Since you asked on the phone, I'll tell you how I solved the Pera case before the police or the newspapers, in fact, while the body was still cold at the morgue. As my personal attorney, you ought to know. Also, it will give you something to say if you're hounded by reporters.

I got here Monday, quite late, but that's how I like it. The moon rides over the marina and a breeze carries fruit scents up and down the streets.

I was late for dinner at the *pousada*. The dining room was packed. My usual table was taken. The crowd was boisterous. There was a samba band in the street—one of those makeshift affairs, all drums and people smacking matchboxes around—and the windows were open. But it put me in a cheerful mood.

Gunther scuttled to my side. He put his big Germanic face close to mine and offered to set another table just for me. But I spied an empty seat at my usual corner and decided to be adventuresome.

That's how I met, if you can call it that, João José Pera...and his wife and father-in-law.

They were pretty far gone. I introduced myself. They ignored me. I sat down anyway.

Pera was in a—literally—terminal state of glumness. He was one of those tall, fun-in-the-sun types. Thirtyish (not a hint of baldness). He had a big mustache but smooth, even baby-like facial skin.

The old man sat at the head of the table. He was sixty-ish, bald, with that grey chicken skin I hate. He was smoking a cigarette in a holder. What a horrid little device! It was the kind of holder that looks like a duck hunter's whistle, brown at one end and yellowed with the gnawing of mottled teeth at the other.

Pera's wife was the reason everyone ignored me.

She was standing on her chair, the better to chat up the samba band in the street. They would launch into a number and she would start shuffling in place, swaying her hips and singing the song (she knew all the lyrics). Then they'd stop and she'd lean out the window for another chat, a sip of vodka, a drag on someone's cigarette and then—bam, boom, bang—the little matchboxes and the big drums were at it again and so was the pretty dish with the long blond hair.

I sat through three rounds of this, letting the waiter bring me my usual cocktail. I picked at salami and olives in a little metal saucer. In the intervals I could hear the old man chuckle, the deep wheezy laugh of the life-long smoker.

On round four, the blond dish climbed out of her shorts and pulled off her T-shirt. This was less shocking than it sounds. For one thing, we were in Paratí. For another, she had a green and yellow bikini underneath.

Soon, she was shimmying and shaking again to the sound of samba. But now she added a new twist. She looked at her husband. She reached out to him, pinching his cheeks in that coochy-coo way some women have of treating their men like babies. He glared at her.

She turned her back to the room, lifting her arms as she danced, showing her body to the samba players outside.

Finally, Pera showed signs of life. He stood up, picked his way wordlessly past the old man, failed to see his wife turn around to flip him a finger, and charged quickly out of the dining room.

The old man laughed, a real guffaw this time, and launched into an obscene pumping motion with his arm, again and again and again like a jack-in-the-box.

Later that night, my sleep was disturbed by a ruckus down the hall. I leaned out the window to see furniture sailing off the balcony of the corner suite. It was Pera hurling lamps, chairs, bedclothes, everything in a drunken spree like Orson Welles at the Copa in 1942.

***

Next morning, Gunther collared me in the breakfast room. He was worried sick. He appealed to me.

You know how I like to dress for the day. I was wearing my white linen suit—open collar—and brown, open-toed sandals. My gouty ankle was acting up so I wielded my mahogany cane. I was garbed for adventure and gladly accompanied our friend to the beach.

Pera's body was snow white and already a little bloated. He was wearing white shorts and a T-shirt. He was wearing only one tennis shoe. The other foot was bare.

There was evidence of a gash to the head and minor injuries to the elbows and knees.

Gunther turned to me and uttered a single word, the word almost anyone would have said under the circumstances: "Drowned."

Most people would have agreed, but the single word—drowned—pulled me up short.

I said, "Gunther, do you mean 'he drowned' or 'he was drowned' in the sense of put to death by drowning?"

I could see Gunther didn't know what he meant, which is typical of hotel managers. (I immediately gave myself a demerit; there goes the great Carlos Cisne trying to be clever again.)

I wish I could say I solved the Pera case then and there, but I can't. And yet it's odd. Often, your mind works at a level of awareness so submerged that your consciousness doesn't grasp it, like a plane flying too low to be picked up by radar.

Gunther asked if I'd have a word with the widow and her father. I agreed. Such delightful people, Oscar!

I spoke to them separately, she in her room, he in Gunther's office.

I was surprised at how unattractive Sra. Pera looked in daylight. Her hair was stringy. Smoking had been unkind to her lips and teeth. One who had seemed young and lithe in the subdued lighting of the dining room became faded and scrawny in the morning sun.

Gunther more or less shoved himself, and me, into her suite with a few polite words and a little pressure from his big right foot.

The senhora said nothing at first. In fact, she turned her back on us and flitted about the room trailing cigarette smoke. We sat down.

Gunther finally got her to sit on a bar stool

"Place is a mess," she said. She was hoarse from smoking and singing.

I stared at her with pity. She was—inside and out—ugly.

Of course, I didn't show any of this. I did what I always do, what you taught me to do when we were at law school together. I displayed only my mask. And what a frightful mask it's become, Oscar, the receding hairline, the dark beard, the black-rimmed glasses with lenses literally as thick as the bottoms of those green-tinted Coca-Cola bottles we used to buy as kids in Copacabana.

"You wanna know what happened last night, right?"

"No," I said. That gave Gunther a start but I elbowed him. "First, I want to know who you are."

"I'm Sylvia Davila...I used to be Sra. João José Pera, but now I'm Sylvia Davila again...thank God." She gave exaggerated emphasis to the last two words.

"How did you become Sra. Pera?"

"Zezinho, my husband...or ex-husband...or whatever he is now...used to be the marina captain here. I've been coming here all my life."

"But why did you marry him?"

"He's a guy."

"A guy?"

"A guy...a hunk...you shudda seen him before he became a lush."

"And your husband, why did he marry you?"

She stared at the floor. She was hunched over. Now, I saw she was desperately thin. She looked like a rag doll abandoned on a stool.

"I dunno."

"Well, there must have been a reason. Who was he, really? Where did he come from?"

"Oh, he came from here, from Paratí. He started off as a fisherman. Then he learned how to handle those big schooners they take tourists in. He was quite a hunk, so the tour companies liked him. You know, he'd take a boat load of tourists around with a lot of middle aged ladies. Eventually, they made him marina captain so the ladies could look at him all the time."

I thought—"And you stole him from the marina crowd to look at him all the time yourself"—but I bit my tongue. The mask, Oscar.

"You said 'Thank God' a moment ago. Why?"

"My husband and I were separated. That's no news. You probably read about it in the gossip columns."

"Why?"

"Zé didn't like Rio. He wanted to live here. I like it here, but not to live."

"That's all?"

"Whaddaya think, mister? Zé was a hunk. Even drunk he was a hunk. But Zé was a failure in Ipanema. You know, high society, The Hippopotamus, Jorge Guinle grinning for the cameras. Zé was a dunce. He couldn't hold a conversation. With either sex. He liked it better here."

"Now I would like you to tell me what happened last night."

She took a deep breath, very cinematic.

"Zé came into my room...he kinda barged in. Like you guys. He was half drunk. He tried to feel me up. That didn't work. He hit me. Look."

She turned her neck so we could view the black and blue marks.

"Is that when he started throwing furniture?"

"Yeah. He threw everything."

"Did you hit him?"

"Hit him? Are you kidding?"

"Then how did he get the gash on his head?"

She stared at me in sincere disbelief.

"What gash?"

"Your husband was found with quite a gash on his head. And lacerations to the elbows and knees. Do you have any idea how he injured himself?"

She turned to Gunther: "You didn't tell me about that!"

Gunther made non-commital squeeking sounds they send hotel managers to schools in Switzerland to learn.

The senhora was a little uneasy after news of the bloody gash to her ex-husband's head.

"I though he had drowned," she said.

"Drowned," I said. There it was again. Now, I had said it in a single word.

***

The old man, Luiz Carlos Gordon Davila, was waiting for us in Gunther's office. He didn't stand up. There was no back slapping or hand shaking. He was smoking a cigarette in that awful holder, and smiling his little yellow smile.

"You're that radical lawyer from Copacabana, aren't you?"

"I am Carlos Cisne," I said. "I am a lawyer. I live in Copacabana. This has nothing to do with politics."

I don't waste time when it comes to a customer like Davila. He's one of these types who inherits a family business—in Davila's case construction—and retires only to make millions more in Brazil's ridiculously easy financial market.

Davila, like me, had heard the ruckus coming from his daughter's suite the night before but he hadn't bothered to investigate. ("They fought all the time.")

I mentioned the gash on Pera's head but Davila didn't seem to know anything about it. Unlike his daughter, however, he immediately grasped its implications.

"Tell me about the divorce," I said.

"Sylvia and the son-of-a-bitch were separated. The bastard wanted money but, of course, he wasn't going to get any, not in Brazil. In Brazil, we kick the son-of-a-bitch out the door."

Davila made kicking motions with his foot.

"Why was your son-in-law sitting with you last night? What did he want?"

This gave Davila considerable wheezy pleasure. "He was looking for his next meal!"

***

Now, at last, I was free, to do nothing, merely to be.

I got Gunther's driver to take me to the Fazenda Banal. It was cool there. The air dripped with the smell of sugar cane.

I dragged my gouty foot around the gardens. I delighted in the thump-thump of the humming birds. With my half broken body I regarded the young men and women, with their perfect bodies, bathing among the cascades.

I had my usual lunch. Then I had my usual rum at the cabana. I was witnessing the ballet of the big blue butterflies when Pera floated through my mind. I closed my eyes and—I swear it, Oscar—each piece of the puzzle came drifting into place until my mind's eye beheld a seamless whole. Suddenly, I knew what had happened the night before and why. (It was perfectly obvious.) Also, I knew what I had to do to prove it.

I could hardly contain myself. I called for the driver. I whispered to no one in particular: "How thoughtful of the truth to wait until I had finished my lunch before stepping into view."

***

There was only one problem. Back in Paratí, the circus had come to town.

TV news crews were everywhere. The hotel lobby was jammed with reporters and rubber-neckers.

Gunther waved me into his office. I got there in time for a cameo appearance on the news. There, beneath the familiar Colaco tapestry depicting cocoa beans and baianas, Police Detective Pães was giving an interview. It was the usual staccato police gibberish. Pães couldn't characterize a crime. There was no coroner's report, no timetable, no suspects, etc. I stood beside Gunther. Together, we stood behind Pães. (I disliked him from the start, with his short black hair, obviously dyed, and big, tinted aviator glasses.)

Gunther introduced me. He offered that I was aiding the hotel. Pães wasn't listening. He brushed me aside to get to Gunther's inner office. He wanted to be alone.

I had work to do.

First, Gunther's driver took me to the fishing village at Trinidade. The fishermen are not educated, as you're aware, but what they know they know well and what they know is the sea around Paratí. I gave them money (too much). I asked them to do a job for me, to locate an object on the seabed. They promised results by morning.

Now, we drove back to Paratí. I spoke to the chairman of the tour company association. He told me exactly what I expected.

Finally, I traced what I surmised must have been Pera's last steps. I began with Sra. Pera's suite. (For a small tip, the chambermaid became very helpful.) I surveyed Davila's room, wandered down the hall and into the street. Finally, on the wooden staircase from the road to the beach, I found what I had been looking for.

Now, I made my way back to the hotel. My heart was light. As far as I was concerned, the case was closed. All I had to do was await the fishermen's report next morning. I was ready for my nap.

But it was not to be.

At the hotel, I found Gunther in a state: "Sra. Pera is having a nervous collapse. The old man is threatening to sue and there's nothing I can do with that detective."

Pães had given father and daughter the third degree. Sra. Pera was under sedation. Davila, unaccustomed to assertiveness by the police, was refusing to comment until his lawyer came in from São Paulo.

I tried to calm Gunther by explaining I had the case all but solved. Gunther was skeptical, not about me, but about Pães.

"The man is beyond reason," Gunther insisted. "He won't listen."

I promised to have a word with him.

Pães was occupying Gunther's office.

I sat down. The detective was on the phone. I waited. Finally, I was able to introduce myself. Pães fiddled with papers.

"I am prepared to offer you my view of the case," I said.

Pães looked up. He strode from the desk, leaned over my chair and lowered his sunburnt little face to within an inch of my beard. With his oversize glasses, he looked like a curious insect.

"I'm only going to tell you this once, pal, so listen up." His tone was modulated. "I'm not going to tolerate interference of any kind from anyone at any time for any reason."

"Thank you for being frank. Now, let me be frank. As attorney for the hotel chain, it will be my duty to contact higher authorities."

Pães short little arms shot out. He grabbed me by the shoulders. His voice was low but it was less modulated now, like a repressed scream.

"You don't seem to remember who you're talking to, pal. I have duties too. I can order jail for material witnesses..."

I didn't like the pressure. I didn't like the insect visage and the bad breath.

Oscar, you know there are two things I hate—lies and violence. Probably, I hate them because, often, they are so useful.

The wide C-hook of my cane came in handy. I swept it across my field of vision, breaking the detective's hold on me at the elbows. He stumbled in mid sentence.

I leaned forward and put my large, hirsute face in proximity to his small, buggish one.

"And you don't know who you're talking to, my churlish friend. As a former member of Congress (true), I enjoy immunity from arrest (false), especially from numbskulls like you (if only it were true). I also enjoy what is called the privilege of the floor (true), meaning I may take the floor of the Chamber of Deputies in Brasilia at any time and move resolutions denouncing Gestapo tactics of incompetent police detectives (utter rubbish)."

My words had some effect. My cane (what a throwback to the primitives) had more. The little man retreated behind his desk.

"Get out," he barked.

I obliged.

***

My sleep last night was uneasy. I had thought the case solved only to find the police had other ideas.

At breakfast I realized why. "O Globo" carried Pera on the front page. Inside was an interview with bug-face. In it, he contradicted everything he had said on television the night before. The gist—João José Pera, poor boy turned playboy, had been murdered. (The case turned on the bloody injury to the head.) Suspects, by implication, were the estranged wife and the arrogant father-in-law.

My anxiety extended through half the morning. I sipped coffee in the breakfast room. I took a walk. Again, I inspected the wooden staircase leading to the beach. I prayed for clear skies.

Then, at last, while I was standing on the beach, it came—the news I had been waiting for. One of the fishermen rounded the point from Trinidade in his skiff just to tell me. (I had been very generous.)

"Did you find it?"

The fisherman nodded. He described the object. It was more mundane than I had supposed but it was enough to square my case.

"You left it undisturbed, just as I asked?"

The boy nodded enthusiastically. I gave him a fortune in bills with instructions to have one of the tour guides, whom I knew possessed an underwater camera, photograph the object as soon as possible.

Now I was ready for Davila and company.

When I got to the hotel, I found they were ready for me as well.

Sra. Pera and her father were in Gunther's office. Gunther offered a genteel introduction.

Before I could begin, however, Detective Pães burst through the door. He was livid. I wheeled toward Davila: "Give me one Real."

Davila understood immediately. He hastened to advance me a crinkled bill. But Pães was slow to catch on. He made an effort to control his voice but his words came out as a muffled shriek: "I told you to stay out of this, pal. These are material witnesses in a murder case."

"Dr. Pães, I am a lawyer. These are my clients. They have hired me to represent them. You have seen them do so with your own eyes. Money has changed hands. You yourself have characterized them as material witnesses.

Therefore, they are entitled to counsel. My clients wish to consult me. Such a consultation is privileged. You will leave."

Pães hesitated.

I tapped my cane: "Dr. Pães, you vex me. I am inclined to denounce you before Congress. I am inclined to ask the president of Congress to order your arrest."

Pães stormed out, slamming the door.

I turned to my new client: "How much does Pães want?"

Davila smiled: "They never quote a figure."

"Sr. Davila, it may hearten you to know I have solved the case."

"Who killed my son-in-law?"

"You did. You and your daughter. You killed him by denying him oxygen."

Father and daughter were silent. Gunther seemed shocked at first but then resigned to more days and weeks of scandal.

"I thought you were supposed to be my lawyer, Cisne. This isn't a very promising start."

"I know. But I don't mean it literally. You killed him by denying him the oxygen of money, home and family."

"Maybe you should get to the point."

"I will. First, let us examine your son-in-law's state of mind. He was a fisherman. But, if you will permit me a small joke, he was a fisherman out of water. You, sir, and your daughter had elevated him from his natural status as a fisherman to an exalted one as...what?...playboy?...He was hardly that. In fact, he was nothing. In Ipanema, he was not Sr. João José Pera. He was Sr. Sylvia Davila. And even that ridiculous identity he was about to lose, along with the financial means it provided. And so he attempted to regain his former identity, the more humble one he had enjoyed as a native of Paratí. But even that avenue was now closed to him. One of the things he had learned in Ipanema was how to deaden his pain. He did so through alcohol. It would not surprise me to learn he also used other, more costly, substances. Perhaps the coroner will enlighten us on that score.

"Yesterday, I made inquiries with the tour companies. They told me exactly what I expected to hear. Pera wanted his old job back. But, after several years in your care, he had become a notorious lush. No one would trust him with a fishing skiff, let alone a tour boat or an entire marina."

Davila seemed genuinely intrigued but he suddenly turned impatient: "The police are threatening us with a murder charge, Cisne. They're not interested in the son-of-a-bitch's mental state."

"Of course not. They're interested in your bank account. They will point to certain physical evidence, chiefly the injuries apparent on Pera's body, especially the gash to the head. They would have you believe he died from that injury and that his body was then disposed of in the sea."

"Neither I nor my daughter had anything to do with that injury."

"I know. The police will find no blood stains in your suite or that of your daughter. I've looked. In fact, they'll find no blood stains or other physical evidence on the hotel grounds. They will, however, find stains on the staircase leading from the road to the beach."

"What's the point, counselor?"

"Your son-in-law's anger Monday was more feigned than real. He wished to create a scene full of sound and fury, especially sound. The more who heard it the better. By hitting his estranged wife, he hoped to invite retribution. But even failing that he had, at least, left a record, the black and blue marks on his wife's neck, pointing to physical violence and tempting the observer to conclude he, too, could have suffered injuries, even fatal ones. His wife, however, through frailty or fear or lack of opportunity, did not attempt to injure her husband. Therefore, he injured himself. He did this at the first opportunity by throwing himself down the wooden staircase. He may have done this repeatedly. There are bloodstains on those stairs. It is the only place in the vicinity, as far as I can tell, where there are any such stains. But the stains there are generous.

"Now, he advanced his plan one more step. No doubt he had a boat waiting at the beach. The boat contained an object. Unfortunately, I have not yet located the boat. When I do, I have no doubt it, too, will show blood traces. I have, however, found the object. It is resting at the bottom of the Paratí Channel and in a most suggestive place, precisely where, when the tide comes in, it brings with it any solid matter it finds in its path, depositing this flotsam and jetsam on the beach in front of the hotel, in short, exactly where Pera's body was found. This dialog between channel and tide is well known to fishermen in these parts, as I discovered talking to some yesterday."

"What was the object?"

"Something quite common: a cement parking stanchion, a lump of cement with a metal bar protruding."

The widow was turning deathly pale. I addressed her directly: "Your husband, having left persuasive evidence of a struggle and of physical injuries to himself, now completed his plan. In his mind's eye, he saw his own body washed up on the beach, covered with bloody wounds, only hours after a violent struggle with a wife and father-in-law known to harbor him thoroughgoing ill will. He had created a scene ripe for an adventurer like Pães to exploit. How easy for the police to call it murder. These were the thoughts he nurtured as he threw himself over the side, tied to the cement block."

"But how did he know he would float to the surface in time for the morning tide?"

"For the first and perhaps only time in his life, your son-in-law used his head. The rest he got by instinct: his despair, his hatred of life. Even his plan was mostly instinct: the row, hitting his wife, the business of the boat, the channel, the tide. These were things he knew by heart. But the timing...that took brains.

"A missing tennis shoe called my attention when I first viewed your son-in-law's body. It set off a chain of thought. Pera affixed himself to the metal bar in a most peculiar fashion by tying one end of a shoelace to the bar's eyelet. Later, as the tide came in, it gently tugged at his body. It tugged and tugged, slowly loosening the dead man's sneaker until, *voila*, the sneaker was freed and the corpse could float freely to the surface."

The widow gasped in horror.

"What should I do, counselor?" Davila was neither somber nor particularly relieved.

"Nothing."

"Nothing?"

"You can forget about Dr. Pães. When the coroner's report comes in, it will cite cause of death in a single word—drowned."

Case closed. See you Sunday, Oscar.

Yours,

Carlos

Pamela Yorston

PAMELA YORSTON is an Anglo-South American. Born in Argentina of British parents, she has lived in Chile, which she considers her permanent home, Uruguay and Brazil. She and her husband Gordon have four sons born here and there.

The things she likes best about São Paulo are the people and the driving. What she dislikes most are the crowds and the traffic.

This is her second short story to be published in a book.

Temporary Accommodation

by Pamela Yorston

I turned on my side, fighting to hang on to the last vestiges of sleep which were being dragged from me by the steadily increasing noise of traffic. The ground shook continually. It must be nearly six. I kept my eyes shut tightly and thought about tonight. A surge of excitement ran through me. Tonight was the party! Suddenly, an acrid sweet cloud of smoke engulfed me and I abandoned the struggle and opened my eyes to the early morning mist. It was raining lightly and although I was sheltered, the wheels of trucks, passing no more than eight feet from my head, threw up a fine spray which, I noticed, was settling on my brother Nelson's cheeks and eyelashes. I lay on my back and looked up at the superstructure of the bridge. I could see it vibrating as the cars rolled over it. My mother called to me over the steadily rising noise of traffic.

"Hurry up, Nilde, it'll be broad daylight soon. You'll be late for school."

Mother had two purposes in life: making sure Nelson and I went to school and somehow finding a way for us to go back and live in the *favela*. I missed the *favela* too, but I was only partly sorry to have to leave. I had escaped Sr. Sérgio's eyes.

I threw back my blanket. The edge was wet and muddy. Picking my way over the sleeping figures of my family, I squeezed in behind the supports of the bridge and washed as best I could from a half-filled tin basin, supported on an upturned apple box. This was the worst of living under a bridge. The concrete pillars offered me little privacy from the anonymous eyes behind the tightly closed windows of the passing cars.

"Mother," I called, "I'll be going straight to Dona Gloria's after school today. She's having a spring cleaning and she said she needed me early." Mother looked up suspiciously.

"Don't you dare go and miss school! Your head is full of this party tonight. I know you can't wait to get together with Fátima to talk about it."

"No Mother, I promise I won't but I'll go straight to Fátima's after work and we'll go to the party together from there."

Mother didn't need to warn me. I loved school, not only because I enjoyed the work and did well, but because it was like a holiday for me. At school I could relax. No one expected me to do more than one thing at a time. Mother always made sure I had something nice to wear. But I had no friends there. None of the girls of my age from the *favela* were still at school. Most girls of seventeen were working full time and earning more than their mothers and sometimes their fathers—those that had a father. Fátima could never understand why I hadn't left school at the first opportunity, as she had. Of course, she didn't have my mother, who talked to me incessantly about the importance of school and the doors which would open to me and also about our imminent return to the *favela.*

"When your father goes to his new job, we'll be back. You'll see. This is only temporary."

We had lost our house two years before. It had been washed away in a torrential storm one night. It was also about that time that Father lost his job. I wondered when Father would go to his new job. He went away some times during the day, but mostly he sat up against the wall, under the bridge. I didn't like to go near him at such times because he could be moody and become violent.

Fátima lived in the *favela* with her mother. It was she who had found me the job at Dona Gloria's as her mother worked for a neighbour. It was Fátima, too, who had introduced me to Jair. I had met them together one day the previous week and Jair told her to bring me to the party. He lived in the apartments beyond the *favela.* I had never been to the apartments, although I had always wanted to. I didn't know anyone who lived there, except Jair. Fátima knew several apartment people from her job at the factory. She and Jair were old friends and I often saw them together. I was in love with Jair.

****

Dona Gloria was the richest woman in the world. Her house was like a fairy tale. The floors were smooth and shone like glass. She had all sorts of furniture covered with the most beautiful and delicate materials. I had never seen such curtains, heavy, thick and soft and on every table there were beautiful treasures. A box covered with thousands of pieces of looking glass, a huge pot of multi-coloured plastic flowers that never dropped their petals or had to be changed, dozens of little porcelain figures painted red and gold and my favourite, a big glass plate with a pink rose painted in the centre. I'm sure that even the people at the apartments did not have things like these.

I came to Dona Gloria three times a week. Today was payday. I had skipped lunch to be there early and I had managed to eat a few cold potato fritters from the fridge while Dona Gloria was doing something at the back of the house.

"Answer the bell," she called from her bedroom. It was the beggar, the same one I saw most mornings on my way to school, huddled on the steps of a neighbouring store. He had long hair and a beard and his clothes were stiff with dirt. There were many different rumours about him. People said he was well educated, maybe because he was often seen whiling away the time doing a crossword puzzle. Some said he was from a rich family who had disowned him and stolen his inheritance. Others said he was a Russian noble who had escaped to Brazil in his youth. Up close he was younger than I had thought. I only knew that he must be very poor because he had nowhere permanent to live, like my family, but wandered around with his belongings in a sack. I approached the gate slowly.

"Yes?" I asked tentatively, but I already knew what he wanted—money, or failing that, leftovers from lunch.

"I don't think we have anything. I'll ask the senhora."

"Come inside!" called Dona Gloria. "We have nothing!" she said to the man impatiently and slammed the door. "You give him something once and he'll be back every day and bring his friends too." I didn't think he had any friends but I kept quiet.

"Is he one of your crowd from under the bridge?" went on Dona Gloria.

"Dona Gloria! He's a beggar!" I stammered. I was dismayed. Who had told her about the bridge? I had never said anything to Dona Gloria. I never actually lied about it but I had always given her to understand that I was a neighbour of Fátima's.

"Well, don't sound so offended, don't your people beg, too? Your friend Fátima was next door with her mother this morning. She told me all about you."

I felt sick. How could Fátima do this to me. Why? She knew that it was my secret. Now Dona Gloria would fire me. I could hear her voice droning on:

"...and I wish you and your friends would take your stuff and go somewhere else. It makes the neighbourhood look so run down to have all of you and all your junk lying around. Why don't you go and live in the *favela*? Can't you pay a rent between the lot of you?"

We did pay a rent—of sorts. We had to pay Alvaro Moreira's men every month or they would make us leave and let somebody else live under our bridge. Mother was worried because Alvaro Moreira said we would now have to pay more because it was a very good spot. The pavement area under it was spacious and flat. We also had a water tap close by.

"It's only temporary." I muttered, echoing my mother. Dona Gloria shrugged and went to the back of the house. I could hear her talking across the passage to her son, Sr. Célio. He was quite old, about forty. He occupied the second bedroom . He muttered something to her, which I didn't hear, but I heard her answer.

"That's all very well but I can't afford a better maid. Don't tell me about maids. When I lived in Higienópolis in the old house we had several servants, let me tell you."

"So you keep saying," Sr. Célio came to his bedroom door, "and you had a gardener, too. And your great uncle was first secretary in the embassy in Prague. But my only memory is this house, which wouldn't be so miserably depressing if it had some paint on those damp patches."

"Paint!" screamed Dona Gloria, "Are you going to pay for it? You never put a cent into this house. Look at all the tiles falling off the wall in the bathroom. No wonder you are too ashamed to bring your friends here." Sr. Célio came towards me down the passage.

"What friends?" he muttered. He shouted down the passage, "I already give you most of my salary, have you forgotten?"

"What salary! You give me hardly anything. Don't tell me the government doesn't pay you well. Why are the papers always complaining about government employees being paid so much?"

"Some government employees, mother. I work in the local post office, have you forgotten?" He came into the kitchen and told me impatiently to get him some coffee. I could hear him muttering under his breath that he would rent a room somewhere else, if he could afford it. I could understand Dona Gloria's anger. It wasn't fair for him to treat her like that. After all, he was rich.

"You're just like your father, just like all his family! All barely scraping an existence. At my time of life I should be taking things easy." She came lumbering down the passage and I quickly removed myself to the front room. Dona Gloria saw me however, and went on at Sr. Célio. "That girl! I bet she makes sheep's eyes at you when I'm not around. All she thinks about is men. The maid next door...her daughter Fátima told me she's been flirting with some man from those apartments beyond the *favela*. Those flats are full of drug pushers and addicts. Next thing she'll be pregnant. They're all the same, these people."

I felt tears of anger running down my cheeks. Her suggestion that I fancied Sr. Célio was silly. My anger was for Fátima. Why was she trying to humiliate me? How could she! I wanted to kill her. I wanted to leave my job, run away and hide. But today was payday and I was going to the party. Killing Fátima would have to wait. She was taking me to the apartments. One good thing about the afternoon was that Dona Gloria gave me a beautiful flowered scarf she no longer wore, when she paid me, later on that day. It was perfect to wear as a belt with the trousers I had for the party. When I told her this, she advanced me some money for some shoes that were on offer at the supermarket.

****

From the outside the *favela* was a mass of patches in browns and greys creeping up the hill. I loved the *favela*. You knew where you were, there. You knew the people. Two access roads wound their way in from the "Marginal"—the riverside highway—with dozens of narrow paths leading off them. The houses in Dona Gloria's neighborhood were shaped and molded by the layout of the roads. Here at the *favela* it was the opposite. The roads curled round and followed the contours of each house and wall, which had been built by adding one onto another with boards, corrugated iron, cardboard or sometimes bricks. The result was a collection of irregular paths of hard packed earth which proceeded erratically, widening and narrowing as they twisted and climbed and sometimes doubled back on themselves. We called the main accesses the 'avenues'. This was where the better families of the *favela* lived. Some prominent people actually lived on the front, overlooking the highway. But there were very few houses left there now. Most of the space was taken up by businesses, like the bar with the billiard table and the tyre repair shop.

The *favela* had sprung up overnight, about twenty years before. Well before I was born. There were still a few of the original settlers. Dona Júlia was one of them and César, the owner of the bar. They had arrived one night in three trucks loaded with clapboard and metal sheets and by morning they had set up a row of shelters along the front of the municipal vacant lot. My grandmother Sule, who was dead now, had been there. Her house used to be the one on the corner where the tyre repair shop was now. Mother told me there had been a great uproar at their arrival. The people from round about were furious; it was even in the papers.

"But you managed to stay," I said.

"Yes, but the *Prefeito* tried to have us thrown out. We swore we'd fight to the death with sticks and stones, which were the only weapons we had. The newspapers reported it all. Fortunately, the Governor of the state of São Paulo was on our side. He accused the *Prefeito* of systematically forcing poor, working class people into a state of homelessness and despair."

"He must have been a good man." I commented.

"Yes, he was. Mind you, when his party won the *Prefeitura* in the next elections, he refused to see us when we tried to complain about police harassment."

"He used you!" I said cynically.

"Maybe....we used him too. " Mother smiled.

"Where did all the other people come from?" I asked.

"They trickled in over the next two years, from Bahia, mainly. It wasn't easy at that time. We had fought for the land, but these new people were taking over all the space and selling it to our own relatives who were arriving. We almost had an open war at one point."

"It must have been frightening."

"Yes, I was afraid all the time. My brother, Raimundo, had small children. But we managed to put together a sort of neighbourhood committee and they stopped new people arriving unless they had some friend or relative who would cede them some space. Land became valuable and people started selling out and moving to legally owned lots on the outskirts of São Paulo, near the factories. Of course, there were no title deeds or anything in the *favela* and sometimes there were gun battles over the land. The police never interfered. They were afraid to go in there. It went on like that till Sr. Sérgio restored order. No one dared challenge him."—Sr. Sérgio of the eyes I didn't like.

"Was he one of the first settlers?"

"No, he came from Rio de Janeiro. He had business there. He still has, they say. He travels back and forth a great deal." I looked at mother sideways and said tentatively:

"They say he controls all the drug traffic in the area..."

Mother was angry. "Who says so?" she exclaimed sharply, "You listen to too much gossip. Sr. Sérgio is a good man. Look at all the people he has helped. Where would we be without him! Can you imagine what would happen if he were not here?"

"Anarchy?" I inquired, rather pleased with this new word I had learned at school. Mother looked at me suspiciously.

"Whatever!" she snapped and refused to talk about it any further. I knew she was right. Sr. Sérgio was the supreme authority in the *favela*, but by the age of eleven I instinctively kept out of his way. I wasn't sure why, but I preferred to remain anonymous, just one of the crowd of children. By fourteen I'd heard some stories about him. Fátima thought I was silly. If Sr. Sérgio approved of you, your family was well taken care of. But I thought his eyes were greedy when he looked at me.

There were constant quarrels and feuds in the *favela* but there was a code of rules which we all more or less followed. These were enforced by threats and attacks but ultimately by Sr. Sérgio. I suspected, as a child, that he was the most powerful man in Brazil. I remembered Chico da Ribeira's relatives who had tried to build a room, squeezed in against the side of Dionício's house, blocking part of his window. There had been a lot of shouting and screaming which lasted for two days, until Sr. Sérgio returned from Rio. The next morning all Chico's relatives' belongings were strewn along the Marginal.

****

In the end I said nothing to Fátima when I reached her house. I didn't want to have a row with her before the party. We took great care with our clothes and our hair, especially Fátima, who put on a very tight pantsuit and so much eye shadow it made her look strange. We set out while it was still light, but it grew dark quickly so that as we approached the apartments, we had to pick our way across the field by the light of passing cars, trying to avoid stepping on rubbish or in potholes. I could hear the music of the *Samba* and the *Batucada*. The music was recorded but there were obviously several people playing the drums. I felt a rush of excitement. I loved to dance. I could now see the flats more clearly. Four blocks, about seven stories high. I wondered what it would be like to look down from up there. Perhaps Jair lived at the top. The blocks were long and narrow with two flights of concrete stairs, one on either end of the building, rising to the upper floors. The blocks were joined at the level of the fourth floor, by wide catwalks which crossed from one to another like bridges. The party was being held on the farthest catwalk.

We walked round to the far stairs to avoid several youths who were sitting smoking. They called out to us but their voices were slurred and we ignored them. As we climbed the stairs the noise grew louder and my pulse raced. We could hear shouts of laughter. We kept pressed to the inside of the stairs because the smell of urine was strong and I didn't want to step in it with my new shoes.

We emerged onto the catwalk. Everybody from the apartment appeared to be there and I recognised many people from the *favela*. Jair was standing halfway along, talking to another man. He was wearing jeans and a long sleeved cream coloured shirt, unlike everyone else, who were in T-shirts. He was laughing at something and I caught my breath as I saw his profile and the line of his throat.

Fátima was right next to me as I approached Jair. I wondered why she was so animated, why she talked so loudly and laughed so much, but all the while Jair looked at me and I didn't take in anything Fátima was saying.

I have vivid memories of bits of conversation and scenes from that party, but for the most part it is just a blur of faces and noise and laughter and drums and flashing lights and Jair. I remember we danced. We walked up and down the gallery which ran the full length of the front of the apartments. And we talked and talked and talked. I sparkled. I felt amusing and clever like the time Nelson and I had drunk sweet wine with fruit in it. But I neither ate nor drank anything that night. I found myself telling him about my family, the school, Dona Gloria and the bridge, things I thought I would never tell anyone. And I told him about Sr. Sérgio's eyes.

Jair also told me about himself. He was a football player. Football had been his whole life since he was a child.

"Did you go to a football school?" I wanted to know.

"Yes, the best. The beaches of Rio de Janeiro. I played there winter and summer, in all weather."

He understood about Sr. Sérgio.

"It was a bit like that for me in football," he explained, "When I started to get good, at about fifteen years old, an official from a local club offered me a place in his team. It was a great opportunity for me at that age and I knew I was good. But I was expected to stay in favour with the team official. I was his man. He used to send me on errands delivering packages, which he said were medicines, to a nearby *favela*. One day, one of my team mates was stabbed on one of these assignments. I left the team after that and the official used his influence to stop me playing anywhere else in the area. I moved around playing wherever I could get a game for the next two years. I never stayed in one place. I didn't want to draw attention to myself again, until I was good enough for my place on the team not to depend on the favour of some official."

We were standing at the far end of the gallery when we heard the explosions. Then came the smell of smoke and the wail of sirens. Everything was happening at once. A glow appeared over the favela and intensified. There were far off shots.

Suddenly dozens of spotlights were turned on the apartments from all directions. The glare blinded me and I heard screams and running footsteps. I remember very little of what followed. At one point I was knocked on the side of the head by some hard object. I fell down and felt myself dragged to my feet. There were people pressing up against me and hands clutching at me. Later I was crammed into the back of a police van with about twenty other women. Rumours flew back and forth. They argued and speculated. This was the police. This was the army. This was the government. One woman said something about the CIA. But one rumour persisted: Sr. Sérgio was dead.

Later at the headquarters, I huddled in a corner of a dank grey room. About eight other women were there with me. Some nervously pacing up and down. Some sitting on the bench along the wall taking in low voices. I sat on the floor and hugged my knees.

I was cold and frightened, my head was throbbing. I grew more afraid every time the door opened and the military policemen came in. Afraid of their eyes, afraid of their hands. They were calling us one at a time and taking down names and addresses. I absolutely could not tell them where I lived. We all knew that girls with no fixed address were an easy target.

"So what?" said one girl I knew slightly from the *favela*. "If it gets you out of here faster what's the odds?" I hid my face and cried.

Later, another group of women were brought in. One had blood all over her. I heard them talking about how Sr. Sérgio's men had woken up everybody in the *favela* when he knew of the raid. The military police were received by a virtual army.

There were only three of us left when one of the police popped his head through the door and beckoned me. "Come this way, Miss." As I passed him I pressed myself well against the wall trying to keep as far away from him as possible, but without looking back, he went ahead, leading the way to the front reception area. I could hardly believe it when I saw Jair waiting for me. Relief flooded through me and I felt lightheaded as he supported me into the waiting police car.

"Let's go home," he said cheerfully.

Later we sat on the steps on one side of the apartment block. The sky in the east was beginning to lighten.

"What did you say to them to make them let me go," I wanted to know.

"I told them you were my future wife," he answered simply.

"Of course, why did I ask? Naturally they summoned a car at once to take us home. And why is your supposed future wife so important?"

"Well," he grinned, I hadn't noticed his dimples before, "I told them that I played football for "São Paulo Football Club", which is almost true as I start playing for them next month."

"Ah, yes, and fortunately they were all "São Paulo" fans."

"As a matter of fact most of them were "Corinthians" fans but somehow I managed to convince them that I would be in the national team by the next World Cup. I said that my wife would be interviewed on television whenever I made a goal just like Bebeto's wife and I hoped that my wife would have nothing nasty to say about the military police."

I giggled, "How on earth did you make them believe all that?"

"Because," he said seriously, "It's true."

"Which part is true?"

"All of it. Come, I'll take you home."

"Home? Where?" I asked uncertainly.

"To your mother. Your bridge is probably the safest place in town at the moment. If Sr. Sérgio is dead the *favela* is going to be extremely dangerous for some time to come. If the military police are to be believed, a battle of succession is raging right now and there are quite a few old scores to settle. If I were you I'd rent out space under the bridge to the people from the *favela*. It's your chance to get rich," he grinned.

****

Jair started to play for "São Paulo" the following month. You will know all about his subsequent transfers within Brazil and abroad over the years.

A long time has elapsed since the night of that party. My eldest daughter, Agatha, is now twenty two. She's a journalist with "O Globo" in Rio and in no hurry to get married. She says she hasn't the time since her promotion. There is talk of her moving to Paris as a foreign correspondent. She speaks perfect French, of course, from the time Jair was with Paris Saint-Germain. Jairzinho is at the University of São Paulo. He's almost an engineer. Marcelo is still at school. He is a dream on the football field. I think he'd like to try it professionally but Jair is against it. He says he would never be good enough. According to him there are too many options open to Marcelo. To be really good at football, he says, it has to be your only chance as it was with him.

As for me, I didn't finish school that year but I took up my studies again when the children went to school. I have never worked outside the house. Being the wife of a prominent man, like Jair, is a job in itself. Sometimes, on talk shows on television, I'm asked about my life in the streets of São Paulo. I don't know why people are so avid for that sort of information. It wasn't all that interesting. I tell them that we were never really street people anyway. As my mother said, it was only temporary.

MANUELA LARANGEIRA is a fourteen-year-old student at the Pan American School of Bahia. Born in Salvador, she still lives in this unique city which inspired the following poem. Manuela has only recently begun to write poetry. She enjoys listening to music and playing the organ, and participates in sports such as tennis, volleyball, and swimming. Fond of languages, she is now studying French. This poem, her first published piece, is dedicated to her parents.

Dwelling

By Manuela Larangeira

A distinct panorama
of the tempestuous ocean in Salvador.
It seems like a volcano
that erupts in the darkness.

The ocean is far away,
but it seems like it's by my side
as mysterious as ever.

There's no sand at all,
nothing covering its body,
exposing its purity
like a nude person.

Ungenerous waves, high and merciless,
unplacidly they hit huge rocks,
the water splashes on the streets,
again and again.

Turbulently...
the process repeats itself one after another,
like a clock that never stops.
Not a single creature in the water -
menacing.
However, some people on the rocks,
fishing -
carefully protecting themselves from the possessive
waves.

Water at the horizon,
transparent as glass
making a peculiar contrast
turquoise sky -
full of white undulating clouds,
silk pillows to angels.
Breaking nature's beauty,
towering twenty-three floor building,
the "Meridien"
in blue smoke letters,
bothers my view.

This view that I have contemplated everyday,
and now staring at it
as if I have never seen it...
like an amazed tourist.

FULTON BOYD is an American living in São Paulo. He arrived in Brazil in 1952, spent most of his career in venture capital companies in Brazil and Argentina, and is currently a partner in an executive search firm. His articles have appeared in magazines and newspapers, and this is the second anthology to publish his short stories.

When God Made Brazil

by Fulton Boyd

Thank God the Financial Director had left today. A wizard with numbers, maybe, but a man of vision, imagination and tact he was not. In fact, Antonio thought, what a negative S.O.B. he was! In just three days this miserable man had destroyed the morale and motivation that Antonio had spent that many years building up among his underpaid staff. Slowly but surely these overworked, dedicated individuals had succeeded in lowering costs, improving quality, increasing market share and turning the company from losses to profits. Antonio had orchestrated this whole process in just the three years since he had taken over as General Manager. In March the company had remitted its first dividend ever.

Most important, he had proven that you can make money in Brazil if you use your head and work your butt off.

Antonio felt justified in proposing a modest expansion program, to be financed not from new money but from reinvested profits. The Financial Director said he was going to recommend against it. Remit this money, don't invest it. Antonio said they needed to expand in order to consolidate their newly achieved market position and keep growing. The Financial Director said that Brazil was not an attractive country for investment, never had been, never would be. In his opinion growth was unlikely.

Then he had dropped the hatchet. In a meeting with all of Antonio's top managers just before leaving, the Financial Director had said that, given the bleak prospects for Brazil, he was going to recommend a reduction of fifteen percent in staff, across the board.

Now Antonio had just arrived home from taking this unpleasant creature to the airport. He was exhausted, physically and emotionally. He poured himself a tall, stiff drink.

"How wrong can a man be?" he asked himself out loud. Was there anything more that he, Antonio, could have said? Was there any way he was going to convince this guy and those cynics in Cleveland that Brazil was moving forward?

He took a long pull on his drink and sat down.

"Great God!" he exclaimed to himself as he leaned back deeply into his chair, "with everything that is happening here, how can this man not believe in Brazil?"

Maybe he could use some divine guidance.

"Please, God," he looked upward, "help me explain this country so they can all understand it."

He took another long pull on his drink. The warmth of the alcohol was spreading soothingly through his system.

Beginning to enjoy his solitary conversation, he continued, "Why, God, did you make Brazil such a complicated place?"

Antonio's voice faded as he drifted asleep.

* * * * *

(A conversation which took place in 1440 A.D.)

God was gently spinning a large globe of the world, humming to himself, when Jesus walked in.

"Welcome back, Father," Jesus said. "Boy, is it good to see you. It's been a long, long time. Anyhow, I got your message, so here I am. You must be up to something."

God turned around slowly.

"Hi, Son," he acknowledged. "Thanks for coming by. I dropped in because, while I was gone, things here on earth didn't go the way I'd hoped. I'm afraid I left you with an almost impossible situation. We'll have to make a few changes. I wanted to tell you what I have in mind."

He pointed to the globe.

"First, behold! I've made the earth round again. That flat business didn't really fly, did it? I was losing my credibility."

"Your credibility! How about mine? I told you right at the beginning it wasn't going to work. That was back in 540, remember, nine hundred years ago, the year you disappeared. Letting that idiot Cosmas get so carried away by the phrase from the Scriptures, 'the earth is a tabernacle',...that was bad enough...but when he insisted that 'a tabernacle is a table, so the earth is flat'...now that wasn't what Paul or even Moses had in mind at all. It was the kind of statement that flew right in the face of everything people already knew. In fact, it made the Church look really stupid. Then you took off for almost a millennium and left me to handle the situation. A flat earth? Pfaw! Why did you do it? It was crazy.

"By the way," Jesus went on, "where have you been all this time? I needed help."

"Look, Son, I had my reasons for the flat earth. Things were moving too fast in the European-Mediterranean theater back then, exactly when I was having start-up problems with another universe. It was a full-time job. I simply could not afford to let the human race get ahead of me back here on earth while I was away trying to get this other project under control. I had to slow people down. So, we burned the library at Alexandria, sent in the Huns and made the earth flat. Hey, don't look so shocked. It worked, didn't it? Scientific inquiry ground to a halt. Progress was paralyzed. I needed the time, and I got it.

"Now we can think about moving ahead again," God went on. "And incidentally, thanks for keeping a lid on things while I was gone. You did a great job."

"So that's what you've been doing. You were out there starting a new universe and you left me to deal with this mess! Look, I did not do a great job. I tried, I followed all your instructions as best I could, but I just couldn't handle it. It's been a disaster. The Church split in two. Then Mohammed came along and set up a new shop. Now we've got some real tough competition. Same with the Far Eastern religions. We're in the minority now.

"Then look what happened," Jesus went on. "The Moslems invaded Europe. There was a moment when they could have wiped us out completely. I had to arrange for Charlemagne to stop them, the Crusades to distract them, and the Black Plague to scare them off, but they're still in the Iberian Peninsula and fighting to hang in there. This has been a nightmare."

Jesus was about to complain further about his problems when another thought occurred to him.

"Incidentally," he asked, "where are you putting your new universe? I thought this was all the space we had."

"It's all right here, Son, in exactly the same space, just in a different time warp. That's my little secret. None of our other competitors have discovered it yet, so we have to get our little business going in these other universes before they're onto it.

"Here's how it works," he explained. "You'll see on earth in a few hundred years how people will learn to send messages to each other broken down into tiny segments. Between the segments of one message you can squeeze in the segments of others, so that many different messages can be sent simultaneously through the same medium. The segments are put in a certain order at the sender's end and disassembled in the same order at the other end. Each is then delivered intact to its proper destination. The pieces are so small and the operation is so fast that no one is aware of the existence of the other messages. They only hear the one they are supposed to hear. The human race will discover how to do this in about 500 years.

"And that," God went on, "is exactly what I can do with universes. Each one exists only within its own time pulses, entirely separate from the others. Eventually I'll be able to make up to eight of them in the same space. I've got six going right now, counting the start-up, so that leaves two to go. The one you happen to be in is number four. My very first universe in fact is getting close to final implosion, so when that happens we'll have three to go. The newest one, the start-up, is just going through its 'Big Bang' stage. That's the one that has been giving me so much trouble."

"Wow! How come you never told me about this before? You mean, all we're made of is little time pulses? And right alongside us, or inside us, we have one universe collapsing into a black hole, another making the Big Bang, plus three others."

"That's exactly right, Son. Exciting, isn't it?"

"Golly," Jesus exclaimed, "I don't even want to think about it. It makes my intestines shiver. And how about you, Father, you can skip back and forth between these eight frequencies at will, into eight different universes, only you and no one else. Hah! How about teaching me to do that?"

"We'll get around to that when the time comes, Son. It won't be far off."

"Why are you doing all this, Father? We've got enough trouble right here. What do you need all these other universes for?"

"We couldn't do without them. I call them breeding grounds and pastures. You might call them reservoirs, or holding areas. I can migrate souls between them. Where do you think humans come from? And where do you think they go when they die? Soon I'll have another planet very much like this one, with human equivalents on it, ready to learn about us. Oh, we'll have plenty of work to do."

Jesus considered this. Then he asked suspiciously, "When you say 'we', where do I come in? Am I going to have to go down to some of these places dressed in swaddling clothes and run through the same routine again? It wasn't fun, you know, especially the crucifixion bit. That hurt."

"We'll cross those bridges when we come to them," said God. "Meanwhile, let's get on with my plan.

"Here's the problem. The way we've got things structured, there's too much power at the top and none at the bottom wherever you look...in the Church, in Governments, all over. Even when the top folk are all angels, which they're not, this doesn't work. Man was made to be able to solve his own problems, not to be taken care of by a giant organization. So there's a conflict here, and that's why you've been having all these problems.

"We're going to change all of that, Son. It won't be easy. The folks at the top won't want to let go of their perks. They want things to stay the way they are. In fact, many of them sincerely believe the people at the bottom of the pile don't know how to take care of themselves. But if the world is going to move ahead, the top dogs will have to be unseated and the bottom dogs will have to learn to fend for themselves once again."

"As long as you're going to change all these things, how about finding some substitute for the reproductive process?" suggested Jesus. "You can't imagine what trouble that has been causing."

"Sex?" asked God. "You want me to get rid of sex?"

"Why not, Father? It gives Satan carte blanche to corrupt everybody. If only human beings reproduced like the amoeba, without all this temptation and stuff, you'd be rid of ninety percent of the problems of the world."

"Oh, come on, Jesus. I can handle Satan any time. So can you. And as far as sex is concerned, that and survival are the greatest motivators people have. The world can't do without these drives. Think about it, Son, and ask yourself, what's so great about the amoeba? No sex, and where has it got him? Nowhere. His is the most boring, unproductive life in the world. When the day comes you can show me an amoeba doing something useful or simply having a good time, then I might reconsider. Not now."

"All right, but how are you going to change things then? I've been trying to run a tight ship, but it keeps springing leaks."

"That's my fault, Son, not yours. At first I thought a top-down, military structure would be good. The generals give the orders, everybody obeys, and things get done. But what if the general isn't perfect? So far I haven't been able to create a perfect man."

"Hey, how about me?" asked Jesus.

"Well, let's not go into that. I had to get personally involved, mind you. Your image with the Romans was terrible, but that wasn't your fault."

"Touché. So, where do we go from here?"

"We're going to flip things upside down, Son. First we're going to let people learn what's going on. This business of keeping them ignorant and dependent has to end. So how am I going to solve this problem? Behold, Son. In just a few years now a fellow called Gutenberg will invent a gadget that will make knowledge available to everyone. People of all levels will be able to learn enough so as to know when they are being deceived.

"Next I'm going after the Church. They're ruling by fear now, not by competence. Imagine, selling indulgences! So, pay attention: in about forty years a child will be born in Germany who's going to make some big waves when he grows up. Keep your eye on him, Son. His name will be Martin Luther. He'll cause a lot of changes.

"After that we go after governments. This is a different problem. What it needs is new space for people to try something unconventional without stepping on others or getting wiped out in the process. Here's where it's going to happen."

He spun the globe around and placed one hand on North America and the other on South America.

"A lot of people know these lands are here, but because of our friend Cosmas they haven't been able to say so. Now that we're making the earth round again, the Americas can be officially discovered. That will begin with a fellow called Christopher Columbus, in about half a century.

"Right about then," God continued, "just to put your mind at ease, the Moors will be driven out of Spain. We'll give Europe back to the Christians. That will complete the fine job you've been doing these last few centuries. And incidentally, Son, their invasion has not been all bad. They gave Europeans the Arabic numeral system. Now that the Age of Discovery is starting, arithmetic will become important. Can you imagine doing calculations with Roman numerals?"

"That's good planning, Father," Jesus said admiringly. "But tell me something. How did you work it out so that Arabic numerals read from left to right, when their script reads from right to left? That was really fantastic!"

God winked at him.

"Let's say I have my diabolical moments, Son. Mohammed still hasn't forgiven me for that one.

"Soon," God went on, "the Iberian Peninsula will be divided up into two countries, Spain and Portugal. It's important to the whole plan that they be separate, and different. You followed my instructions perfectly in putting the Celtic tribes into the western part of the peninsula, what will become the Portuguese area, and the Visigoths into the Spanish area. That is a key factor. The Celts are gentle souls, some may be stubborn and not too bright, but they don't have a trace of arrogance. The Visigoths are different. They're fighters, they can be mean, and they tend to associate cruelty with manhood.

"These two nations," God continued, "will beget great explorers, great discoverers. They will open up new colonies, particularly," he patted South America, "on this continent.

"Now here's what I'm going to do. I'm going to send the Spaniards to the places where there are already some thriving civilizations—Aztecs, Mayas, Incas and so forth. The Spaniards will fight and conquer the people in these areas and plunder their riches. It will be a cruel process. Later on of course this will all come back to haunt them."

Jesus looked at him balefully. "You're going to plant all these time bombs and then disappear again, so I'll have to deal with the fall-out," he said.

God ignored him and continued, "The Portuguese will have a different destiny. They will go to the eastern and central part of this continent, a vast area where there is nothing but a handful of Indians living at subsistence level. They will start a new country, and it will be called Brazil. Believe it or not, the Pope himself will assign this land to the Portuguese and the others to the Spanish, through a treaty, the Treaty of Tordesilhas. That will be the last thing the Church will do based on a flat earth.

"Now behold, this is what I am going to do. The Portuguese men will go to Brazil without wives and families. They will settle in with the races they encounter, and they will intermarry. Soon they will beget a beautiful new race of gentle and happy people, a mixture of whites from Portugal with the native Indians and blacks from Africa. This will be an extraordinary mixture, by the way, the first time I have mixed white, black and Indian races. Later on I will throw in a bit of the Oriental, just to complete the cocktail.

"And you wanted me to eliminate sex! Listen to me, Son. This is what makes it possible for me to turn Brazil into my first true melting pot. It will be a genetic masterpiece. The result will be a tolerant, creative, musical race of people, with a culture of its own."

God then smiled as he said, "As you know, some of the most important elements in the culture of a nation are its music, its cuisine, its humor and its women. There are few places in the world that have more than one or two of these items. Brazil will be highly endowed in all four."

"It sounds like you're aiming to make a paradise. Aren't you giving a lot of goodies to just one nation?" asked Jesus.

"This is an experiment," God replied, "but I want it to work. It will be the first time I have brought predominantly outsiders into a tropical country. It will probably take several centuries for them to get their act together, but I'm betting that they'll make it work. I've set aside some wonderful resources, the biggest river complex in the world, and an exceptional climate. Plus some extraordinary human talent. Given time, they will become one of the most productive and influential nations on the earth. The technology they develop will not be scientific, it will be in human relations. Brazil will teach the world tolerance and give the world a sense of humor. And it will be by example, it will be imitated, a bottom-up process, and not by imposition.

"Now, Son, you will have to excuse me. I'm going to have to dash off again to my Big Bang. Do you have any questions?"

"Hey, not so fast!" Jesus exclaimed. "I have dozens of questions. For example, you mentioned resources. I understand petroleum will one day be the mightiest resource in the world. If Brazil is going to be so wealthy I suppose it will have a lot of petroleum?"

"No, Brazil will never have all the petroleum it needs. You will see when the time comes how corrupting it is for a country to have such easy wealth. Brazil will get off to a good enough start with gold and sugar, and eventually with agricultural products including the second most important world commodity—coffee. But these are things that require hard work to produce, year after year. The country will have earned what it receives in return."

"Another question," said Jesus. "You keep emphasizing the word 'tolerance', the fact that the Brazilians will be very tolerant people. This could backfire, couldn't it? We've already seen in many countries, particularly in tropical countries where survival is easy, that excessive tolerance leads to corrupt and evil governments. How will Brazil get around this?"

"Good question, Son. The answer is, it won't. I don't see much of a problem with evil, though, for these will be gentle folk, but I do see a problem with corruption. Here's why. The Portuguese culture comes from the Roman empire, still a top-down sort of thing. It will lead to structures where there are lots of rules and regulations, where people have to ask permission to do anything. That's a breeding ground for corruption. The rich can buy their permissions, and the poor cannot. Their tolerance, as you pointed out, will induce them to simply accept this condition. It's going to take a lot of time to correct. You'll just have to deal with this as best you can, to experiment with whatever comes to mind. In the long run what it takes are some things you haven't seen yet: a strong middle class; good education; and a vigorous, independent press. Whenever and wherever you manage to put all these things together, then you can have an effective bottom-up style of government.

"Incidentally," God continued, patting the North American part of the globe, "you will have a lot of good inputs from this hemisphere. That's where I am going to be carrying out a totally different and independent type of experiment, one in the government and economics of free people. I can't overemphasize the fact that the top-down ones just plain don't work. And wait till you see what I'm going to do to get this point across. It's going to be dramatic!"

He rubbed his hands together gleefully.

"You will see the emergence of a giant, top-down monster, a powerful nation, at a moment in history when people all over the world will be desperate. They will have lost confidence and will want someone to take care of them. They will be drawn to this monster, even people in the best of the bottom-up countries. Then, just when everybody thinks this system is unbeatable, all its rotten vices will surface and it will collapse in a spectacular way, like a super nova. And that, my Son, will finish top-downs on earth for a long, long time. To tell the truth, I'm trying to figure out how to avoid them completely in my new universe. They waste too much time. Speaking of which, I really have to run. Any more questions?"

"Yes. How do I contact you if I need you?"

"I'll be in and out, Son, don't worry. But don't you call me. I'll call you."

"Wait a minute, Father. Now the earth is round again, and we'll have exploration, science, philosophy, everything's going to get out of control. Excuse the expression, but all Hell is going to break loose! How do you expect me to keep a lid on it this time?"

"You can handle it. You got through the last millennium just fine. Fact is, now people are going to start learning, and the more people learn, the less they need us. Don't try to control them too much; their independence is a good thing. We'll be around to help when they have tough problems. But you won't have to get involved so much in the day-to-day details any more. You'll be able to concentrate on over-all strategy and crisis management."

"Yeah, yeah, I know, you make it sound like fun and games. I know better. But before you dash off, just one more question about Brazil. That seems to be your special baby. Assuming I can't get in touch with you, how will I know if and when I'm making the grade there?"

"Easy," God replied. "You will have made the grade when Brazil becomes a serious, bottom-up country, when it turns from a nation of passive subjects into a nation of concerned citizens. I'll send you a clear signal when this happens, one you can't miss.

"One day there will be a gadget called the 'radio', through which people can broadcast all sorts of things to the public in their homes. Politicians will discover this and convert it to their own use, especially in Brazil. There they will take one hour of prime time every evening on the radio, all stations, and they will call this '*Hora do Brasil*'. It will be the only thing you can listen to. My signal will be when public opinion prevails, when the politicians finally throw in the towel and convert '*Hora do Brasil*' from compulsory listening on all radio stations into a competitive, optional program. People will then be able to listen to it if they want to, or to something else if they do not.

"When you see this signal, you will know that corruption, evil and misuse of power have been virtually eliminated in Brazil. It will be the last step in the long and tortuous path to maturity. Then, my Son, and only then, will you know that Brazil has passed over the threshold and made the grade for good."

Burglars

by Fulton Boyd

Eduardo had been locked in the bathroom with his wife, daughter and maid for forty-five minutes when one of the burglars knocked on the door and said, "Okay, we're finished. Now we need the *senhora.* Just her. Don't try anything. We have three guns pointing at you."

"What do you want with the *senhora*?" Eduardo shouted through the door, a cold chill running through his chest.

He heard the key turning.

"Back up, back up against the wall, all of you," the voice commanded.

Eduardo herded the females into the far corner of the bathroom and took his position in front of them. It was a large bathroom. There were more than five meters between the corner they were huddled in and the door.

"Okay, we're ready," he shouted. His voice was higher and more quavery than he liked. Luisa, his wife, noticed this and whispered, "Just do what they say, Eduardo. I'll be all right." His daughter and the maid were tongue-tied.

The door flew open. An arm reached in and pressed the door against the wall to be sure no one was behind it. Then Eduardo watched a wild, three pointed head emerge slowly into the room, the extremities first—a beard, a sharp nose, bristling eyebrows, all jutting out from a chiseled face. Just below it a nervous pistol. Bright eyes darted around the bathroom. The pistol aimed quickly at corners, at potential hiding places, then swung around towards Eduardo and the family as the entire burglar materialized. Physically he was small, unthreatening, but the pistol and the blazing eyes sent a warning. He might be crazy or on drugs. Eduardo could make out the other two in the dim light and shadows of the corridor beyond. Their pistols were at ready.

"*Senhora*, please, come with us," said the burglar, gesturing with his pistol.

"What are you going to do with the *senhora*?" Eduardo asked again. His voice had gone a bit higher, quavier.

"We won't hurt her, *senhor*. Don't worry. We just need a ride. It won't take long."

Luisa had already stepped out from behind Eduardo and was starting towards the door. Eduardo grabbed her arm.

"Wait a minute. They're not taking you anywhere."

He turned to the burglar. This might not be as bad as he feared.

"Look, where are you going? I'll go. Don't take her."

"It's already been decided. She will take us to the bus station. You stay here. The *senhora* will be our insurance policy."

"The bus station! What bus station? The nearest one is half an hour from here. My wife doesn't know how to get there. She doesn't drive at night. Please, I'll drive you there. I'll be your insurance policy."

The burglar hesitated.

"Just a moment," he said. He backed out the door, locked it, and went into conference with his comrades.

Luisa was livid. "What do you mean, I don't know my way to the bus station! What do you mean, I don't know how to drive at night! What are they going to think of me? They're going to think I'm helpless."

"It's better if they do. There's no way I'm going to let you go out at night with three desperate men. You stay here and take care of Luisinha and Lourdes. I can handle these men."

"Handle them? How? Look, Eduardo, there are three of them. They all have guns."

"No, I don't mean that. I only have to drive them down to the bus station and that will be that."

Just then the burglar shouted through the door, "Back up, back up, I'm coming in again."

The same man entered. They were still in the far corner.

"You," he pointed the pistol at Eduardo, "you come with us."

Eduardo turned to Luisa.

"Don't worry, my love, I'll be back as soon as I can."

"Please don't resist," she pleaded. "Just come back alive."

Eduardo left the bathroom. The two other burglars backed away, keeping their guns pointed at him, as the bearded one pulled the door shut and locked it.

"Don't worry, *senhora*," he shouted as an afterthought. "He'll be back."

This could be much worse, thought Eduardo. He hadn't relished the idea of being stuck in the bathroom with his daughter and the maid. What if one of them had to... Eduardo could make out the other two burglars in the dim light of the hallway. They looked young, probably about twenty years old. One had a full mustache, neither had a beard, both were unshaven. Eduardo designated the bearded man "Number One", the man with the mustache "Number Two", and the other "Number Three". It occurred to him suddenly that all three of them were as frightened as he was.

Number One was running the show. "Let's get out of here. Zé," he gestured at Number Two, "you go first. Then you," he indicated Eduardo. "We'll keep him covered from behind," he said as Number Two hesitated. "Go on down the stairs, out the door to the garage.

"When we get to the garage," he explained to Eduardo, as they moved down the corridor, "we want to go in the big car, the same one you drove in with. I'll sit in the front seat with you. My friends will sit in back."

"No problem," Eduardo replied. He was feeling calmer now, but it did not occur to him to try any heroics. The ordeal was almost over now. How lucky, he thought, that his fifteen year old son, Miguel, was spending the night at a friend's house. Miguel was into body building. He watched a lot of television and fancied himself a Stallone-type crime buster. If Miguel had been there he would have got them all shot.

They got into the car. The garage door was electric and opened right on to the street. Eduardo had once thought this was the best possible protection against bandits when one was entering or leaving, because it opened and shut so quickly. Yet these three had appeared out of the shadows at the exact moment that he was entering the garage and trotted in alongside the car, guns pointed at him. There was nothing he could have done. Then they had followed him into the house, rounded up his wife and daughter from the living room—just then the maid entered.

Number One, startled, pointed his gun at her and gestured for her to join the herd. He didn't want there to be any surprises.

"Is there anyone else in the house?"

"No, this is everybody", Eduardo had answered.

"Where is your son?"

This had surprised Eduardo. How did they know he had a son?

"He's not here. He's spending the night at a friend's house."

"Are you expecting anyone to drop in?"

"No," Eduardo replied. Number One had looked into the dining room and seen just three places set at the table. He was satisfied.

The burglars then had guided them at gunpoint to the large upstairs bathroom. The only comments from his family had been a wide-eyed "What are they going to do to us?"

from his daughter Luisinha, a terrified whimper from Lourdes, the maid, and a "Damn, we're going to miss a good television program," from his wife.

****

As the garage door closed behind him, Eduardo no longer felt threatened. He decided to strike up a conversation with burglars, keep everybody calm. They had asked where his son was, he suddenly remembered.

"How come you picked my house?" he asked Number One. "You seem to know a lot about us."

Number One was sitting almost sidewise in the seat, his sharp features and the pistol pointing at Eduardo. He seemed less nervous now.

"We did our homework. We know you have a son and a daughter, that you send both of them to an English speaking school. We know that you are going to Disney World next week for vacations. We figured that you would have a lot of cash in the house because of the trip. By the way, we didn't take your traveler's checks, just your cash. It wasn't hard to find. We didn't take any jewelry or anything else."

"How much cash did you take?" asked Eduardo. He didn't remember how much he had.

"All of it. Eighteen thousand dollars. That's six thousand for each of us."

"Damn!" said Eduardo. It was more than he thought. "I needed that money."

"So did we," Number One replied.

"Yeah, I know, this will keep you in drugs for a month or two, then you'll do the same thing to somebody else."

"No, *senhor*. We're not into drugs, none of us. We're working men. Each one of us needed this money for something special."

"Like what—women, a car, something like that?"

"No, *senhor*, nothing like that. Look, we live a long way from here. We're not city people. Zé, here, and his brother, they both work on a big chicken farm. It's the only job they can get. They can't leave town because their mother needs them there. The owner of the farm is the big shot in town. He's a politician and a crook. He knows these boys are stuck there. So he pays them very little.

"Zé and his brother are good workers," Number One went on, "the best on the farm. They know all about how to mix feed, how to manage the chickens and keep them healthy. They deserve a lot more than they're getting."

"So how is six thousand dollars each going to solve their problems?" Eduardo asked.

"The business is the following. They have a chance to become partners in a local feed company. It's just a little thing, but the man who owns it is old and tired. It could be a lot bigger. These feed companies don't need much capital, you know. You just have to work hard and know how to handle your customers, and don't let them get behind on payments. You buy on thirty-sixty-ninety days and sell on fifteen-thirty-fortyfive days, the life of the chicken, so all you really need money for is to keep some inventory."

"How come you know so much about their business. Do you work on the chicken farm too?"

"No, *senhor*. I run a little bar in the town. Zé and his brother stop by. We've gotten to know each other pretty well. This was all my idea, by the way. The only other way they were going to get out of the dead end they were in was to win a lottery ticket, and after they take care of their mother they don't even have money to buy one."

"Why do you need money? You probably do pretty well at the bar."

"More or less. I make out. So I'm going to put half my money in their business, as a silent partner. They need fifteen thousand dollars to buy in."

"Then you'll still have three thousand dollars left over," Eduardo commented. "What are you going to do with that?"

"Yes, *senhor*. I'm going to put that into a savings account. Every month I'm going to take out some of the interest, not all of it, so what's left will keep up with inflation. Every month I will be able to buy a lottery ticket. That way, if I never win anything, I won't have lost anything. But if I win, well, then I'm going to buy my own bar, make it into a nice restaurant too, maybe even into a small hotel. I have a girl friend. We can get married and run the business together."

Eduardo found himself believing Number One. He was even wishing these fellows were all going to succeed.

They were getting near the bus station.

"Look," Eduardo said to all of them, "I don't know how you guys got all this information on me, and I'm not going to ask. You're obviously pretty smart to have planned things the way you did."

Zé spoke up from the back seat. "Raul," he said, indicating Number One, "is the smart one. He put this whole thing together, and it worked, and nobody got hurt. We were scared somebody would get nervous."

"What I wanted to tell you is this," Eduardo went on. "Maybe you know it anyhow. But when you buy into a partnership with the old man, make sure you have control, over fifty percent. Will you have that?"

"Yes, *senhor*. With my three thousand dollars they will have sixty percent," Number One, Raul, replied.

"Good. Now, does the old man have any family?" asked Eduardo.

"Yes, three daughters. All married. None of them or their husbands have any interest in the feed business."

"Then you should try to get some sort of option to buy the rest of his shares. If you're going to make the business grow, and if one day they still have forty percent, they can become a nuisance."

"How can we do that? Maybe they're not interested, but the old man wants to stay in the business. It makes him important in our town."

"Oh, you can fix that," said Eduardo. "I did a deal like this recently, took over control of a family company, something a little bigger than this, and we kept them on the board so they still looked as if they had something to say about management. They didn't of course—they were incompetent—but we are making them look good. They're nice people. And, we have an option to buy them out completely."

"Good idea," said Raul. "We'll have to work something out like that with the old man."

"Look, when we get to the bus station, I'll write out the formula we used. It's simple. I can do it in two minutes. But still you should get a lawyer."

"That'd be great. I hadn't thought about the other forty percent. We'll use a lawyer. There's one in town."

"One other thing," Eduardo went on as they pulled in to the bus station. "If you're selling rations and feed concentrates, you ought to be selling veterinary products and maybe agricultural chemicals to the same market. You should get some other representations. Then you can really grow."

He parked the car. They all got out. Enormous buses were maneuvering about. The noise was deafening.

"Just a minute," shouted Eduardo. "Let me write out the option formula."

He got a tablet out of the dashboard and looked for a hard surface to write on. Zé handed him his own briefcase.

"Hey, wait a minute," said Eduardo. "You can't take this. This is a Pierre Cardin briefcase. It has my initials on it. It cost five hundred dollars. This thing will be much too conspicuous in a small town. Look, I've got an old Varig bag in the trunk. You can use that."

He opened the trunk and took out the Varig bag. Zé didn't argue. He climbed into the back seat and transferred the cash from the briefcase to the Varig bag. Eduardo wrote out the option formula.

He suddenly realized that none of the burglars had a gun.

"Where are your pistols?" he asked.

"We left them in your car. We won't be needing them any more," Raul answered.

"Good God, what am I going to do with them?" Eduardo exclaimed.

"Don't worry, they aren't real. Look, we've got to run. Thanks for everything. You've been great. Please tell the *senhora* we're sorry to have inconvenienced her."

One after another, Number One, Number Two and Number Three gave Eduardo a big *abraço*. Number Three hadn't said a word. He was still trembling. They disappeared into the crowds, carrying the Varig bag.

Eduardo watched them leave. He was going to have to get rid of the toy guns on the way home. He decided he would not describe the conversation, and certainly not the *abraços* at the bus station. After all, what would Luisa think?

The Supreme Elixir

by Fulton Boyd

Both before and after work you should do something stimulating, something that gets your juices flowing and focuses your mind on subjects other than the tribulations of the office. A twice-daily self renewal.

Certain things don't work. Turning on your radio to hear the news, for example, is a no-no; it is too much like a replay of the bad things that go on in the office. Listening to music, on the other hand, is a fine, uplifting tonic as long as the music is not hard rock. Planning a devastating chess move or two ranks high on the charts. A few moments daily spent learning a new language is even better. Physical exercise is one of the best, especially if it is a violent exercise like squash.

The supreme elixir, however, is none of the above. The supreme elixir is the act of driving to and from work in São Paulo traffic. This single act combines many of the best therapies: the fast moving, three dimensional aspects of a sport like squash; the symphony of blaring horns and growling diesels; and the use of a special, highly descriptive language dedicated exclusively to this activity. There is a nice content of strategy and tactics involved, too. The strategy concerns your daily selection of route so as to avoid street fairs, road maintenance projects, and children's schools. The tactics relate to the competitive aspect of driving in São Paulo. These can be tuned up or down to suit your mood—today a strong measure of aggressiveness, tomorrow a compensating dose of courtesy.

It has been observed that some of the world's top multinational executives are bred in Brazil, because they have acquired exceptional skills in managing the unexpected. This harvest of geniuses is attributed to the fast changing business environment in Brazil. What the experts don't realize is that these skills are acquired principally from the executives' exposure to driving in São Paulo traffic on a daily basis.

As you deal with the surprise element of São Paulo traffic there are certain items for which to look out. For example, if the driver in front of you is wearing a hat, beware—he is a farmer from the interior, accustomed to open spaces and unaware of the traffic around him. He is probably lost. His moves will be random, unpredictable.

Another tricky item is the Combi, the van itself. It is dangerous partly because of the way it blocks visibility but mainly because the driver is perched in a higher seat, right in the front of the vehicle. This positioning automatically eliminates the need for caution, and the Combi becomes a menace.

Female drivers are on the hazard list, too. Now, before you females get offended, listen up. Female drivers cover a broad spectrum of competence, and many are far better than their male counterparts. Others, however, see the car as a weapon with which to assert themselves, to compensate for the unkind stings of a male chauvinist society. There are yet other females who are prone to window shop in heavy traffic, and who are likely to slam on the brakes when they see an attractive display. The point is, you have no way of telling which of these creatures is driving ahead of you.

Finally you have the Japanese driver, whose reflexes are tuned to a different rhythm, and whose fine oriental culture disintegrates when he is behind the wheel.

What, you may ask, should you do if all these threats unite and you find yourself behind a Combi driven by a

Japanese woman wearing a hat? The answer is, pull over. Get off the road as fast as you can.

There are frequent moments when you will be stopped in a traffic jam. What then? Under no circumstances can you let your thoughts drift back to your workday. Such a regression is not permissible. On these occasions there is a useful game you can play with yourself: look into your mirror and try figuring out what is going on in the car behind you. You will discover a rich theater, full of drama and variety.

The most frequent fare on this menu is a female twisting to see herself in the rear vision mirror, retouching her hair or lipstick. Next comes the male, same position, smoothing his mustache. These are mundane activities. In terms of interpretive challenge they can be ranked down at the bottom of the list, along with the driver lighting a cigarette or pretending to talk into a cellular telephone.

The fare becomes more interesting as you flip down the screen. You are likely to see:

- a young couple flirting lewdly with each other. That's always exciting to watch. Sometimes you wonder if they're going to make it to the motel before losing control.

- if you're lucky, a large bearded man singing an opera in accompaniment to his radio. Why, you will wonder, is a giant like Pavarotti driving a little Fiat in São Paulo traffic? Don't laugh. Stay with this man if traffic permits, and switch your radio on to Radio Cultura. Soon you will be happily ensconced in a full blown performance of La Traviata.

- a middle-aged couple arguing. This sounds boring, but wait: arguments can be exciting. Take, for example, the case of an angry wife cursing her husband for, let's say, a recent indiscretion or infidelity. Right in the middle of her diatribe the poor fellow has the misfortune to be caught yawning. Furious, she tries to slap him, but her seat belt catches her. For a moment her hands stop gesticulating in order to unfasten the seat belt and complete the assault, but just then the light turns and traffic starts moving. Whether she actually hits him or not is lost in the shuffle. The screen goes blank; the outcome is a mystery. But it is better so. The skit you have just watched will provide grist for the imagination the rest of the day.

- children in the back seat of the car behind you can provide pathos, nausea or wild drama. This brings to mind a series in three parts, at three long stoplights. At the first light the children are raising hell, and both parents simultaneously turn and shout at them. It seems to have worked. At the second light there is no motion at all in the back seat, just two small heads bent over some common project while the parents talk calmly to each other in the front seat. In the third episode smoke is rising in the back seat, between the children. The parents haven't seen it yet. But suddenly they do, and they will pass you wildly on your right side somewhere along the next block, driving as fast as traffic permits, panic on their faces, smoke billowing out of the rear windows.

As you gain experience, what you will really be looking for are scenes like the following:

- two ladies discussing something that amuses them immensely. At first you will bet your boots that it has something to do with a male coming to grief in some illicit adventure, but perhaps this conclusion is too easy. Just then your engine stalls, your mirror stops vibrating, and you can clearly see the sinister look in their eyes as they laugh. You've got it! These innocuous ladies are planning a murder. But wait a minute, why are they laughing? Elementary, my friend. One of them has just come up with an extremely clever way to dispose of the corpse.

- a man explaining something carefully to a youth, who is paying strict attention. How nice, you think. A father taking a son into his confidence, explaining things about his business, and the son is fascinated. Wrong again. They are not father and son, but bank robber and accomplice planning a major heist. Didn't you notice how small and wiry the youth is, how perfectly-sized for slipping through air ducts?

- a man alone in his car arguing a forceful case, with appropriate facial expressions and gestures. Is it something he wished he had said yesterday instead of being such a wimp? No, this man is rehearsing for an upcoming meeting in which he is going to challenge the Chairman of the Board in a proxy fight. He is going to take over control of the company.

- two scruffy men in a shabby car with a ladder tied to its roof. Painters? Plumbers? Electricians? You know better. Look at their furtive eyes. These men are well disguised terrorists, but they can't fool you. They are about to plant a time bomb in a public building.

Two or three days a month you hit real pay dirt. This is the exhilarating moment when a single male, in his early twenties, an intense look on his face, pulls up behind you and starts tailgating. You are on a major thoroughfare. He wants to pass you. You don't want him to. He does not have a BMW or a Porsche, so the playing field is level. The game is on.

You will use the moving traffic ahead and alongside you as pawns in this match. You will observe your adversary switching lanes to race past you, only to have to slam on his brakes as you, with uncanny timing, accelerate, close ranks with the car ahead, and leave him stuck behind a delivery truck in the middle lane.

As traffic patterns change he works his way back, once again on your tail. Now you analyze what's up ahead of you carefully, and when the situation permits, you shift to another lane, letting him pull triumphantly alongside. Then you slowly cruise ahead of him as your lane picks up speed while his doesn't. The car right behind you has caught up, and the car behind it, so your adversary can't duck in. He is stuck in his lane for several blocks.

He won't give up. For a while he may not realize that there is malice in your maneuvers. Assuming he is not a complete idiot, though, soon he will know what he is up against. Then begins war. Faster than you thought possible he will once again be on your tail. If your rear vision mirror is clear enough you will see specks of froth around his mouth.

By now you have time for just one more trick before turning off. Once again, split second timing is of the essence. Speed up if you can, entice him into a dangerous velocity for tailgating, and flick on your parking lights. He sees your tail lights go on and panics, thinking you have stepped on the brakes. He screeches to a stop. You accelerate and run the next light, just turned red. Then you turn off the main drag to your destination. The game is over, and you have won. Your adversary is still back there, pounding on the steering wheel and gnashing his teeth in frustration. Dangerous fellow, that.

Yes, São Paulo traffic is hard to beat. Many people complain about it, but they aren't the real drivers. They perceive the automobile as a means of locomotion to go from point A to point B. While driving they listen to the news, which is depressing. From time to time they look at their watch, which is frustrating. Then they daydream themselves into the left lane when it's time to turn right, or vice versa, and soon they have traffic backed up and honking, which is humiliating. Now, do you think Ford, General Motors and the rest of them manufacture cars just to make you miserable? Never! They spend fortunes to make driving fun. Get out there and enjoy yourself. After all, if you pay that kind of money for a car, you have the right to some satisfaction.

Author of four published novels, a feature film, a London stage play, several television plays and numerous articles, SANDY HUTSON grew up in Los Angeles, lived in Amsterdam for one year and in London for the following ten. After returning to Los Angeles for a period of time, she moved to São Paulo where she has lived with her husband, Luis Cuza, since January, 1992. Currently working on a novel, she teaches Creative Writing, is a contributor to the *São Paulo Village News* and was included in Brazil, Brazilonia.

Edie and Lolita

by Sandy Hutson

"*Lolita la bonita! Chiquita Lolita! Levántate viejo!*," she croaked loudly, drumming her feet repeatedly on his kneecaps.

On the edge of sleep, trying desperately to cling to a magnificent dream of retirement in Valhalla where dozens of nubile maidens fanned his brow and peeled his grapes, Larry Gorman batted at the sheet with eyelids still squeezed shut.

"Die, Lolita," he grumbled conversationally.

"*Yo vivo. Viva Lolita!*" she responded in a monotone.

I give up, he thought wretchedly, peeping hopefully at his world through tiny slitted lids. Unfortunately, the scene never changed. At one end of the room, his wife Isabel trained her eyes on the video screen and together she and Jane Fonda huffed and puffed, jumped and thumped in some sort of morning routine that was supposed to guarantee them twenty year old silhouettes forever. Outside, São Paulo was tuning up for the day with birds verbally jousting and trucks in physical combat. And, in his direct line of vision, marching purposefully up one leg and onto his abdomen, one cold black eye fixed on his nose, was Lolita.

"Dad, where's Lolita?" With a noisy bang, the door was flung open and Edie Gorman, eighteen years old, tanned, leggy and ever enthusiastic, leapt into the room. "Oh, there you are, you naughty old lady."

"La Cucaracha, la cucaracha, ya no puede caminar," Lolita cawed hoarsely in response, *"porque no tiene, porque le falta marijuana a fumar."*

"Isn't she just the most darling pet?" asked Edie as the parrot turned and flew to her shoulder.

Larry sat up abruptly, frowning crossly at the pair and even Isabel paused for one disbelieving instant.

"A parrot that speaks only Spanish after all these years in Brazil is not darling."

"Pendejo," croaked Lolita.

"You should wash out that witch's beak with soap, Edie."

"She didn't mean it, Dad. She just gets homesick sometimes."

"Let's send her back to Venezuela, then, where she can communicate freely," Larry suggested with a nasty grin. Edie stroked Lolita's brilliantly hued head and gave her an affectionate kiss on one feathered cheek.

"That's not funny. Did you get her exit permit yet?"

Larry glanced at the clock, then stared. Eight? Already? My God, he'd never make it. Thrashing his way out of the tangled heap of sheets, pillows and crocheted bed spread, the Chief Executive Officer of São Paulo's largest international marketing firm flopped to the floor and executed three half-hearted and hasty push-ups. From the very beginning he'd been torn between the thrill of getting rid of this disgusting bird, a present he'd impulsively bestowed on his eldest daughter several years ago when the family was briefly posted to Venezuela, and resentment over the difficulties, vast expense and bureaucratic obstacles to be overcome in obtaining permission for Lolita to accompany her mistress to the University of Arizona. It had become something of a life work and, had it not been for Edie's tearful pleas, threats and stormy scenes, he would have given up long ago. Lolita and her plight had somehow become his main occupation.

"Not yet, sweetheart," he grunted. "But we're hot on the trail. Actually, I've got an appointment at nine thirty with João Carvalho at the Instituto Biologico, so shove Lola in her cage while I take a shower."

"Her cage? Why does she need to go?"

"For a physical exam."

Edie's eyebrows pulled together over her hazel eyes and her lips lifted in pain.

"What?"

Larry struggled to his feet and rushed toward the bathroom door.

"Don't even think it. Just get the bird in the cage."

****

"But...where is the psittaciforme?"

"Right here, *Doutor*."

Larry stepped inside the sloppy, miserably unkempt office of *Doutor* João and beckoned Edie, winged pet perched demurely on her shoulder, to follow. The ornithologist frowned at the odd group, his day clearly unsettled.

"He's not in a cage?"

"She. Lolita's a lady. Her home is full of our Christmas ornaments right now," Edie explained with a glorious and winning smile. "She hardly ever uses the cage anyway."

"I see," he responded disapprovingly, stepping forward. Obviously in his opinion there was a place for everything and all things should be in their respective places, which excluded storing Yuletide treasures in a parrot cage. Silently, the humorless scientist peered at Lolita, viewing her from all possible angles without touching so much as a brilliantly hued feather.

"Her wings aren't clipped."

"They will be soon," Larry assured him.

Doutor João took his red and white plastic pen with Residence Inn inscribed on the side and smacked Lolita sharply on the beak a couple of times.

"This parrot looks fine to me," he pronounced, moving away.

"*Pendejo*."

The man paused in his struggle to extricate an official form from an enormous mountain of apparent trash on his desk.

"Spanish?"

"It's her native tongue."

"Pity. I'm going to give her a certificate of good health anyway."

****

"What a jerk."

"Don't be judgmental, Edie. We got what we wanted."

Larry trounced vigorously on the accelerator and swerved away from the curb without glancing once at the heavy São Paulo traffic. Horns blared and brakes screeched but twenty-seven years in Brazil had taught this *gringo* to drive like a native. He squeezed between an aged bus loaded with exhausted workers and a bent and broken truck precariously piled with a towering heap of pineapples. Both side mirrors scraped paint from the other vehicles before Larry raced ahead, his eyes trained on the dashboard clock.

"Today is shot, Edie. Ruined. I've just got time to get to the Minister of Flora and Fauna. If we hurry."

Larry pressed heavily on the gas pedal. Dramatically, his daughter leaned her head against the passenger window, closed her eyes and ruffled Lolita's feathers reassuringly with one finger.

"Flora and Fauna? Surely you jest."

"If you want to take the bird, we follow the rules."

An amazingly short time later, they were seated in the very plush office of Gaetano Andrade, Minister of Flora and Fauna.

"You see, *Senhor* Larry, we can't allow just every bird and animal to be taken from Brazil on the slightest whim. We wouldn't have any wildlife left."

The esteemed minister tapped Larry's business card on his polished, mahogany desk, then studied it carefully. His visitor remembered the mobs of monkeys, alligators, and raccoons that had assaulted their rustic hotel in the jungle last summer vacation and the crowds of parrots, tucans and smaller birds that patrolled noisily overhead. Adjusting his initialed cufflinks, Larry glanced at the Minister and pondered his approach.

"I appreciate the threat of extinction, but this is a special bird, my daughter's companion, as you can see." Father and daughter exchanged affectionate smiles. "Edie's grown up in Venezuela and Brazil and needs the parrot to help her feel at ease and less lonely while she settles into university life in a country she really doesn't know." He extracted a sheaf of signed and stamped official documents from his briefcase and placed them in front of Gaetano. "I think you'll find all the necessary forms are in order."

The Minister's face curved into a patient, puzzled smile signifying difficulty in understanding Larry's fluent but accented Portuguese. He didn't even glance at the papers.

"Yes, of course, but the parrot would also be lonely in such strange surroundings. And my chief concern is the fauna of this country. Flora, too."

"Edie's not keen on exporting any flowers. Just the bird."

Minister Gaetano's eyes strayed back to the card.

"I see you're CEO of IEM do Brazil. Just what is that?"

"Import Export Marketing. We specialize in merchandising national and imported items."

"Yes. I see. You realize that these documents must go to Brasilia for confirmation?"

Larry hadn't had the slightest clue and his heart and fists clenched in frustration. At some point in his life he had to return to work. Earn a living. Pay for Edie's college tuition. Expenses for his other children. Jane Fonda's other videos,

Lolita's meals, Isabel's trips to Miami, the maid's vacation in Bahia, maybe get himself a therapist.

"How long will that take?" he asked pleasantly.

Gaetano shrugged.

"Oh, possibly several months. Who knows?" He smiled as Edie, seated at the far end of the room with Lolita on her shoulder, gasped noisily. Months? His daughter left for Arizona in seventeen days.

"Do you think there might be a way we could work together and solve this problem?"

"Possibly, *Senhor* Larry. Why don't we complete this document and then we'll talk."

Picking up his pen, the minister vigorously shook a form as though dislodging invisible microbes and dust particles, then diligently bent over the printed questions which Larry had answered innumerable times to countless other officials. It could be a questionnaire about a human being, and included the complete name of pet, current residence, owner, age, and a vast amount of trivia. Gravely, *O Senhor* Gaetano progressed through the interrogation, duly noting Larry's thoughtful responses.

"Place of birth?"

"I'm not sure."

The minister looked up, frowning.

"Certainly you must have some idea."

"Of course. Lolita was born in Venezuela in the outskirts of Caracas but precisely where I don't know."

Obviously relieved, *O Senhor* Gaetano tossed his pen onto the desk and stretched back in his leather armchair, allowing himself the luxury of a broad smile.

"But then she's <u>Venezuelan</u>."

Larry and his daughter exchanged guardedly hopeful glances.

"Yes, that's right."

"If she's not Brazilian there's no problem." With an air of beneficence, the minister picked up a number of rubber stamps and his ink pad and began viciously whacking at the permit. "Of course we care a great deal about the fauna of the world but we have <u>authority</u> over only Brazilian. Lolita is free to leave the country."

"*La cucaracha, la cucaracha ya no puede caminar,*" rasped the parrot.

****

"*Lolita la bonita. Chiquita Lolita*".

Why was every morning the same, he wondered. Larry gradually opened his eyes and stared at Jane, Isabel, Lolita and Edie. In the hallway he could hear Jureçe, the maid, herding the younger Gormans out the front door and onto the school bus. Time to break the latest tidings of great joy.

"I've found an airline that will take her."

"That's <u>terrific</u>! Which one?"

"Air Amazonia."

"What?"

"Don't even think it. You and I have to accompany her on this rinky-dink line, a prospect that doesn't thrill me at all. Plus, I'm having to pay for Lolita's own individual seat, distribute tips that would probably settle the national debt and go update my will, activities that shall undoubtedly fill my entire day. Or week. So don't say a word, just get her cage ready for this adventurous voyage. And clip her wings, please."

Bird ensconced on her shoulder, Edie strutted huffily to the door.

"Would <u>you</u> like to have your wings clipped?"

Glancing first at Jane and Isabel, then at Edie and Lolita, Larry tried unsuccessfully to recall the nymphets of his dream.

"Mine were and hers should be."

****

Larry smiled encouragingly at the beautiful, young ticketing agent in her prim, trim, official navy blue uniform.

"That's it, then? We're all set for two adults and a bird?"

"Not quite."

Impatiently, the international marketing mogul checked the time on his burglar-proof, cheap watch with the plastic band and florescent numerals and his smile vanished.

"What?" he snapped.

"Your parrot hasn't been vaccinated."

"No one mentioned it before. Who requires this?"

"Our airline. Amazonia can't take wild creatures unless they've had their shots."

"This is a pet, not a wild creature."

"But it's a parrot, not a dog or cat. So it has to be vaccinated." She shrugged helplessly, her smile captivating.

Drawing his eyebrows together in an ugly frown, Larry unleashed a masterful glare that invariably toppled his adversaries. Undaunted, the clerk began work on her computer.

"We haven't finished," stated Larry, feeling his neck growing damp and hot inside the Egyptian cotton collar.

"Until the bird's vaccinated we have." Another ravishing smile, her dark brown eyes pleading with him for understanding.

Larry leaned over the counter, his voice dropping to a frustrated snarl.

"Where do I have Lolita...vaccinated?"

"At the Instituto Biológico."

"I was just there." His voice rose perceptibly. "That's where I got the Certificate of Good Health."

"You need to go back."

His vision clouded briefly, then Larry reached across the counter and lifted the telephone with one hand, flipping his agenda open with the other. The agent was deeply alarmed.

"This phone isn't for public use," she announced, reaching for the receiver, prepared to physically defend company telecommunications equipment.

Dialing quickly, Larry hunched possessively over the phone.

"I'm not the public. I'm trying to be a customer. Hello, *Doutor* João Carvalho?"

"Yes," responded the male voice.

"*Doutor*, this is Larry Gorman." Silence. "The one with the daughter and parrot?" he prompted desperately.

"Ah yes. *Tudo bem?*"

The appropriate, in fact the only, permissible response to this polite Brazilian greeting is an affirmation of one's well being followed by a smile and a similar question. For the first time in many years, Larry was politically incorrect.

"No," he hissed. "Nothing's all right. Air Amazonia has agreed to fly the parrot but wants you to vaccinate her. Do you know what they're talking about?"

The scientist gave a quiet chuckle. "Yes."

"Well, should I come back with Lolita for the vaccination or is there another way to do this?"

"Unless you want a dead bird you'd better figure out something else. If I give her the shot it'll kill her."

"Kill," Larry repeated quietly, watching the clerk who now bustled efficiently from one computer to another.

"That's right."

"Thank you *Doutor*."

Hanging up, Larry dropped the telephone with an enormous clatter on one of the computer keyboards and barked, "I want to see the manager of this pitiful airline."

"*O Senhor* Geraldo? I'm afraid he..."

"Now. Right now. Immediately. Before we have serious problems here."

After a brief glance at her tormentor, the agent led Larry down a corridor, her hips swaying while her feet moved to an inaudible samba beat. Opening the door to her supervisor's office, she graciously introduced the men, bestowed another luminous smile on each, and withdrew, presumably to her computers.

The two executives exchanged business cards, eyed one another warily, and then sat down on opposite sides of *O Senhor* Geraldo's large desk.

"What can I do for you?" inquired the airline official.

"I understand that my parrot needs to be vaccinated before flying to the States."

"That's right."

"I also discovered that the shot will kill her."

O Senhor Geraldo nodded in sympathy, then shook his head.

"Yes, that's probably true. But maybe we can find a solution."

The word was *"jeitinho"* and it brought an easy, relaxed smile to Larry's terse lips. This was familiar territory. All Brazilians, and others who had spent more than three and one half minutes in the country, knew that anything could be fixed, any difficulty resolved. A *jeitinho* was the Brazilian way.

"You know," he began, "You have a wonderful airline here with all the ingredients for success. But you have something of an image problem."

"Yes?" The manager studied Larry's card, then leaned forward, his forearms on the desk. Larry followed suit.

"The public needs to learn about your product. Every Brazilian should know what a wonderful airline you have...its safety record..." Geraldo's face clouded and Larry hurried on, "...its fine cuisine...." Geraldo looked as though he might burst into tears, "...the friendly staff..." Geraldo angrily lit the wrong end of a filter cigarette as Larry eased back in the armchair. "You might regularly appear on television yourself. Let the public know Amazonia through you."

Geraldo straightened, his face self consciously urbane.

"A kind of star, like in the *novellas* and *Aqui Agora*?"

"Uh...yes. The Board of Directors would be so grateful to you for popularizing the company. Ensuring its success. Who knows the direction their thanks might take?"

"You're right."

"Of course. Marketing is my business."

O Senhor Geraldo stood up, moved around the desk and slipped one arm around his new friend's shoulders.

"What's a parrot shot? We'll make sure the ticket agents know this bird's already been vaccinated."

****

"Welcome to Los Angeles Airport. What's that in the cage?"

"My mother-in-law."

The customs inspector smiled grimly and glanced at Larry's passport again, then stared into his eyes, searching for any trace of dishonesty, drug addiction, intent to commit mayhem, hidden perversions, concealed weapons or elaborate plan to defraud the U.S. government and stash the cash in Switzerland. His scrutiny turned to Edie and he graced her with a small, thin-lipped leer.

"Betcher glad to be back home. See a baseball game and grab some hot dogs and a coke."

"We have those things in Brazil," she announced frostily. Larry placed his foot on hers and pressed down very firmly.

"*Pendejo*," added Lolita. The inspector stared at the pet.

"Hey, the bird talks foreign."

"My daughter's here for college and we have a connecting flight to catch in forty-five minutes," said Larry sternly.

"Not with that bird. He has to be cleared by the USDA and Dell's off 'til Wednesday."

A nerve beside Larry's left eye began to twitch. Was there a chance that the *jeitinho* concept had reached L.A.?

"Well, could we somehow get Dell to come back especially for this inspection?"

"It's fifty bucks extra."

Hope rose. "Fifty's okay," he said easily.

"But not on Sundays, not even for fifty. He lives way down in Diamond Bar and he goes fishing every weekend. You'll have to leave the bird here."

Obviously *jeitinho* hadn't made it this far north.

"Just...leave the bird? By herself until Dell comes back in three days? She needs to eat, you know. Like humans."

"Oh we got plenty of grub. All the stuff I confiscate like bananas and pineapple...you wouldn't believe what people try to smuggle."

He shook his head in disbelief while Larry stared at him blankly. Edie leaned forward and spoke loudly and impatiently.

"How is my parrot going to get from here to Phoenix?"

"Don't be so feisty. Jeez. What airlines you flying?"

"South Inter-Air."

"Just go talk to them. You'll have to buy the bird a coach ticket but they'll take care of her and fly her down on Wednesday just as soon as Dell's made his inspection."

"*Porque no tiene, porque le falta, marijuana a fumar*," sang Lolita lustily.

Edie kicked the bird cage.

****

"Sure everything's okay?" Larry asked anxiously.

"Don't worry, Dad. Lolly and I'll do just great."

"I wish you'd had that bird's wings clipped."

"Tomorrow, first thing. It's a promise."

Larry enveloped his daughter in a massive bear hug, his chest tightening with anxiety and worry over this separation. For a long moment they clung together, then he kissed Edie on the cheek, his face inadvertently grazing the bird perched on her shoulder. Taking a deep breath, he moved across the tiny dormitory room that Edie would soon share with another student.

"Let us know if you need anything."

Taut with an unexpected grief, Larry opened the door to the small, carefully landscaped garden around which the dormitory had been built. As he stepped outside, there was a sudden rush of air and he felt the brush of brilliantly hued feathers as Lolita soared over his right shoulder and sailed upward into the clear sky.

"Dad! Oh, no!" wailed Edie as she dashed into the garden. Stunned, father and daughter watched as the bird skimmed the red tile roof and began a steep ascent.

"*Adios*."

Lolita's faint croak was barely audible. Eyes straining, Larry watched the parrot execute a gradual turn and disappear into the distance. For a long time, neither he nor Edie moved nor spoke, then the girl commented sadly, "At least she's headed south."

****

Clinging to the edge of sleep and the girls of Valhalla, all of whom seemed to resemble Isabel twenty-four years ago when they were married, Larry shifted heavily under the weight of the sheets and crocheted bed spread. Eyes still closed, he frowned, struggling to pinpoint the reason for his uneasiness. Jane and Isabel could be heard firming up together, Jurece was noisily shepherding children down the hallway, Edie had called yesterday to say that, although she hadn't stopped mourning the loss of her pet, she'd pulled herself together and earned all A's and B's in her mid-term exams, and he had been featured in *Veja*, so what was the reason for this apprehension?

He shifted again, startled by the weight of the bedclothes and then unnerved by an unmistakable, persistent drumming on his kneecaps. All traces of sleep vanished as he felt large claws marching up his leg and onto his stomach. Opening his eyes, Larry stared directly at a parrot.

"*Hola! Chiquita Lolita! Lolita la bonita vuelve! Levántate viejo!*" she squawked loudly, strutting forcefully onto his chest. Grinning, Larry twisted his head toward Isabel who had stopped jumping and twisting and stood staring at the bird. Looking back affectionately at the parrot, Larry ruffled her neck feathers.

"Welcome home, Lolita," he whispered.

IVO MARINO FERREIRA, a retired business executive, is a Brazilian from the state of São Paulo. A bilingual Portuguese-English poet and short story writer, he has been published in both languages. Married and the father of two children, he studied engineering and business in the United States and Switzerland. His professional career has included positions in both American and Brazilian companies.

You I Hold In My Arms

by Ivo Marino Ferreira

1. Protection

The Israeli and his wife walked nervously out of the Alitalia plane and barely looked at each other as they joined the passport line. One hour behind schedule, their Boeing 747 had just landed smoothly at Guarulhos International Airport after curving gracefully against São Paulo's morning sky. The couple had never been to Brazil, didn't speak or understand the language, and was definitely somewhat frightened, wondering whether they should have come at all.

Of course they could trust the word of their Israeli connection, whose cousin should be waiting for them outside the gate. Of course they could rely on the successful experience of the other Israeli couple they had personally interviewed. Nevertheless, here, unexpectedly, the responsibility and guilt associated with what they were planning to do in a few hours seemed a lot bigger than back in the village of Binlaat. Behind the avoidance of each other's eyes, lay the fear of facing the coming routine immigration questions about the purpose of their trip and how long they were planning to stay.

How could they answer that when, this very evening, they expected to be aboard a Varig plane back to Rome, with immediate connection to an El Al flight to Tel Aviv? They smiled wryly at the thought that their country's famous military training had failed to toughen their nerves to face calmly these circumstances.

Somehow the man's hand found the woman's and even though it was just as sweaty as hers and his forced smile just as panicky, she felt comforted by his attention and looked back warmly at him.

Their passports stamped, they lost no time at the luggage belt, for they had brought none, and continued quickly to the customs station where he gave her a smile and confidently pressed the random checking button. It buzzed loudly, however, directing them to luggage inspection, luggage consisting of her oversized hand-bag. There, against instructions and without his knowledge, she had brought everything that could reveal their intention. Why had she risked it, she thought, when their contact had made it specifically clear that his Brazilian cousin would provide them with everything they needed?

When the customs inspector asked, "What are these for?" she froze, unable to answer.

"Gifts, ... for friends," he stammered, hoping the questions, "Who are these friends," and "Where do they live?" wouldn't be thrown at them as they certainly would, for tight security reasons, had they been landing in Israel.

Once out of customs, the smile on the friendly face of their contact's cousin relieved most of the tension, but not all. For their minds, now, refused to quit wondering about how many more attacks on their emotions the day still reserved for them.

"We have to rush," the cousin was saying, "your plane was late and it's almost nine o'clock already. Did Julian tell you we have to catch another plane and fly some more to the south of the country? No? I've made the reservations. Did you bring the money? Plus some extra, just in case? Good! Let us exchange just enough currency for the round trip plus incidentals. I'm accompanying you and will gladly answer any questions once we're in the air."

Judge Boaventura was leisurely shaving in front of the large silver-lined Rococo mirror of his own private bathroom. He was happy with the two-bathroom master-suite of his new luxurious apartment. His wife had finally lost any reason to complain at how long he took to complete his morning ablutions. Judge Boaventura liked his wife; he would probably buy her a gift worth one thousand dollars, this evening, coming back from Court. Why not? After all, it would amount to only one third of what he was going to make, totally free of taxes, this very afternoon. Yes, a gift, definitely; maybe that aquamarine brooch? Judge Boaventura smiled contentedly as he carefully shaved around his commanding mustache.

Nurse Doriana worked feverishly this morning. It was already nine o'clock and it bothered her to be running late in her schedule. She was a competent and efficient administrator, the head nurse of one of the town's largest hospitals. It ran an exemplary maternity ward for the needy that included counseling and follow-up services for unwed mothers. As busy as she was, Nurse Doriana took some time out to carefully plan her activities up to two o'clock in the afternoon. By then, with a maximum allowance of fifteen minutes, she had to be totally available to take care of the Israelis. And to make two thousand dollars. Free of taxes.

The healthy-looking blonde young woman was still in bed. Early this evening, if everything went as promised, she would catch a bus to distant Passo Dourado to spend a month with her parents. No need telling them any more than that she was on vacation. She would rest and recover under her mother's care and then come back for another year of call-girl work attending ranchers and rich coffee growers. She planned on taking plenty of presents to her parents. After all, she should be one thousand dollars richer this afternoon.

Nurse Lina was a pietistic Catholic, a fervent devotee of novenas and benedictions. She was also quite a humble and almost illiterate soul. For this reason many people, including Head Nurse Doriana, mistakenly judged her to be not very intelligent. That explained why she had been recruited to be the new day janitor of the nursery ward.

At first, Nurse Lina had refused to believe what embittered ex-janitor Lucenda told her, down at the janitor supply room.

"I know why they are promoting me out of this hospital," the old woman had said. "They suspect I know what they are doing. Thank God they only suspect it, for, were they sure, I don't know what might happen to me. You be careful; that's my advice to you."

Head Nurse Doriana had pointedly warned the new janitor about Lucinda's constant griping. So, more in compassion than curiosity, Nurse Lina had asked why she had to be careful.

"They sell babies in this maternity," was the answer. "The head nurse and the judge at the Children's Court in town, they do it all the time. They sell them to Jews that can't even speak Portuguese. I've seen it with my own eyes! The other nurses are either too afraid to speak or are getting paid to keep their mouths shut. You be careful. Don't let them know you know it."

Nurse Lina was intelligent enough to reason that the involvement of the judge meant that the dealings, though immoral, would be perfectly legal. She also did not consider the babies as being sold. The money involved was probably just expediting the Israelis down the long international line that waited for prime adoption babies from the southern states of Brazil. She remembered hearing something on television about the subject. So, she did not let her mind dwell on most of the information she had just been given. Except for the part about the Jews. How could they put a child in their hands? Jewish people did not believe in Christ! How could the head nurse give them a rejected infant? She had hoped she would never see it happen.

Regardless of her wish, she had now seen it happen enough that she had even learned the routine, could identify the prospective babies, and sense the pick-up date.

Though not exclusively, she found out, the dealings concentrated mostly on male babies, ten to fifteen days old, born to the descendants of German, Eastern European and Italian immigrants, who comprise the major ethnic group of Brazil's southern state's population. The parents to be, at least in this hospital, were mostly Jews, Israeli citizens, occasionally even those with the peculiar hats and dark overcoats. Nurse Lina could recognize them as they waited by the cars outside; she had even seen the head nurse giving them babies to hold.

The knowledge that the infants were being delivered, unprotected, into the hands of non-Christians had so pained Nurse Lina that she had made a decision to do something about it. Except that the opportunity had not come. Being a janitor nurse only, she could not get close to the cribs at her will; besides, she had never found herself alone with the babies to do what she thought she must do. Except today.

She knew it was delivery day, for the baby in Crib 5 had been receiving special attention from the assistant nurse all morning. Also, the taxi with the Israelis was already outside; one of them had even come to the door to ask for the head nurse. Doriana, however, was nowhere to be seen, so the assistant nurse decided to go search for her. When she asked Nurse Lina to watch the babies awhile, Nurse Lina knew her opportunity had arrived. She just had to act quickly.

As soon as the assistant disappeared down the corridor, she took the fifteen-day-old sleeping baby in her arms. As she rushed past three lines of cribs, to the sink with the water tap by the wall, she hoped the child wouldn't wake up crying before she even got started. Upon reaching the sink, she glanced back and ascertained that she was still alone in the nursery.

She turned on the water tap and started lowering her charge into the sink. It was only then she realized that the baby hadn't been given a name yet and she hesitated, for she was sure she had to call his name before continuing. The sound of a distant door told her to act or she wouldn't have time to dry the child, return it to the crib, and still behave as if she had never been close to it.

Suddenly, the thought came to her that she could name the baby herself and, in a flash of inspiration, she knew what name to give him. She held him up and said to him: "I name you: 'You I Hold In My Arms'."

Relaxed now, she went on to give the baby permanent protection against the unchristian Jews, the only protection guaranteed to last for eternity. As she let the cold tap water run over the top of the child's head, she pronounced, with fervor, her Catholic two-thousand-year-old salvation formula:

" 'You I Hold In My Arms', I baptize you in the name of the Father, the Son and the Holy Spirit, Amen."

2. Mara

Nurse Doriana kept the baby tight against her as she walked slowly towards the car. About one third of the way down, she stopped to comment on something to the gardener; then she greeted one of the doctors as he walked by, and showed him the child. She knew the Israelis would be anxious and impatient, but she had to show them who was in charge, regardless of who was paying. She also felt that the minimum she could do for the baby and for his future parents was to accentuate the child's value in their eyes. She had, further, to keep a door open for herself and Judge Boaventura to refuse to grant the adoption in case they considered the couple unfit, this being the limit of the professional responsibility they felt they owed to their charges.

"Senhor Marcos," she said to the cousin as she approached the car, "I have to pick up some papers for the judge to sign. Please take the baby to the court, walk directly to the audience room and wait for me. Tell your friends not to worry if they do not like the child. This one is so special that I can easily place him."

"What is special about him?" the cousin asked.

"The girl had made up her mind that she wanted to be a single mother, so she chose the father very carefully for his looks and intelligence. She told me he is a successful business man."

Mara, the Israeli woman, received the child from the cousin and held him clumsily in her arms just as he started crying. When her husband tried, awkwardly, to rub his middle finger on the baby's nose, she discouraged him with a severe look; they had scared the poor thing enough already. Then she complained about the way the chauffeur started the ride; the baby had responded to the screeching sound of the tires by crying even harder.

She wondered if they had fed him at the nursery, for, if they hadn't, what could she do? Things were definitely not going the way she had thought they would. No wonder. It was clear now that she had thought only about how happy she would be to have a baby, in spite of having lost her uterus to gunfire. Not once had she thought about whether the baby would be happy to have her. This one certainly wasn't.

He was in pain, scared and uncomfortable. She felt she was responsible for his unhappiness and she didn't know what to do. All the silly castles she had built in the air were falling down into nothingness, but their sharp edges pierced her heart as they fell. To make things worse, both her husband and the cousin were staring at her stupidly, as if her past training had qualified her for these circumstances, although it consisted mostly of shooting at terrorists and climbing up walls. Feeling totally unqualified, she, too, started crying.

Through her tears, she asked the child's forgiveness for cheating on him, trying to pose as his mother. She also promised to take him back to the nurses, who knew better than she how to treat him. Not sure at all about what to do, she patted him a little and started humming, poorly, the only Israeli nursery song she remembered. When the baby stopped crying, she felt so happy she hardly heard the enthusiastic shouts of joy uttered by her husband, the cousin, and the taxi driver.

She bent down to thank the little thing for having been good to her and then she saw, as if meant exclusively for her, the flash of a smile going through the baby's face. Was it possible? Had this fifteen-day-old child smiled at her? It was certainly an involuntary muscle contraction. Wait! Another one! This time he seemed to mean it.

Strangely, the warmth started where she least expected that it could: in her lower abdomen, where she didn't have any feminine organs left. From there it crept up quickly through her belly and chest to her head. It felt like sickness but she knew what it was, and her gratitude to the tiny being that had provoked this feeling in her had no limits. She took her husband's hand. He was smiling at them, closing and opening his eyes as if they were smarting.

She bent down to the baby again and for the first time put her lips to his face. She then held him upright, looked at him and saw how beautiful he was. As she felt the warm wave start again, she hugged the child and, barely moving her lips, whispered her first secret to him: " 'You I Hold In My Arms', I love you."

All through the rest of the taxi ride, she watched her anxiety grow, worried should anything come up that would separate her from her son.

3. The Name

As the Varig plane cleared the Brazilian sky and settled on its great-circle course to the Italian capital, Mara's husband, Yussef, felt the weight of their long and tense day and fell asleep, his head cocked towards her and the baby. His wife, on the other hand, kept herself alert, ready to fight with coffee any sneaking sign of fatigue.

At the Court, the judge's requirement that they come back with the baby in one year's time, to be issued the permanent papers, hadn't bothered her the least. She was already developing a liking for her son's country and, besides, she was glad that his country's legislation took this much care of him, for she felt he certainly deserved it.

She had finished cleaning and feeding him one hour ago. He was sleeping now, but seemed irritated that he couldn't quite direct his thumb to his mouth. She was going to help him when the thought occurred to her. With a pinch of impishness in her face, she calmly considered whether it could be termed immoral and she concluded that it couldn't. She also took into account that this baby of hers was making her feel like a young girl again and, as a young girl, she was known for being daring and capricious. Besides, now that she had thought about doing it, she was going ahead with it and repenting later, if at all.

She quickly unbuttoned her blouse and bra, took her right breast out and offered it to the baby who immediately started sucking it, in great peace.

Mara hadn't covered her breast; she wanted to watch. She wouldn't be doing much of this in the future, but the prankster in her was glad she had done it this time.

"What a beautiful baby you have! What is his name?" The solicitous Varig hostess was bending over her.

They hadn't talked about it yet, Yussef and she, but she didn't hesitate. She knew her husband was certain to agree. For Fate and Jewish tradition—that the first grandchild should be named after his grandfather—had conspired to allow their son to be named after another baby that, reasons notwithstanding, had also been abandoned by his mother to be cared for with love, also by a stranger, thousands of years ago.

"Moses," she said proudly. "His name is Moses."

The Factory of Blessed and Sacred Holy Oil

by Ivo Marino Ferreiro

The Factory of Blessed and Sacred Holy Oil did not have that name. In fact, the factory of blessed and sacred holy oil didn't have a name at all. The closest it got to a name was "At Seu Carlão" or "With Seu Carlão" and the closest its employees ever came to expressing where they worked was "With Blessed Oil". So, if you went to my hometown of Aparecida, pilgrimage center of Brazil, and asked my cousin Benjamim the standard western post-introductory questions "Where do you work?" and "What do you do?", you would hear that he worked "at Seu Carlão" and "with blessed oil".

More specifically, as he told me, my cousin worked at the end of the filling line, his responsibility being to glue the labels on the 20ml bottles. That the labels read "Blessed Sacred Holy Oil Burned In The Lamp Of The Altar Of Our Lady Aparecida" and that the cooking oil at the beginning of the line came from 200 liter steel drums didn't seem to bother Benjamim or Seu Carlão at all.

It did bother me, though, so I told my cousin to ask Seu Carlão how it could be that the drums of oil could be filled from the two half-liter lamps at the foot of the image. Instead of complying with my request, Benjamim told his boss that I had asked him to ask the question. The next morning, Seu Carlão came to my father and said I was telling people that he was not an honest man.

Not only did Seu Carlão come from a respected family in town, but he was president of the Sons of Mary Association, he belonged to many charitable societies and he was always one of the first in processions or in the leading of novenas. Therefore, my father concluded that he was an honest man and also that I had been slandering an honest man's name. As my father later told me, Seu Carlão had explained that he made a point of burning some of the oil in a lamp he held in his hand while he prayed at the altar. He never revealed, however, and my father never asked, how he had discovered the scientific laws governing the relationship between blessings and infinite dilutions.

Unfortunately, in those days my father for many reasons was already mad at me, just needing a good excuse to punish me and now, having found one, decided to do it in front of that veritable pillar of righteousness. This demanded a confrontation and, though I wasn't afraid of Seu Carlão, I was afraid of my father.

So, when Father said, "Why have you been telling lies about Senhor Carlos?"

I said, "Seu Carlão, I'm sorry, but it was only because Benjamim said you had many drums of oil that I asked how the lamps could fill them."

Those were war times. Cooking oil was rationed—one liter per family per week—bought with coupons at the municipal school, under strict control of the military authorities. I hadn't made the connection at the time, my only concern being the mathematics of one-half-liter lamps versus 200-liter drums, but the information fell like a bomb and held my father's further recriminations in the air.

"Drums? Where do you get drums of cooking oil, Carlão?" he said, forgetting the pretense of "Senhor Carlos".

"Well, it's like this, you know, it's like...." and a long explanation started which Wisdom whispered in my ear not to stay to hear.

Suspicion of Wealth

by Ivo Marino Ferreira

1. The Banker

Two weeks ago, as my wife and I faced a possible budget deficit, she suggested that we should try to sell a rather heavy gold ring that she inherited from her father. I decided to make a call to a jeweler whose shop was next door to an international bank branch that I had managed years ago. As many people do, in Brazil, he used to call me "Doctor" because I had a university degree. He had been an occasional client of the bank and we had always been mutually courteous although we never developed a friendship. When I called him, I had to mention the bank before he remembered who I was, though I told him I was not in banking any longer. He asked if I could come just after his business hours; he would be glad to weigh the ring, determine its gold content and pay me promptly. We agreed to meet the next day as I had an afternoon business engagement fairly close to his address.

I walked into his shop at six o'clock sharp. He greeted me warmly, showed a last client out, and closed the doors. He then took my ring, excused himself, and went inside to determine its weight and purity. At this moment, someone knocked at the door insistently at the same time that a feminine voice called his name. I told him what was happening and he returned from the back. Happily saying, "Oh, my darling, oh my darling," he opened the door and let in a beautiful smiling woman whom he kissed on the cheeks three times. She was a rather well known stage and television actress to whom the jeweler introduced me as being a director of the international bank. He then said how proud he was that his shop supplied the jewels she wore on all occasions.

I meant to explain that I was not with the bank any longer and had not been a director but, at my first word, she insisted that our host continue attending to me as she could wait a little; after all, she had come in late. He went inside again and I thought I'd better take my eyes off her and hide my embarrassment at her dominating presence. I smiled, turned to the table showcases, and made as if I was looking at the jewels.

She came up behind my right shoulder, let me feel her closeness and the wisp of her perfume at what I'd call the very minimum of the proper distance, and asked, "Is it going to be for a lover?"

I remember thinking that if I answered the question poorly, or let her know that I was not a banker, her disappointment would make me feel more embarrassed than I was already. I took a slow deep breath to gain time, and said, "Why would it be for a lover?"

"Because for a wife you have to give what she likes," she said. "Only for a lover can you give what you'd like to see on her."

I felt that my next sentence would determine whether she would think of me as a man or a mouse, so I took another deep breath and said smiling, "I wouldn't know that, since I do not have a lover. I was just thinking which of these would please a beautiful woman."

She smiled as she breathed, asking for her time out, while inside I shouted, Touché!

She was too smart to walk into the trap, however. "My advice," she said, "is that you get to know this beautiful woman well, and discover what pleases her."

At that moment, I thought that if the jeweler came back right then to pay me, and she discovered that I was selling a ring for its weight in gold, her spite might make her kick me as I crawled out the door. I had to run out, and do it quickly. I called to the jeweler that we could not let the lady wait any longer; she certainly had thousands of demands on her time.

"I will call you tomorrow and come back," I said. Deep inside I prayed that he would not insist for me to stay.

Through the back door, he showed his friendly face, and said, "Any time you wish, Doctor."

I smiled at her, said, "Sorry, I have to go; it was pleasant talking to you," and ran out of there as quickly as I could decently make it.

At home, that evening, I disinterestedly joined my wife as she watched the top-rated TV serial melodrama. When the right scene came up, I said, "Do you know who tried to seduce me today?"

"Who?" she asked.

I touched a spot on the screen three times.

"How come?" she said.

Then, I told her. I did not lie to her, but I didn't tell her the whole truth. I let her think that it had happened because of my good looks.

2. A Prospective Provider

She couldn't wait to get home and call her best friend.

"Myrna," she said, "you can't imagine what happened!"

"Wait!" said the other, "The way you sound, this is going to be good. Let me bring my cup of coffee to the telephone... All right! Now, tell me everything."

"Myrna, do you know the jeweler that I merchandise jewels for? Those I wear on my stage plays and TV serials, and the real ones that I wear at receptions and parties? You must remember him; I took you to his shop once."

"Oh... Sure! The big store at the avenue."

"Exactly! I had to be there today and couldn't make it on time. They had closed already and I had to knock to get in."

"And?"

"And, inside, there was one of these special clients, you know, one of those busy ones who can only come after hours?"

"And?"

"And, Myrna, Myrna, guess!"

"You tell me."

"I think I'm in love!"

"In love? What about Mario?"

"Oh, silly, I don't mean in love that way. Mario is my passion, though sometimes I wish he wasn't. I pay his expenses, you know. But I think I could love this guy enough and treat him very specially. Oh, it would be a change from the last two, you know, both rude and loud mouthed, the last one a miser always wanting to show me off. No! This one is a banker. A doctor banker! And intelligent. And smiling all the time. You should see the jewels he was looking at! I bet they were for a lover."

"How come?"

"Oh, and he is also charmingly shy! He couldn't take his eyes off me, you know. He tried not to show it, but his face went red! He couldn't hide that he was impressed with me."

"What about this lover of his?"

"Well, that was interesting," she said, as she explained that, before the jeweler could show some of the pieces he kept inside—"You know, where he keeps the really expensive ones?"—the banker had given an excuse and left in a hurry. "And I know why. He didn't want me to see the pieces and recognize them later on some socialite's neck."

"What are your chances?" asked the other.

"Oh, they are excellent. I know he liked me. After all, I am beautiful, alive, sensual, filled with fire! And he is such an educated man, you know."

She had decided to play it coyly, so she hadn't asked the jeweler any questions. The banker knew her name and she was sure he would call. If he didn't, she would casually drop his name around; she had friends; they could arrange a chance meeting.

"Well, bye, bye, for now," she had to go to a party. As she lowered the telephone, she thought that she was getting a bit tired of just modeling the shop's necklaces and earrings and rings and brooches.

LEE CARVER has made a career of being an ex-pat wife and mother in five foreign countries. Now an empty-nester, she recently published a humorous anecdotal book about the ex-pat experience entitled Did I Just Kiss the Waiter?, and has several short stories and magazine articles in print.

A Ph.D. drop-out in biochemistry, she can now slaughter nine languages and is currently dragging her feet into yet another area of the world. In her spare time, she tries to help others in making the international adjustment, plays golf and sacred music, and is working on a collection of short stories set in the American southland.

The Inconvenience

by Lee Carver

"Look, the reason I called was to ask if you can get me the name of a good abortionist," said Patricia. "I'm about three months pregnant and I just can't handle this."

"Well, I don't know, abortion isn't legal in Brazil," I stalled.

"Yes, but you must know someone who does them. Women have them here all the time."

"I do have a couple of friends who have had abortions, but are you sure you want to do this?"

"I never wanted more than two children. I mean, a new baby is just not what my life is about right now. The thought of going back through diapers and kindergarten after Sarah and Stevie are in school....It's just too awful." Patricia now sounded rattled and on the verge of tears. She was experiencing a typically emotional pregnancy.

"I could call around and see what people say. I'll get back to you when I know something," I said, less than happy at the prospect.

"Thanks. I knew you could help me. You know everything in this city. Bye. Gotta run." Thus the weight of her problem had been shifted deftly to my shoulders in three minutes or less.

My father had come to Brazil as a businessman from England before he and Mother were married, so I had dual English and Brazilian citizenship. As such, I had made and lost hundreds of friends as families moved in for a few years and then moved on. They needed support in the daunting city of São Paulo as much as I needed contact with the outside. But I also had my forever friends, the ones for whom São Paulo was home. I started calling.

When the same doctor's name popped up three times, I rang Patricia again.

"That's great. That's super. Can you call him and make an appointment for me?" she asked.

"You want me to make an appointment for you to have an abortion?" I was incredulous.

"I can't speak enough Portuguese. Not even in person, and it's harder by phone."

"Sure, I can make the call, but when do you want it done?"

"As soon as possible. As soon as he can take me," she answered. Did this sound like she was scheduling a haircut? I got a few details, made the appointment, and rang her back the same afternoon.

"Okay, you're on for next Tuesday. If you decide to cancel or need to talk to his office, here's the number..."

"I'm not going to cancel. Thank you, thank you, thank you. You're a life saver."

Somehow that comment went against the grain, but I let it pass.

The next day, a fantastic floral arrangement of tiger lilies, orchids, and antheridia arrived from Patricia. Every glorious color of the tropics was included. I was her dearest friend, the card said. But when my husband asked what they were for, I ducked by saying simply that I had done a favor for a new acquaintance.

"Patricia, this is Laura," I said by phone that evening. "Thank you for the gorgeous flowers. They will be sensational for the company dinner we're doing tomorrow night."

"What great timing," she said. "Look, Laura, I need to ask you one more favor. Would it be possible for you to go over there with me Tuesday?"

"To the clinic?"

"Yes, I know I should have been studying Portuguese more, but cram as I may, I won't be proficient enough to do this alone by Tuesday. Besides, I need someone with me and my husband will be in Buenos Aires next week. It won't take long. Please say you'll come. There's no one else I can ask."

So I agreed, got a substitute for tennis, and picked her up in my car at eight o'clock Tuesday morning. How do I let myself get drawn into these situations?

The clinic was like any other doctor's office in most respects. There was a small front reception area, but we were shown into a larger, somewhat more comfortable waiting room. A Brazilian man sat silently, nervously, on a dark plastic sofa. He was hunkered over his cigarette as if it were a drug that he desperately needed.

Soon a coarse faced, heavy nurse brought out his wife. The patient walked clumsily, leaning a bit on the nurse, but she looked more relieved than pained. The couple left together, and the nurse in the nearly-white uniform turned to us. It was obviously Patricia's turn.

Patricia stood with a breezy, "Well, here we go." The nurse's smile came close to a sneer.

I went back with them to an examination room for a little question and answer session. After a simple blood pressure and stethoscope routine was performed, I translated the instructions for Patricia to undress and mount the table in the next room. To my intense relief, I was told to go wait in the front room.

I sat, urging my watch to move faster. What if something went wrong? Could I be sued? What if Patricia got AIDS having the abortion like a certain friend-of-a-friend two years ago? I had stopped smoking some five years before, but this was the worst I had ever wanted a cigarette in my life. Maybe the receptionist had one. Perhaps there was a magazine stand on the corner that had cigarettes. No, don't put your foot in that trap again, I thought. Get out the novel you brought.

Trying to read, I was unable to keep the plot going from paragraph to paragraph. A torrid love scene held my attention for a few minutes, but I began to wonder if the protagonist was going to get pregnant. Would she be presenting herself at a clinic like this in about fifty pages?

How long had I been waiting? How long would it take?

And then the nightmare happened, the thing that I shall never forget as long as I live. That hideous nurse tromped out to the waiting room with something bloody on a piece of plastic, held out to me in both hands.

"Look, it was a little boy," she said.

I had heard of the family of surgical patients being shown an appendix or some such, but never this. My eyes locked onto the fetus in horror and fascination. Even with his dead blue color and the torn arm and side, he was the most precious thing I had ever seen.

I knew, with a stunning clarity, that this was not an inconvenience. This was a baby.

A Simple Plan

by Lee Carver

"You just got a boarding pass for this flight to São Paulo, didn't you? Look, they're overbooked and I've got to get out tonight. I'll trade you my ticket for tomorrow night and five hundred dollars for your boarding pass."

David Simmons shifted his backpack and tried to size up the prosperous-looking businessman making him the desperate offer. There was no problem delaying his flight out of Miami, but was it legal? Why would someone be in that big a hurry? David's hesitation netted him a higher offer.

"Okay, a thousand dollars, in cash. Here, see? A thousand dollars and my ticket for tomorrow night for your ticket and boarding pass tonight. I've got a business deal that's going to crash if I don't get there tomorrow morning. What do you say?"

Thinking fast, David realized the deal wouldn't work for him. "The airline clerk just checked my passport and visa against my ticket. If I try to fly on your ticket tomorrow night, I'll probably get arrested for stealing it."

"All right, what are you flying? Coach? That's maybe twelve hundred dollars round trip? I'll give you twenty-two hundred cash. You buy your own ticket for tomorrow, and give me this one."

"What about the bags I just checked?" countered David.

"No sweat. They'll be waiting for you at the airport. Tell you what: get back in line and check in my two bags, too. It'll be extra, but it doesn't matter. I'll pay for it. Then I'll pick up mine in Brazil, and leave yours at the baggage claim. Okay? Sound good?"

It sounded about like in-state tuition plus books for one of his last two semesters at the University of Texas. If he could get a decent summer job in Brazil, he could graduate on schedule after all. That, simply stated, was his plan for the summer. "Done!"

David grabbed the handles of the heavy, real leather suitcases. "Say, what's your name?"

"My name? Tom. Uh, Small. Tom Small. I'll just wait right here for the other two ticket stubs. Don't worry. You won't regret this."

David got in line and checked in Mr. Small's two suitcases, tagging them with his own name, thinking that "Small" was an ironic name for a man who stood at least six feet two and acted as if he were accustomed to having people agree with him.

Returning with the baggage claim stubs stapled into the ticket folder, David noticed Mr. Small's good suit and perfect grooming. He's not going to like my tourist class seat, he thought. David gave the round trip ticket folder with boarding pass and the latter two suitcase stubs to Mr. Small. The two men shook hands, both smiling at having gotten the better deal, and wished each other good flights.

Okay, what do I do now? thought David. Lucky I've got my backpack with a change of underwear and stuff. And I'm in my favorite jeans and knit shirt. Glad I don't have to travel in a suit and tie. Oh, yeah. I need a ticket for tomorrow. It wouldn't be a good idea to get back in the same line. Mom and Dad always want me to fly on a U.S. airline, but I've got all this money from Mr. Small. Maybe I could save another couple of hundred.

From the beginning of the evening's encounter, his father's favorite maxim had played through his head like a broken tape: "Make a simple plan and stick to it." But he pivoted from his father's choice airline and went to the VASP Airline counter.

Asking first if there might be a seat available that night, he was put on the stand-by list. Two hours later, he was given a ticket for the flight arriving in São Paulo soon after he had planned. On the way to passport control, he had just a minute to do the first wise thing of the evening: find an automated teller machine and deposit the surplus cash into his savings account.

Meanwhile, George Mastroni (a.k.a. Tom Small) breezed through the security line and sat anxiously smoking down a pack of cigarettes, eyes scanning the crowd. The boarding call was made, and then followed by a request that passengers have their passports available. Two stewardesses were tearing off boarding pass stubs. The passengers entered the tube to the plane door, and someone inside was looking at the passport but apparently was not comparing the name with the ticket. It was going to work.

Once on the plane, Mastroni folded his suit coat, wedged his body into the tourist seat with knees touching the seat in front, and put his briefcase under his feet. In two minutes he was either asleep or putting on a very good act.

Back in the Miami departure lounge, David Simmons found the telephone number of Kirk, the friend with whom he would be staying in São Paulo. They had been buddies since their fathers both were posted to the Portuguese Embassy. He made a quick call and gave Kirk the changed flight details. Then he pulled out his Fala Brasil book and settled down to study the language and wait. Soon he was chatting with other young travelers, using the Portuguese of Portugal. Their names had lots of vowels to roll around, like João, Paulo, and Aparecida. This was fun, being the center of a circle of people teaching him just the right way to say the current Brazilian buzz words, like *"otimo"* and *"legal"*. The camaraderie continued onto the plane and sporadically throughout the night flight.

By the time David arrived in São Paulo, he had some casual invitations to visit the new friends in Rio de Janeiro. They had given him a quick Brasil 101 course, and he now knew he could at least get some English teaching and translating jobs. Without a work permit and on a visitor's visa, that might be the limit. Nevertheless, it was going to be a great summer/winter.

George Mastroni stirred and tossed restlessly. He had hoped he would not have to go to the tiny toilet during the flight, because it would be too obvious if he took his briefcase with him. He couldn't wait. Nearly all the passengers were asleep anyway. He pushed the briefcase well under his seat, stepped high over the snoring man to his side, and made his way to the rear toilets.

The only person who noticed him was the sleepy fellow standing in the back space with a plastic cup of bourbon or something. As Mastroni entered the cubicle, the fellow stumbled drunkenly and sloshed the smelly liquid on the back of Mastroni's shirt. Mastroni cursed. The guy apologized and shuffled unsteadily down the aisle.

The fast and deadly solution of concentrated nicotine, made from old cigarette butts, was absorbed directly through Mastroni's skin. He was dead for an hour before the steward unlocked the door. *Another heart attack victim,* he thought. *Well, let the ground crew find him. It takes hours to fill out the forms when a passenger dies.* The steward put up an "out of order" sign and started preparing breakfast.

As soon as he felt sure that Mastroni was not going to get out of the restroom, Roberto de Sousa left his seat again and retrieved Mastroni's briefcase from beneath the seat. Breaking into the combination lock inside the restroom, he found the first twenty counterfeit Eurodollar bearer bonds of the thousand he hoped to eventually get. They were well printed. It would be easy to pass these off as the real thing.

Mastroni's passport in the name of Thomas Small was in the briefcase, but so was a set of tickets printed as David

Simmons. Roberto took the baggage stubs and left the broken case behind the last row of seats.

Claiming Mastroni's luggage and getting it through customs was the risky part. Roberto had to believe that the rest of the bearer bonds were well concealed in a false bottom, but it was hard to look bored when his heart rate was so high. He didn't know what the bags would look like, so he had to unobtrusively check all the tags of suitcases not being claimed by other passengers. Possibly the greater risk was in picking up the other two bags Roberto had also noticed were tagged to David Simmons. No one was checking the baggage stubs, so he could have walked out with any number.

Roberto attached himself to a large Brazilian family and walked past the customs area without being directed to enter and open the bags. His nondescript appearance and worn clothing were carefully cultivated professional assets. No sweat. He was through the crowd and into a taxi in no time.

Taking a room in a lover's motel on the Dutra Highway, the anxious murderer rummaged and then ripped through the con man's leather suitcases. His activity produced only 480 more bearer bonds, and panic gripped his heart. Okay, so that's why he had the other two suitcases, Roberto thought. A thousand bonds are too bulky to conceal. He turned on the rumbling window air conditioner, poured himself a scotch from his duty free liquor, and sat on the bed of the musty, sweat-smelling room.

Roberto broke open the other two suitcases and was soon swearing in fury. There was nothing here but the clothing of a much smaller man of modest means: tee shirts, jeans, and worn out underwear!

He destroyed the simple cases and came up with nothing better than a letter from a guy named Kirk who lived in the Higienópolis neighborhood of São Paulo. The scrawled English indicated that David Simmons was going to be staying with Kirk Norton. So that must be the contact: this David Simmons, a smaller and probably younger guy, had the other five hundred bonds and was going to be passing them off to Kirk Norton.

Taking a camera and a few other items from the leather bags but only the letter from the second two suitcases, Roberto neatly stacked the 500 bonds in a black plastic bag. The rest he left for the room maid, who would not enter before his pre-paid hours were up. There would be no police, no questions.

His partner met him in front of the *churrascaria* next door, and they were already driving before Roberto gave him the news.

"So we have to stake out this address in Higienópolis and find out where the other five hundred are. What I can't understand is who else is in on this. I thought we were the only ones besides Mastroni's group who even knew about the bonds coming in."

"Yeah, right. The deal that couldn't go wrong," retorted Oscar.

Things got very complicated for David Simmons after he arrived on the VASP flight. Kirk met him, and they went together to the American terminal to get David's bags. David had already realized that he couldn't enter the baggage area, so he had decided to present the two stubs to an airline employee and process a lost baggage claim. Then, when the bags were discovered in the terminal, he could just act as if he hadn't seen them in the baggage claim area and proceed more or less as usual. What he didn't expect was for the airline employee to call security, who told David that, lamentably, David Simmons had died on the flight. David was taken for questioning by a completely unnecessary number of security police, while Kirk slipped away to call his father at the Consulate.

Kirk's father and the Consulate legal officer arrived as soon as possible, which was not soon enough for the weary and stale young man. "Is it illegal to trade boarding passes? I mean, he goes, 'Here's a thousand dollars and enough to get a new ticket.' I didn't give him my passport or anything."

"Did you then travel under his name?" the lawyer wanted to know.

"No, I just got a standby ticket with a different airline and came on without luggage. Because, like, my luggage was already checked the first time before the guy offered me the deal."

"I don't think you've broken any laws, but the first airline isn't going to love you any more," the lawyer wisecracked.

David commented about the many times an overbooked airline had made offers for volunteers to wait until the next flight in exchange for passes or money. He had just agreed to do the same on a private basis.

The lawyer continued, "FAA might have something to say about it, but I think we can proceed with getting you out of the airport."

Whatever the airport security and military police knew about Tom Small / George Mastroni, they weren't telling David. He knew he was being watched and sometimes followed, but he had nothing to hide.

Eventually, he had a much more positive attitude. "I was hoping to have a great summer and maybe come back with a thousand dollars saved for next semester," he told Kirk. "I'm already a thousand two hundred ahead, so let's have a great summer! (Or winter.)"

Kirk's family took them all to the American Society Fourth of July celebration at Chapel School. They ate hot dogs and apple pie and played American sports on this midwinter day with hundreds of displaced Americans plus David's Brazilian shadow.

"I can't believe you, David!" exclaimed Kirk later. "You're on the court with the basketball, with your access to the net blocked, and you shoot the ball to the guy on the sidelines who's tailing you. You shoulda seen the look on his face."

"Well, I know he's there. His eyes are always on me. I can feel it. I just wanted him to know I knew he was there."

Having done the family scene, David and Kirk got permission to take a bus to Rio de Janeiro for a few days. Upon arriving, David immediately called Aparecida and the rest of the bunch he had met in the VASP departure lounge in Miami.

It was much too cold for swimming, but never too cold to be on Copacabana Beach in a string bikini. What a place! His new friends howled with laughter and pointed at his conservative bathing suit borrowed from Kirk. Then they got down to some serious beach volley ball and worked up a sweat. The shadow posted himself at the drink stand and had a few beers.

Interesting, thought David. A cop doing a stake-out in the U.S. wouldn't be drinking beer on duty in a public place. But hey, this is Brazil.

That night David and Kirk left the hotel to meet their new friends for *feijoada* at a little place that had a good samba band. The first time David went to the men's room, Roberto's partner Oscar followed him in and blocked the doorway. "Enough of this. I want the bonds. What kind of deal are you trying?" he said.

"Bonds? What bonds?"

"Look, we've wasted enough time. Maybe you don't realize how serious this is. If you've got a proposal, let's quit playing around. Where are they and what do you want?"

João and Paulo, two of his new buddies, came into the men's room. They saw that some kind of scene was underway, and pushed the man aside with the door.

"I'll get back to you," said David to the threatening man. Hoping to get more information, he asked, "What's your number?"

"Humpf. I know where you are." And he left.

David, Kirk, João and Paulo finished up the night at Aparecida's family's apartment overlooking the beach. The fun and dancing were over, and David was still being watched. He was getting worried.

The group started brain-storming the situation. "But what kind of bonds would have value if they were stolen?" asked Kirk. "Bonds have someone's name on them, right? So nobody else could cash them in."

"Not bearer bonds. Bearer bonds are paid to the bearer—anybody who has them," said David, softly. He was thinking out loud, and trying to remember what the professor had said in his international finance course. "So they're stolen bonds, or maybe counterfeit. They could be sold to legitimate investors. We're talking big money here."

"Enough to get Tom Small killed," added Paulo. "Let's say he was bringing in some bearer bonds from the U.S., or maybe Europe. Someone finds out and kills him for the bonds. They get his suitcases and yours, too, but either they don't find the bonds or don't find all of them. They're coming after you, my friend."

"What do bearer bonds look like? How many can you hide in a suitcase?" asked Aparecida.

All eyes turned back to David, the resident expert on bearer bonds. "Well, I think they're like, you know, a heavy printed official-looking paper in an envelope. Sort of like a thick letter. If there were a lot, you'd have to split the batch up to hide them in suitcases, or maybe make more than one trip."

Kirk was tired, and David was exhausted. Kirk suggested that they call his dad after daylight to pass on the bond idea, but they needed to get back to a safer setting. "This is all right in the movies, man, but I don't want to die for some stupid bonds."

"Volley ball tomorrow on the beach? One more time before you go," Aparecida said specifically to David.

"Yeah, we're taking the overnight bus. Kirk's taking me up to see the Christ statue tomorrow morning—in a few hours—and we'll meet you guys on the beach after that. Same beach as before? About three."

David wasn't so relaxed about being followed anymore. It was clear since last night that not all the shadows were police. He and Kirk were followed to the hotel, then to the Christ statue on Mount Corcovado the next morning. They stayed away from public men's rooms.

They were sitting on the sand waiting for the rest of the group when the rough guy from the men's room appeared again. He stood with his back to the sun so David and Kirk were squinting up at his face. His right hand was in his pocket, and it might have been closed around a small gun. "Let's talk about the bonds," he said. "What are you trying to pull?"

David was trying to evaluate whether he should fake knowledge about them in order to get away, or would the simple truth work? No, he's got nothing to gain by believing me, and probably nowhere else to look for them, thought David. Then he saw João and Paulo walking up behind the man. They realized another confrontation was happening and backed off.

David and Kirk started making up lines as if they had a script. "Yeah, like, we think we know where they are...." started David...

"...where Small stashed them...."

"...on his first trip," they said alternately, bouncing ideas between them.

"His first trip?" asked the big shadow in the sun.

"He couldn't bring them all in at once..."

"...they were too bulky to get them all in on one trip, you know..."

"...so he had to bring some and go back," concluded Kirk.

"You mean the first five hundred were already in Brazil before he got killed?" Oscar was confused, thinking about dates and flights; but where would "Small" have left them?

David and Kirk were quickly deducing that "first five hundred" probably meant there were a thousand total, a neat number to counterfeit, and that Tom Small had not had a heart attack on the plane. They needed to lose this man.

João, Paulo, Aparecida, and a bicycle beach policeman came barreling up behind Oscar, who spun and ran for the sidewalk. Thinking fast, David threw the volleyball with all his might, hitting Oscar in the head. Stunned, he wobbled a bit. Kirk dove in with an American football tackle and the tee-shirted beach policeman whipped on the handcuffs. A police car screamed up with its siren on full, and the South American market in counterfeit Eurodollar bearer bonds silently began to crash.

There was much laughing and shouting in the group celebration that night as the capture scene was told and retold from each angle. Everyone was a hero. Kirk said that David should change his major and become a spy or international crime investigator.

"No, man," countered David. "I'm going to finish my economics degree and apply for a job in diplomatic service, just like my dad."

"Economics and diplomatic service? That's boring!" protested Kirk. "Come on, you could be America's answer to James Bond. You could..."

"I could make a simple plan and stick to it. Just don't ever tell Dad I said that."

Living in Brazil for fourteen years, NADJA VENEZIAN is a native New Yorker. A graduate in Psychology from Lycoming College in Pennsylvania, Nadja got the better part of her education in the seventies. In those freewheeling years, she hitchhiked throughout the United States, spent a year skiing in Colorado and for several years was a door-to-door salesperson in San Francisco.

Now in São Paulo with her husband and two children, she loves to travel and play ragtime music on the piano. She is currently working on a surrealistic novel.

The Ranch

by Nadja Venezian

Driving through the blaring sights and sounds of the city, Louise frequently remembered the still dark nights on the ranch when time seemed to take on another dimension. "Reach up," she would say to her tiny daughter, Jessie, as they stood in the damp grass looking up at the sky. "Reach up. Try to grab a star."

It took Louise a long time to explain to Jessie why the ranch had been sold. Jessie was attached to that piece of land almost as much as her Brazilian grandmother, Claudia, who had grown up there and who dropped into a deep depression after she signed the papers that finalized the deal. In Louise's tiny São Paulo apartment, Claudia and Jessie would sit together reminiscing while they gazed out through the windows at the cloudy concrete landscape.

The last time the family went to the ranch was for Jessie's eighth birthday. The party was complete with friends and relatives, a big cake, dozens of balloons, and a tugging nostalgic feeling that they would never again set foot on that land. By evening the pool seemed alive with rainbow-hued balloons. The young children swam late into the night while the older people looked on and Louise frantically took pictures as if she could capture that moment forever.

The party was embarrassing for Dona Claudia, whose brother and sisters owned land nearby and took it as a sign of failure that the farm was to be sold.

A week before the party, Louise, her Brazilian husband, Carlos and their two children arrived at the ranch after dusk, numb from the eight hour journey. Turning off the highway, the car jolted as they passed under the wooden entrance and on to the potholed dirt road that was part of the ranch. It was about a half mile drive to the farmhouse and Carlos made a point of driving this last long stretch very slowly. Tall grass brushed against the side of the car and the headlights caught moths and reflected against the eyes of cows resting on the road.

"This is it, isn't it?" Louise said glancing sideways at her husband. "This is the last time we're coming here."

Carlos slowed the car almost to a standstill, turned and looked at his wife. "What do you mean by that? Are you glad? Relieved that you'll never have to come here again?"

"I don't know. I guess I have mixed feelings." Louise answered, ignoring the hurt and the hostility in his voice. She looked at her children that were sprawled out over the back seat sleeping. She shook her head sadly. "I feel bad for the kids. Living in the city like we do, they'll miss this place so much. but this is probably harder on your mom than anyone else. She loves this place. She feels more at home here than in her apartment in São Paulo."

"Yeah, I know, but I can't keep supporting the ranch any more. I don't know what my father and brother do with the money but between them they're running this ranch into the ground. The interest rates don't help either. We are paying the bank back double what we borrowed to plant the coffee. This farm could be making a fortune but we're dirt poor."

The grandparents were outside the house waiting to greet them and their huge dog ran circles around the car. Kisses and hugs were exchanged and smiles were forced. The children ran into the house to the room that they usually shared to make sure that nothing had changed.

Louise walked into the house alone feeling forever the outsider. She sat down on the couch in the darkness of the living room and overheard the conversation between her husband and his parents outside.

"I wanted to leave this land to my grandchildren," Claudia was saying. "I wanted this land to stay in the family."

Louise grimaced. It seemed to her that ownership and any sense of belonging to the farm was the right of her husband's family and then bypassing her, passed directly to her children. It hurt her and at times like these she felt like an intruder. It probably didn't help being a foreigner either. Maybe there were some subtleties of the language that were still lost on her, but she doubted it. The language was a problem the first few years. Yet after that, when she became fluent in Portuguese, she used it as a barrier, continuing to speak English with her husband and children as if in doing that she could claim a space that was still hers.

Carlos and his parents had walked into the grass and were looking up at the sky. But within moments the conversation, outside the window where she was sitting, resumed. It had turned to money and Louise, resentful of checks that she had seen her husband give his father, got up and went to look for her children.

Dinner was tense that night. Carlos, who couldn't support indecision, snapped at his mother. Claudia looked around the table as she served a supper of chicken soup. She looked worn and tired; all of this was too much for her. The pink flowered shirt that she was wearing contrasted horribly with the gray pallor of her face.

Jessie looked at her grandmother intently, unaware of the pregnant silence at the table. "I want to have my birthday here next year, too. I love coming here."

Claudia looked at her granddaughter and blinked her eyes tightly, shaking her head. "I don't want to sell the farm. There still must be something that we can do so we can keep it." She looked at her husband and her son but they both avoided her eyes. Tears filled her eyes and she retreated to the kitchen, questioning the values that she had instilled in her son. She emerged shortly afterwards, carrying a tray of food as if to excuse her absence. Her eyes were red.

The TV hummed throughout dinner, playing out other people's problems on the evening soap opera. The kids curled up on the couch in their pajamas and, after their beds were checked for spiders, they went to sleep. The slatted shutters closed, the windows open for air, the scent of night flowers seeped into the house.

The following morning, as she was lying in the hammock after breakfast looking out over the vast expanse of pasture, Louise thought how much she would rather be at the beach. They rarely went to the beach because of the farm and the obligations that it entailed. Closing her eyes she remembered the lavender of the sea when it reflected the setting sun and the sensation of her feet sinking into the sand as foamy waves broke around her ankles.

She liked the farm, greatly appreciated its beauty and knew that it meant a lot to her husband's family, but she had been in Brazil for eight years and hadn't really seen anything of the country except the farm and the road leading there.

Dona Claudia pulled up a chair next to where Louise was stretched out in the hammock; close enough to talk but not too close so as to be intruding. She had a large bowl and a big papaya which she began cutting into pieces to make a sweet dessert.

Even with her eyes still closed, Louise knew that her mother-in-law was there but she waited a few moments before she turned and looked at her.

"If I sold my apartment in São Paulo", Dona Claudia began, "we could keep the farm. I don't know why Pedro is so attached to his law office in Sao Paulo. He never brings any money home."

Louise listened as she watched her children swimming and splashing in the pool silhouetted by the never ending pastures of the ranch. She had heard the same story countless times before. Many more times than her husband who, although he was a good listener, didn't like to hear anything negative about his father.

Louise suspected another woman in her father-in-law's life. It didn't seem possible for so much money to vanish without an explanation. It was a suspicion that she had never voiced to Claudia and they both pretended along with the rest of the family that Pedro was a pillar of respectability and propriety.

"I know how much you love this place." Louise turned and faced her mother-in law. "I know you will be miserable if you can't come here anymore. It's your decision."

"If I don't sign and things don't work out it will be my fault. I don't want that responsibility."

Louise could see her point. She had always realized that Claudia didn't stand a chance against the men of the family. Louise remembered the first time that she had seen Dona Claudia's handwriting; it was like that of an elementary school child. At first she had been shocked but after settling deeper into the family she came to know that Claudia had stayed home from school, helping with the house work, as her parents amassed great stretches of land. Louise had once thought it was because of this lack of a formal education that her opinions were not taken seriously. Later she realized that it was mainly machismo and her father-in-law's insecurity that perhaps his wife knew more about farming than he did.

The night before the party when the maids were in the kitchen cleaning up the dinner dishes, Zé, the tall lean manager of the ranch, appeared at the kitchen window. He asked one of the maids to call Pedro who was in the living room watching TV.

Pedro went outside carrying two glasses and a bottle of Brazilian vodka made from distilled sugar cane. He motioned for Zé to sit down at the table with him and then he filled the glasses.

The two men looked out at tall grass in the pastures illuminated in the moonlight. They sipped their drinks. "This is a beautiful piece of land, Pedro," Zé began. "The soil is so rich, so good for growing things. The weather is perfect for cattle. You're making a big mistake."

A drop of water, a tear perhaps, fell from near Zé's face and made a tiny dark spot on the wood of the table. He quickly rubbed it away. "What will happen to my family and the other six families that live here?"

Pedro looked down shaking his head, "I don't know but if I ever have a farm again, I'll look for you." Then he got up slowly and walked back into the house.

Heading back to São Paulo was always a hectic experience. At the last minute, Dona Claudia would always send her maids to the orchard near the farm house to pick succulent oranges and mangos and lemons to bring back to the city. She would slice off a big hunk of her freshly baked bread and wrap it up for the ride home. She would take out frozen slabs of beef from a recently slaughtered cow and put them in a Styrofoam container. There would barely be room for the suitcases of clothes with all the farm food that was crammed into the car.

The day after the party, it took longer than usual to leave the farm. Dona Claudia was frantically filling the car with foodstuffs and long forgotten treasures of the past that had to find new homes. The sales contract hadn't been signed yet and there was still the faintest glimmer of a possibility that something extraordinary would happen and the farm would remain theirs. So there was a pinpoint of hope inside them as they were leaving the farm for the last time. The maids were outside the kitchen door saying good-bye and the grass waved greenish gold in the midday sun. Tears ran down the grandmother's face as her husband stood stoically beside her.

Then Louise, Carlos, and the children drove past the pool and the big tree with the swings, past the grazing cows and onto the burning highway with its promising mirage of water that retreated forever into the distance.

ALEXANDER "SANDY" REED is a retired North American banker, married to a Paulista and living in São Paulo. He has just completed a textbook for beginners in international business and for interested observers about the world's monetary infrastructure and how, why, where and with what results its 160 different moneys move and meet in the global marketplace. His short story herewith is a collage of three vignettes from a novel he has just begun about a young international banker.

A Banker's Afternoon

by Alexander Reed

Rain had poured steadily for two days on the cement city of São Paulo. The quick run-off created floods everywhere but particularly in streets, factories and houses near the rivers. This confined my activities to paper shuffling in my office in the financial district located, by design I suppose, along an avenue in the highest part of the metropolis. But today the drenching had ebbed to sporadic drizzles and mist. I therefore took advantage of the lull this morning to dodge through the wet, visiting the international departments of several Brazilian banks, which are my major customers. In the afternoon I again retreated to my comfortable, dry office slightly above the watery confusion along Paulista Avenue, and I awaited one interesting caller and one fantastic one.

My first visitor had made an appointment for two o'clock, and he came in almost on the dot. He was Sergio Oliveira, the Secretary of Finance of a small northern Brazilian state. I had sat beside him at an evening dinner of financial executives in São Paulo a few months ago, and we became instant friends, if that is possible. Despite the mediocre food that night, Sergio added it gustily to his robust physique as we talked. He was a short, balding fellow with silver rimmed glasses and an open, amiable face. My secretary, Flora, brought him into my office and quietly retreated.

We backslapped and complained about the rain as Sergio plopped into one corner of the long couch facing my desk, and I took an arm chair under the picture window. His dark gray suit was made of an artificial fiber which, somewhat disconcertingly, reflected light easily. This fabric was heavily favored by certain politicians, since any flashbulb picture of the material created a respectful aura about the person. A long generation earlier Sergio would have been wearing a white linen suit favored by all of Brazil's northern elite at the time. This practice kept thousands of people employed from Rio de Janeiro to the Amazon, washing and ironing these garments which wrinkled like broken accordions a half hour after being donned. Although Sergio had his tie pulled down and off-center, this did not distract me from his intelligent eyes and quick, perceptive approach to our conversation. I estimated his age as pretty close to my thirty-eight years.

I was what is known basically as a correspondent banker. Our headquarters in New York City carried bank accounts from people, businesses and governments from all over the United States and the world, but it specialized in handling the business of other banks. Any bank in Brazil which engaged in foreign business had to carry accounts at large banks in New York, London, Paris, Tokyo, etc. We in turn loaned dollars and pounds and yen back to these banks for productive purposes in Brazil. My work was to monitor those relationships, develop new ones, and try to help my New York headquarters and the Brazilian banks understand each other. I therefore had a fair idea about the purpose of Sergio's visit.

He seemed mildly agitated and hurried, perhaps the result of dodging sidewalk puddles and low umbrellas. He began, "Peter, I know you are quite busy and I'll only take a few moments. One of your assistants recently visited our state bank at its headquarters in our capital. I want to encourage you to approve a line of credit to our bank, specifically to help us finance the export of fruits and vegetables up there. The output is growing fast. Three million dollars U.S. would be about right."

"Sergio, first I'm pleased to see you again. Sorry about our weather. As to credit facilities for your bank, yes, the request is under consideration here. But the possibilities of our approving anything are almost nil. I want to tell you why, although I think you certainly understand. You are a professional financial executive, not a politician. The government owned banks in Brazil, and I include all thirty-four of them, each defy the fundamental universal principal of banking which is not to engage in <u>self-dealing</u>."

"Enough, Peter. I don't need a lesson in economics."

"I know that, Sergio, but your political friends up north certainly do. Look, I am a banker. I'm proud to be one. We take the public's money in trust and must loan it out in a reasonable and prudent manner. That implies that we can't lend it to <u>ourselves</u>, meaning effectively the shareholders of the bank. If we could do that, all the rules of reason and prudence would tend to be ignored over time. Brazil's politicians are unaware of the explosiveness of disobeying this simple rule or they don't want to know. The shareholders of these banks are your states. But politicians don't look on their banks as banks. Somehow they think the deposits come from the public, belong to them as representatives of that public and can all be used for politically oriented purposes in their states. All they know is that when the big loans can't be paid, Brasilia will always print the money to bail them out. But banks are banks, not toys for politicians. This type of self dealing has destroyed thousands of banks over thousands of years, including just about every government owned bank in Brazil at one time or another. You know as well as I do that most of them should be closed."

"You express that very well, Peter, and I am actually going to write that thought down later. It's a good argument. Self-dealing? That's a good expression and puts it all in a nutshell."

Was he being sarcastic? Probably unnecessarily I continued. "Well, you can add to the argument that the state banks, and unfortunately every state of the Republic has one, are an enormous source of inflation. Every time one of them is in trouble the Central Bank pumps in huge resources to keep it alive, meaning money that didn't exist before, thus increasing the country's money supply.

"Listen, Sergio, this is getting a bit heavy. The fact is that I can not justify a loan to your state bank." His poker face surprised me, but his eyes reflected a disoriented understanding. I was compelled to add, "We could make a loan to one of your state companies, like telephones or electric power, but I'd have to have a federal government guarantee." The last was tossed out to be friendly, but we both knew a guarantee for Sergio's almost bankrupt state was presently impossible.

This was uncomfortable, and Sergio was twisting his large bulk on the couch, further rumpling his suit and moving his tie down another inch. I, too, felt uneasy. We therefore switched to a review of the dinner where we had met and the extramarital proclivities of a northern governor who locked his wife and children out of his mansion and carried on a number of publicized affairs with budding showgirls eager for the press coverage. But it was time to end our meeting. As Sergio stood up he mumbled something about lunch if I came through his capital city but indicated he was fully booked for his two days in São Paulo. He picked up a well-traveled black briefcase and finally, somewhat grim faced, shuffled out my open door. I accompanied him through our reception area, where I noted out of the corner of an eye a well-dressed visitor, and then out to the elevators, where the wait was, fortunately, only a moment.

It is time to mention that my Muncie, Indiana wife gave up on me a few years ago. The constant moves and changing cultural environments were just too much, aggravated by her inability to have children. We parted reasonably good friends and I'm hoping she will find a nice doctor to settle down with in the mid-west USA. I must admit, coming to a new country as a bachelor was far easier than setting up with a wife. The language, the professional culture, the business and social contacts, and the long hours of business, were all more easily and quickly absorbed by being alone. But being alone was lonely. I didn't like it. I had had my eye out for the right mate for some time, both in New York and in São Paulo. Particularly, I had my eye on Bettina Janos, a Hungarian/Brazilian lady of exceptional good spirits, charm and empathy, and I would see her this very afternoon.

As the gray metallic elevator doors closed, I turned back towards our attractive glass entrance with the name of our bank and its well-known globe logo displayed discreetly in precise, squared-off letters to one side of the door. I looked through to our comfortable reception area of heavy carpeting, large couch and stuffed arm chairs. A coffee table held some of the latest magazines and today's newspaper. No three year old Newsweeks and Vejas for us.

I knew the man sitting there and that he was here to see me about some banking problem. He was Oswaldo Bacelar, wealthy owner of a large chain of pharmacies. He came from one of the traditional São Paulo families, referred to by the envious as the "Four Hundred", and he and his wife for many years had a joint account at our New York headquarters. He had come in two or three times to complain about some irrelevancy or ask about procedures for using his account. Generally long and meaningless conversations.

I hesitated outside our door. Bettina was to arrive in about half an hour and I certainly wanted nothing to interfere with my interview with her. I would have to attend to Sr. Bacelar and resolve his situation with utmost haste.

I pushed our door open and walked over to greet him. He was a rather thin, small man, immaculately dressed in a navy blue pin-stripe suit bought somewhere abroad. No shoulder padding, straight hang, thin lapels, accompanied by a maroon tie with white polka-dots. For men who dress this way there are obligatory French cuffs and a small handkerchief matching the tie stuffed in his left breast pocket. Sr. Bacelar reacted to my admiring glance, not with a greeting, but with the words, "Chipps, New York." Startled, I could only nod in recognition. With my reasonably normal height and build, I was wearing a similarly conservative gray wool off-the-rack suit of a minor New York haberdashery, making mine a genteel but poor cousin to his finery.

Sr. Bacelar and I were not familiar enough for a major *abraço*, so as he arose I shook his hand firmly while patting his back lightly, and then escorted him down our hall to our office. He, too, sat in a corner of my long couch and I again took the arm chair under my picture window. Bacelar was a quiet, timid man, seemingly rather unworldly, but smart enough to let a well-known, tough, honest accountant run the pharmaceutical business he had inherited from his father. I believe he spent a great part of his time at a small coffee plantation he owned in the interior of São Paulo state, and I knew that he and his wife traveled extensively. I had heard in the trade that he had made several unfortunate investments over the years through equally well-dressed, articulate sons of other, traditional Paulista families, who gathered in the money of their friends and quietly disappeared. Our relationship had never gone beyond the account in New York.

Bacelar addressed me with a pleasant smile, mumbled a few amenities and then began. "Mr. Reynolds, I am here with a rather unusual request for information. I think I have to become involved in the black foreign exchange market, but I don't know how to go about it."

I cut in quickly. "Sr. Bacelar, I represent a large international bank. You understand I can't get myself or my institution involved in illegal operations."

Bacelar put up his small hands in protest and explained, "No, Mr. Reynolds. I am not asking you or your bank to do anything like that. I am only here for information. Just listen to my story."

I nodded, and he proceeded. "My wife's mother died a few months ago, leaving a considerable amount of real estate to my wife and her sister. The girls are not interested in this real estate, and we have been selling it off for cash. Now Celeste, that's my wife's sister, wants us to send her her share of the money realized to date. She lives a great part of the time in Europe and wants the money in an account she maintains at a Swiss bank. I thought there would be legal means of transferring the funds to her, and I consulted our lawyer about this. Unfortunately Celeste has no permanent residence abroad and is in Brazil a good deal of the year, so the Central Bank will not authorize a transfer."

"The problem is fairly obvious, Peter, if I may call you that. Celeste wants about US$800,000 outside Brazil, and I suppose we must use the black market. The money is already here in São Paulo in two accounts in different banks in my wife's name. You may think that as the owner of several businesses and real estate I should know about the exchange markets. The truth is, I have never touched the black market. The money in our account in the United States comes from some investments my father made there years ago and from occasional swaps of currencies with friends of Celeste. We pay their expenses here."

Bacelar shifted his position on the couch, adjusted his tie, crossed one leg over the other and twisted the tip of one beautifully tasseled black shoe up towards his knee-cap. I let him continue.

"I can not afford to have anything come back at me or my wife as connected to this kind of business. In your position you must have had situations like this. Do you have any ideas?"

Yes, I had ideas, but I didn't like them. The constantly changing regulations in this area of business create an Alice in Wonderland kind of atmosphere where rules are merely impediments in the game, and the determined player looks for ways around them, legal, illegal, or in the enormous, vague area in between.

"Maybe you are worried unnecessarily." I suggested, "There are ways to accomplish what you want to do. You and your wife can go down to Montevideo with your check-books and sell those *reais* in the accounts here to the branches of your banks there. They will pay you in any hard currency you want, and they can put the money in Celeste's account in Switzerland with a phone call or telex transmission. Of course you'll have to account some way about where all those *reais* went, but who's going to ask?

"That's one way. Here's another. I've heard that there are financial representatives in São Paulo who will set up an investment holding company for you here. Cost, about one hundred reais. Then their bank or brokerage house abroad will incorporate a subsidiary of the Brazilian company, and the Central Bank will let you remit your funds through the holding company to the foreign subsidiary. Maybe a bit complex for Celeste."

I paused and watched a renewed drizzle out my windows. "Then of course the quick, simple way is to go to one of the black market exchange operators in the city, give him your reais, and he will see that Celeste is credited in Switzerland. It can be done in a few minutes."

Bacelar quickly interjected. "Yes, but I can't afford anything from a black market traced back to me or my wife. That may be the easiest but it doesn't sound too good to us."

I thought about this for a moment. "There is a way you can cut the trail back to your wife's bank. Have her ask for cashier's checks, and you can trade these with your black market operator. He'll give you a fictitious name to make the checks out to. That pretty effectively cuts the trail between you and the black market operator. I can give you the telephone numbers of two or three operators and you can discuss details and probably even better methods with them."

"But US$800,000 all at once! The operator could take my checks and disappear! It sounds strange but I know absolutely no one in that business."

"Bacelar, some of these operators turn over several million dollars every day. No one's going to run anywhere. And you can remit in smaller amounts if you're nervous."

I took a small pad on my desk, and from a battered address book of my predecessor in one of my drawers I wrote off three names and three telephone numbers. I came around my desk to hand Sr. Bacelar the slip of paper. This was his signal to rise, which he did. I was concerned that Bettina might be already waiting in the reception area.

I accompanied Bacelar down the hall, found the reception area empty, and saw him off at the elevators outside our entrance door.

My corner window gives me a long, unobstructed view down mid-town Paulista Avenue. It continued a gray, rainy fall afternoon, and the kilometer of tall buildings created an even darker canyon into which the water fell. The black asphalt and the gloomy tops of the automobiles dispersed weak reflections of a few neon signs and occasional motorist's headlights.

But inside my office there was to be brightness. Flora had made the appointment for Bettina Janos to visit us at 4:00; I had not talked to her, so I had no idea what she wanted. But bright-eyed Bettina always had something interesting to say. Her father, Jorge, had immigrated from Hungary in the late 1940's, started a small machine shop, and when Brazil began automobile manufacturing in the 50's, he went into auto parts. He now controls an empire of three sizable metallic part suppliers. He had been a customer of the Bank since the '60's, and had visited us in New York on many occasions, sometimes with Bettina, whom I met there on one of my tours at Headquarters. I had been immediately smitten, but I was married at the time. Since my arrival in São Paulo as a bachelor I had taken Bettina to several animated dinners and had, perhaps monthly, profound telephone exchanges about business and politics with her, but my work, difficulty with the language, cultural immersion, and frequent trips had kept the relationship at this low level.

Bettina taught European history at the University of São Paulo and had a tough, realistic view of the world. She, too, had been away for extended periods doing research in Hungary and France.

Flora brought Senhorita Janos in on the dot of four and retired down the hall. After the usual touching of cheeks, Bettina performed an unusual act by turning and closing my office door, which I normally leave open all day. I directed her to one of my easy chairs, but she strutted to the hard back next to my desk. I reoccupied my overly flexible, rotating chair behind it. This was going to be serious business. Bettina's figure, which can be categorized as excellent for her considerable height, was dramatized by a slightly mannish, light tan business suit, fluffed white shirt and a paisley bow tie. My office this afternoon had become a fashion show. She swung her lanky frame about and observed me with a slightly nervous smile. Her auburn hair framed a plain, slightly angular face, some attractive freckles, well-proportioned nose, pale lips. But her eyes. No one looked at anything else after her eyes. They were brilliant, exuding an enormous warmth, confidence and enthusiasm. But today they also reflected some inner concern.

In a flash, something perhaps peculiar to mid-life bachelor-divorcees, I suddenly realized this was a girl I could live with forever. What had I been doing not to realize this? This had me tongue tied for a moment, and I did not know how to start a conversation.

"Bettina, this is a real pleasure. My days are quite cut and dried in São Paulo."

"Peter, it has been over a month since we last talked. I only found out a few days ago that you were back from your long visit in New York. Our grapevines don't seem to cross."

I noted subconsciously that her hands were gripping the side of her chair rather than laying delicately in her lap with her purse. Why? Let's keep this light, I thought.

"Well, I can guess why you are here. You want to open a boutique featuring stylish European clothes in the business oriented line that you are wearing now. Your father won't lend you the money, so you're coming to a banker?"

She pretended to laugh, but the gurgle died in her throat.

"Peter, I am here for something much more personal. Yes, I want to borrow something, but not money. I want to borrow your body." Now the eyes flashed a fraction brighter, but with a tinge of what? Guilt?

"Oh, Lord, you have a bazaar out at the University or at one of your mother's charities, and you want me as a bartender?"

"No, I want to borrow you for something far more personal than that." She looked at me nervously and, for me, disconcertingly, because of that same, laughing brilliance in her eyes. "Let me explain a little bit about myself. We know each other pretty well, at least by telephone." Was there a touch of regret in that voice? "You and I have discussed everything from Hungarian black clay pottery to Kant's philosophy and world demographics. But we don't have that much contact. First, I want to tell you that I am engaged to be married within a few months to Fernando Borges. We have been going around together for about six months and it is certainly time for me."

Something exploded in me. Not something violent. But like a brightly illuminated living room when all the lights suddenly burn out at the same time. What had I missed? To let this gem slip away, while I was too busy working! Where was I headed? What were my priorities? And my ego? I must have thought I could leave someone on a shelf indefinitely, to be picked up at my convenience. And Fernando Borges. No need to explain who he is. Ex-Formula 1 driver and now successful auto parts retailer. She must have met him through her father. All this in a horrible flash, as she calmly but somewhat hurriedly continued.

"Well Peter, I have this problem. You know that my father is strictly religious and I attended a Catholic girls' school in the United States. Two girl cousins stuck to me like fly paper through Boston University. My two brothers and older sister have always protected me very carefully in São Paulo and on my research trips, so here I am at thirty years of age and still a virgin. Sure, I have had a number of what you Americans and the French call 'affairs', lots of heavy petting, but I guess I was never quite attracted enough to jump the barriers created by my education and family influence. But, Peter, I am now in a quandary. Fernando, as you can imagine, is a fairly decisive and energetic businessman, but when it comes to individual relationships, he is rather shy, nonaggressive, maybe even a bit disoriented. We love each other deeply. Besides everything else, he brings out a maternal, protective instinct in me. But physically he has never pushed beyond a good bit of kissing and holding me."

Where was this conversation leading? While Bettina appeared less nervous, I began rotating my chair.

She continued, "I think I need some more explicit sexual experience before I marry Fernando." There was a short pause. She looked at me inquiringly. "Now don't jump out of your seat, Peter. When I mentioned your body, that's exactly what I meant. I know you much better than you think. You are a decent and warm person; maybe a bit dull and one sided at this period in your life. But honest and discreet. If there is anyone in this world with whom I would like to have my first real sexual experience, it would be with someone like you."

Her magic eyes kept darting out the window, but I could see her hands grip the chair slowly, relax and return to her lap.

"I would like to spend at least one night with you, Peter. I think it would relieve some hang-ups I probably have and would give me the knowledge I need about how to proceed with Fernando."

Besides rotating, my desk chair also flips backward, and while I didn't go over all the way, I certainly put some strain on the retaining springs. What was this? What a conversation for a business office! No wonder the closed door. Was I to be a gigolo, a male prostitute, or could I put this in the category of what? A wedding present! I suddenly panicked that the interphone to Flora could be in the "on" position, and in twisting my swivel seat, I was relieved to see it turned off. I fumbled for a moment with a folder on my desk and then looked at Bettina again. Damn those laughing eyes.

"Wow," I mumbled in a weak voice. But gathering my composure, I added, "This is the best business proposal all day." I practically choked on the cliché. "Obviously I congratulate you about Fernando Borges." Then like a schoolboy who has lost a friend over a meaningless argument, I added, "You know, I thought maybe you and I would work something out one day."

She came back fast and too accurately. I think she had anticipated my stupid remark. "Peter, you have a way to go before you remarry. It's not the time for you. Besides," and she held up one finger, "you're married to your bank for now." Another finger, "You don't need me." A third finger, "And finally, while I respect and admire you, I don't love you."

Her friendly reprimand, delivered like a lecture, gave me time to compose myself, although I again tilted backward in my chair. I think my heart rate started to return to normal. I inched up the angle of my seat. I suddenly recognized that this had been a very difficult interview for Bettina. I must be compassionate and understanding.

"Bettina, I certainly deserved that. You are right. I still have a few unpleasant scars from my past which I guess I try to obscure by burying myself in numbers and risk assessments."

I sat upright in my swivel chair and turned directly to her side. "Yes. I understand all that you are saying. I am frankly quite dumbfounded, but I certainly am honored by your idea." I could even feel a smile begin on what had surely been my very startled face. The intensity level of her twinkling eyes increased correspondingly.

"Then you don't think my idea is far-fetched or outrageous? I anguished over this for a long time."

"Bettina, you are one of the wonders of this world. Yes, I like your proposition. I want to cooperate." I began to pick up enthusiasm. "Since this is a business proposal, I think we can say we have a meeting of minds."

She stood up, dropping her purse on the floor, and stepped toward me behind the desk. I arose, and as we giggled with relief like children, we had a long, friendly embrace. I was perspiring slightly and I could detect a bit of moisture above her upper lip. She finally stepped back to pick up her purse, pulled her jacket straight in preparation to leave, and stood by her chair.

I adjusted my tie and coat and, finally smiling fully, said, "The only thing left to negotiate is the date, time and place."

Bettina gave me one more tremendous flash of her eyes before she turned toward the door. "Oh, that's the easy part. This was the hurdle for me. Don't worry, I have lots of ideas. I'll be calling you." And she was off down the corridor.

After graduating from the Art Institute of Ft. Lauderdale, Florida, with a degree in photography, KEELY RUNGE ACOSTA went to work in New York where she met her husband, Luis. They moved to Miami in 1988, then were transferred to Brazil in 1991, living first in Rio de Janeiro and then São Paulo. Keely and Luis have recently returned to Miami, where she continues her artistic and creative endeavors.

Birds of a Feather

by Keely Acosta

My husband, Julio and I had been living in Rio de Janeiro, Brazil for about a year when our dear friend came for a visit from San Diego, California. Her name is Sue Ellen but she is affectionately known to us as "*La Pecosita*", which means "the little freckle face". She is a vivacious little red head about five feet tall with an abundance of freckles and a ready laugh.

Rio de Janeiro is famous for being one of the most beautiful hang gliding locations and for their world champion hang gliders. The hang gliders take off from the top of one of a pair of mountains called "*Dois Irmãos*", Two Brothers, in the São Conrado area. They take off and fly on the air currents over the very exclusive homes with pools and gardens built on the side of the mountain and they fly out over the ocean and back in again to land on *Praia do Pepino,* Cucumber Beach.

Julio and I had been watching them since we moved to Rio. On a clear day, there would be dozens of them with beautiful multi-colored hang gliders slowly weaving their way down to land on the beach as softly and gently as a cotton ball falling to the ground.

We had taken *La Pecosita* to see the hang gliders several times. Each time we said it looked like a lot of fun and we should go do it, but then we always did something else.

On a gorgeous Saturday morning, the day before she was scheduled to fly home, the three of us were having breakfast on the verandah. We could occasionally glimpse one of the hang gliders as he popped over the top of the mountain and then disappeared from sight on the other side. *La Pecosita* and I looked at each other and said, "Lets go," and then we turned to look at Julio who quickly offered to be the photographer from the earthbound side. Our respective positions resolved, off we went.

The closer we got to the beach, the more nervous *La Pecosita* looked and the quieter she became.

"Do you want to change your mind?" I asked, "It's still not too late."

"No, I really want to do this," she answered pensively.

After arriving at the beach, we went to the hang gliding Kiosk and asked about the instructors. They told us of a young man by the name of Rony who had been Brazil's national champion. We were instructed to wait on the beach for him to land as he had just gone up the mountain. We were given the colors of his glider so that we would know which one he was, and sat down to wait. Finally, we saw his glider come into view. We were thrilled as we watched him float on the currents and noticed that he stayed up the longest. He made a beautiful, soft landing and we quickly decided he was the one to take us flying.

The three of us walked over to speak to him. He was very nice and spoke English very well which Julio and I thought would be reassuring to *La Pecosita* since she would be jumping off of a mountain in a foreign country.

Rony showed us his hang gliding license, explained what we would be doing, and told us he had a partner named João who was very good. He explained that João could take me as I spoke Portuguese and he could take *La Pecosita* since he spoke English, so that we could both go at the same time. We all agreed that was a great idea.

While Rony packed up his hang glider and loaded it onto his car, *La Pecosita* and I hugged and kissed Julio good-bye and gave him instructions should we meet an early demise. Most importantly though, I made sure he had film in the camera, turned it on, and took off the lens cap. He looked at us both quite nervously, told us to have fun, and waved good-bye as we drove away. I'm sure I saw his hair turning more gray by the second.

All the way up the mountain, we picked Rony's brain with questions about hang gliding. How many years had he been doing it? How did he start? How long could he stay up? How do you know when the currents aren't safe? At what level of expertise was he? How long did it take to get a license? What are the different levels? Had he had any accidents? After all, we didn't want to jump off a mountain with just anybody. We wanted an adventure, not to commit suicide.

He answered all of our questions readily and thoroughly and even offered additional information about how the classes progress and about international license qualifications. He was very interesting and very knowledgeable. I was feeling more and more relaxed. By the time we reached the top and got out of the car, *La Pecosita* also seemed much calmer.

Rony showed us around and introduced us to his partner João, then explained about the equipment, what we would wear, how we would be hooked up to the glider and finally, how we would be hooked up in tandem to them. Everything was going fine until he got to the part about running in tandem up the wooden platform and jumping off the cliff. *La Pecosita* and I looked at each other, smiled sickly and said, "No problem, we can do that!" as we turned a rather odd shade of gray. Rony, ignoring our pallor, said, "Great, then let's practice running to the end and stopping quickly."

By the look on her face, I knew *La Pecosita* and I were both thinking the same thing: What the hell am I doing here? I don't need to jump off the top of a mountain! Am I nuts? But neither of us said anything as we practiced running.

La Pecosita practiced with Rony counting each step, slowly at first and then faster and faster until they were synchronized and could stop at the very edge in a second. I then practiced with João until we could do the same.

They explained to us that the takeoff was the most important part and could be very dangerous if we didn't do it just right. By the time we finished practicing running to the edge of the platform, Rony and João's assistants had both hang gliders ready. *La Pecosita* was to go first with Rony but somehow João had her hooking up to him and I could tell she was very nervous. She was soooo pale, her freckles had all but disappeared! I started to insist that she wait and go with Rony and let me go first with João but she said, "No, I'll be okay." I think she wanted to get it over with as quickly as possible and couldn't wait a second longer or she would run screaming back down the mountain.

They got into position and as they started running, she turned her head and yelled to me, "If anything happens, I want you to have my jewelry!" and then they leaped off the cliff and were flying beautifully. I heard João yell something at her as they jumped but neither of us had any idea what it was.

And then it was my turn. As Rony and I got into position, I was filled with an intense feeling of exhilaration and anticipation of the moment when our feet would leave the ground and we would be at the mercy of the wind. I took a deep breath, we started running, and then we jumped into the abyss.

In the blink of an eye, we were floating on the tranquil breezes. And as we played on the currents, circling over the tiny Monopoly-sized homes on the side of the mountain and the antlike people on the beach below, I felt euphoric gliding in the peaceful silence, feeling the freedom of the birds that flew around us as if we were one of them. We flew out over the ocean and waved to the people in the boats below, then circled back to the beach where we landed softly in the sand.

It seemed as if it was over much too quickly although I knew it hadn't been. I wanted to go back and do it over and over again.

La Pecosita and Julio were there to greet me with huge smiles and big hugs as I landed and Julio promised he had a whole roll of great pictures of us both.

We thanked our pilots profusely and had Julio take pictures of all of us together as proof that we really did go hang gliding. We then left for lunch and to spend the rest of the day laughing at our fear of running and jumping off a cliff and reminiscing on our birdlike flight, having fulfilled at least one of our lifelong dreams.

Being a Brazilian born in Bonn, Germany, culture shock and ambivalent patriotic feelings have been familiar to CLAUDIA LESCHONSKI from an early age. She grew up (and quite tall, too) with a love for books and a passion for horses. After graduating from veterinarian school, she lived mostly on horse breeding farms and at horse training centers.

During her teenage years, Claudia wrote lots of fiction of every kind, but in more recent years an interest in "real life" has taken over. Thus she has been trying to produce a collection of stories drawing upon her professional and personal experiences in the Brazilian hinterland. "A Carter's Story", originally written in Portuguese, is part of this project.

A Carter's Story

by Claudia Leschonski

Everything was ancient at Seu Antonio Nene's place: the house, the fences, the oxen and the mules, and the people as well. Mr. Antonio Nene was in his mid-seventies, a little old man so frail that his skull was well outlined under the skin, tight over the upper half of his face, wrinkled around chin and neck. Wilted and bent over, he still worked all day long, slowly but steadily. And there was something about him, I don't know if it was his expression or gestures, that made it possible to see the boy behind the old man, a little kid who for seventy years hadn't known any other life but this one on the sandy soils between São Paulo and Minas Gerais. Perhaps due to this, or maybe because of his joy for living which he maintained with never-tiring curiosity, he had acquired his nickname, "Nene", which means "baby".

Silvio, the area's main farmer, visited him some Sundays, bringing a cut of the most recently butchered cow, taking his children along to eat cheese with quince jam. When Silvio was still young and worked as the camp cook for his father's diamond prospectors, Antonio Nene used to own all the lands bordering the Santa Tereza farm, which Silvio had now owned for ten years.

The old neighbors would gather in Seu Antonio's kitchen, roofbeams blackened by decades of soot, with glassless windows, where one had to keep shooing at the chicken scratching under the table. People coming at around ten o'clock, Seu Antonio's lunchtime, would be coaxed into nibbling chunks of manioc or strips of pork cracking. Seu Antonio, Dona Ninha, and their son Zito ate with spoons from enamel plates, perched alongside the fireplace.

"Mighty good manioc, Seu Antonio," Silvio would exclaim, licking his fingers which dripped of meat sauce. Silvio had made a fortune selling shoes to *gringos*, and traveled to the States six times a year. But he wouldn't have traded anything in the world for fat ribs, candied figs or whole leaves of lettuce, seasoned and served in large bowls.

Silvio loved large, well-kept vegetable gardens. He would get very mad at those wranglers and herders who proved unable to set up and keep a small green garden close to their quarters at the farm. Since a vegetable-loving work hand is still to be born, life at the farm wasn't always peaceful. But here, Dona Ninha blushed with happiness at their visitor's praise and urged them to eat more of the fat meat.

Antonio's team of oxen, big and heavy-boned, their horns sawed at the tips, was a special beauty. It was easy to imagine their strength. Once in motion, they were slow but impossible to restrain. The eight oxen, tall and mature, certainly close to fifteen summers each one, were a rarity in these days of feedlots and baby beef. They were still strong with lots of work left in them.

In that part of the world there still were working oxcarts called *cantadores,* or singers, so named because their axles and wheels produced a certain whining sound which could be heard for miles around. The song of the *cantador* was as moody as the *berrante*, the multiple horn used to call and drive cattle on the trails, which itself sounded like bellowing cattle.

In the anniversary parade of every town—Patrocinio, Passos, Ibiraci, Nuporanga, even Franca—there were always some bitted or ringed oxen with riders among the many horses. Opening or closing the parades would be teams of oxen drawing carts or hauling giant logs, which left a track of sawdust on the pavement.

Seu Antonio still worked with his team now and them, during the corn harvest or hauling logs. There was something incredible and touching abut the sight of the tiny old man commanding the oxen by voice and rod only, helped by his son Zito.

Zito, poor fellow, didn't talk much but openly laughed a lot, in spite of lacking his front teeth. His age was hard to determine, perhaps between forty-something and fifty-ish. He had lank hair and uncertain eyes. Of Seu Antonio's six sons and daughters, he was the only one who had remained helping his father at the farm, working from dawn to sunset—but I'd be hard pressed to know to what point he was useful; certainly, he wouldn't have been able to do the work without his father's help. Zito wasn't quite right in the head. Luiz Lemos, who used to work for the neighbor Silvio, confirmed what I had suspected already. Luiz concluded that of Seu Antonio's whole brood, no one was in good running order upstairs. "And them all feuding against each other, on top of it!" he said.

Some time later, Silvio told me that Dona Ninha was Seu Antonio's cousin, and that each one already came from inbred families. "They wanted to hold the estate in the family," he muttered, at once pitying and malicious, "and what came of it? Six middle-aged children, not only feeble, but quarreling and selling the lands to the point of having lost almost everything. I hardly want to see what'll come of it after the old man's gone."

And on top of that, Dona Ninha was ill, living downtown at a daughter's home part of the time. Sometimes we arrived to find Seu Antonio and Zito living as bachelors, the dark old house gone to seed even more than usual, with them eating out of pots.

The first time Luiz Lemos took me to visit Seu Antonio, he had explained in a rather uneasy tone which I hadn't heard him use before, "I haven't taken you there before because I thought you'd mind...their place and their ways..."

I had particularly noticed he seemed relieved to see me squatting on their doorstep, chatting away like an old friend. Luiz could hardly know that Seu Antonio's place reminded me of my years as rural veterinarian in southern Paraná, where a few settlers still live in the ways of a century ago. As there, glass in the windows was an exception and running water a rarity.

On the next visits, Seu Antonio would tell me about his bygone days as a mule driver, and I listened respectfully. I had long been fascinated by stories of mulestrings from Palmas to Sorocaba, or of packers trailing up the sea mountain range. But all these things had been, for me, in a distant past. It was hard to imagine that the old man in front of me was living the last of those days. He told about the times he'd gone with his father to Campinas by oxcart to fetch salt: one month on the road, both ways, if it didn't rain.

Even by bus, Campinas nowadays is four hours from Franca; Silvio, who wore out cars as other people do shoes, did the same stretch in two hours. Seeing the oxen's slow, methodical pace, I tried in vain to imagine it: one month on the road, walking beside the oxen, the cart "singing" in my ears. And all this to fetch licking salt for the cattle? It became easy to understand how, long ago, salt used to have value as a currency.

During that whole year, we visited Seu Antonio periodically, usually only Luiz and I, or sometimes everybody on horseback: Silvio on his Texan mare, each child on his pet pony. And always Dona Ninha got all excited about our band's arrival, and we were kindly but firmly coaxed into eating everything there was: caramelized milk with cheese, guava jam, orange candy, manioc, fried pork, biscuits, all with lots of coffee. Knowing that the boss wasn't partial to *pinga*, the sugar cane liquor, Seu Antonio kept the jug for those times when Luiz went there by himself or just with me.

On occasions, in return for so much kindness, I paid a veterinary call on some sickly cow or lame mule, or yet to

Dona Ninha's little old bitch dog. Matriarch of the whole pack, she suffered a vulvar carcinoma, which I did my best to treat as a normal flesh wound—any drastic remedy, from surgery to euthanasia, being out of the question. The little dog was old and didn't seem really bothered by her condition, sleeping most of the time. I recommended and demonstrated the use of a collar fashioned out of a small plastic bucket with its bottom removed, to make it impossible for the dog to lick and worsen the wound; but after a couple of weeks, they removed the bucket, pitying the dog, and everything remained the same as before. Meanwhile, Seu Antonio and Luiz would chat, telling stories and comparing knives and guns.

Sometimes we'd also meet Seu Antonio on the roads, sitting very straight on his old pet mule which paced in small strides, the old man perched atop his sheep-skin covered saddle, reins high in one hand, driving whip in the other, resting its handle on his hip. We'd greet him and chat for a while, with horses and mule eyeing each other suspiciously as rivals.

In early August of that year, during a time of those frosts which freeze puddles and stiffen laundry hung to dry, an old German friend of mine came to visit us. Called "Rooster" because of his scrawny neck and good baritone voice, he was enough of an eccentric to forego the usual touristic Brazil in search of the country which normally remains hidden to foreigners. Reasoning that there hardly would be anything similar in Germany, Luiz and I took him to meet Seu Antonio. As we had hoped, the German and the old farmer immediately established rapport with each other. Seu Antonio asked lots of questions about life abroad, marveling not only at the answers, but also at the sound of a foreign tongue being spoken. I, born in Germany of a Brazilian mother, translated. Seu Antonio was adamant about presenting Rooster with one of those old, bone-handled penknives used for shredding tobacco. It came with detailed instructions for the correct preparation of a *palheiro*, a cigarette rolled in corn husk. Needless to say, Rooster took a special liking to the *pinga*, and we all parted as old friends. At all my visits thereafter, Seu Antonio would say, "Gee, my child, it was such a pleasure for this old man to get acquainted with that foreign lad, and him so nice and well-spoken."

Once, another son and daughter of Seu Antonio were around. They were city dwellers, nice in a superficial way. To me they didn't seem more feeble-minded than most human beings. It seemed impossible that they should be full brother and sister to Zito, and reared just like him. He stared at them quietly from his corner at the fireplace. He left after a little while just to return almost immediately, disrupting the conversation to mention something about the cattle.

"Mom, let's take the calves in. Pa?"

"Your father is going," Dona Ninha answered, talking as one does to a child. Looking at the three of them, I had a sense of time having stopped, forty or fifty years ago, at that farm: Seu Antonio and the oxen, Dona Ninha at her fireplace, Zito frozen in his boyhood. The other children didn't seem to belong to the place. For some reason, perhaps being nervous on account of his visiting brother and sister, Zito kept pestering them about the calves until Dona Ninha sent him outdoors, still as one does a child. His siblings resumed the conversation about the coffee crop and the grandchildren's doings.

At Silvio's farm, sometimes we wondered about the arguments that were sure to rage one day over Seu Antonio's estate, but it seemed still far away. Seu Antonio went on working strongly in the fields with the oxen, making cheese, and in the pigsty. Our major fear was the possibility of Dona Ninha's illness taking a turn for the worse. How in the world would the little old man manage by himself?

I left Silvio's farm in April of the next year. Almost another whole year passed before I visited that area again, and then Lamia, Silvio's oldest daughter, told me of Seu Antonio Nene's end. At first, I thought that the girl was making it up, she with her taste for tragic stories, but other neighbors later would support her story.

I couldn't find out exactly how it happened—and I think that no one is ever going to—but Seu Antonio Nene died trampled by his own oxen while at work in the corn field. Only Zito was with him, and he never managed to put together a comprehensible account of the accident.

It seemed like one of those ballads sung in country music: seventy years working with ox teams, to die under their hooves and the cartwheels! Of course, gossip of all kind ran loose about the children, one thinking him- or herself lesser favored than the others; and above all about Zito, of the easy laughter and uncertain eyes. Lamia told me for sure—her father's own words—that Zito had borne a grudge against his father for his whole life, but this seemed too unbelievable to me. Poor Zito, who was hardly able to shake one's hand and say hello at the same time?

It was some time later that I was able to again do a bit of horseback riding in that area. On the trail, Luiz and I came right across Seu Antonio Nene's farm. The fence remained in half-decay as before, the mules stood eternally, the cows were chewing their cud in the corral, and the half dozen hairy little dogs were impossible to tell from each other. But Zito was all alone at the doorstep. Dona Ninha, Luiz told me, had moved to her daughter's for good.

"Want to stop by?" Luiz asked me, reining his horse in.

"Oh, no," I replied. "It's running late already, isn't it?"

We simply greeted Zito from afar, calling out and waving to him, to which he answered with his same toothless smile. Somehow those gestures summed up all possible conversation we could have had. I wondered how long he would be able to run the place by himself, or perhaps another brother would move in, or they would hire someone. Finally, as I've seen happen so often with inheritance cases, the lands would be left untouched for years, until there wouldn't be one fencepost standing. The woods around would be full of chickens and half-wild pigs, those left behind after most of the stock had been rounded up and moved to another farm.

We left Seu Antonio's lands through an end of the pasture, where only one strand of wire was left. Luiz' well-trained horses used to cross there easily. But that day they snorted and balked at the heap of yellow hide and bones lying close by the road. Slowly, I clucked my horse on, and saw that the long horns revealed the carcass to have been one of the cart oxen.

"Hey ox, if you could talk, what would you tell?"

Luiz laughed for an answer, "A Minas-bred ox; he wouldn't say anything."

While we allowed the horses to set their own pace homewards, I wondered what would come of those mighty oxen. Too old to butcher, no work to do, they would end up wild, roaming the bush, the swamps, the old claims, the overgrown coffee. And little by little they would go, one after the other, and nothing would remain except those little heaps of hide and bone. The old carter's renown would fade like the cartwheels' mournful music, carried by the late evening breeze.

ALMA GARY GORDON DOLE loves her native country of Brazil, if not her home "town" of São Paulo, to which she returned 13 years ago. Her mother and father invested the best years of their lives in Rio Verde, Goias, where they founded a still-functioning hospital and nursing school. Brought up in that small interior town, Alma went to the States for all of her high school and college education.

While a professor at the University of Recife, PE, she was courted by mail and left Brazil to marry her true love, Richard Dole, who today is director of the video department of COMEV. They now have an adult son and daughter. When not busy as a writer, speaker, teacher, handbell choir director or counselor, Mrs. Dole works with street children and their families. As a freelance writer, Alma has had numerous articles published in both American and Brazilian periodicals. This is her second published story. Her next big project is a much-requested biography of her parents.

The Best Exit

by Alma Dole

A gun? She had none. A knife? She might miss her mark. A rope? Too difficult. Alone in her minuscule dark bedroom, Ana sat considering the various ways she could end it all. Now that the play of her life had lost all interest, her dreams burned to ashes, it was just a matter of finding the nearest fire escape, the best exit.

Suddenly she knew. Lye! Mesmerized by the rhythmic sound of the drops of rain dripping through the cracked roof onto the cement floor, Ana remembered several people she'd known or heard about who had walked off life's stage and quit this dreary world's tragic comedy with lye as their secret accomplice. She would join them. Soon.

"Ana! Ana! Are you there? Please, Ana, can you hear me?"

Slowly the insistent sounds penetrated the dense fog that had settled over her mind, and Ana could hear the words. It was Geraldo, Antonio's best friend, whispering as loudly as he dared: "Ana! Open up! I need to talk to you!"

"Go away! I don't want to talk to you, Geraldo. Just go away and leave me in peace!"

But after a little while, realizing he was going to persist, Ana felt she had no option.

"Shut up! Don't you realize you'll soon wake up grumpy old Dona Teresa next door, and she'll make such a scene, all the neighbors will wake up? So quiet down!"

Reluctantly cracking the door to check that Geraldo was alone, Ana then let her untimely caller in. She sat down in one chair, and waved Geraldo to the other one, even as she fumbled for the matches, struck one, and lit the kerosene lamp on her tiny living room table. Even though she set it as low as possible, the four whitewashed walls were so close together that they reflected a surprising amount of light.

"So what is so urgent at this time of night? Go on, Geraldo, out with it!" Ana could now see that Geraldo was uncharacteristically pale.

"Oh, Ana, you'll never believe this. I know you're angry at Antonio, and well, I don't blame you. He certainly had no cause to break off your engagement so abruptly, and not even bother to explain why, the jerk!"

How right you are, Ana thought, her streams of despair now flooded over by rivers of anger. Yes! He is a jerk! she ached to scream. How could he ever do this to me! But quickly building a precarious dam to obstruct the flow, she merely grimaced and muttered through clenched teeth: "So go on, Geraldo. What on earth happened?"

"Antonio was shot early this afternoon, out on the *fazenda* where he's been working. Well, they brought him in by oxcart to the hospital, where they arrived at sunset, and, well..."

"Well what, Geraldo?" Stunned, Ana had to hear it all now. Immediately. But Geraldo was taking so terribly long to tell her this ghastly news, it was all she could do to sit there, waiting...

"And the gringo doctor operated and took out the bullet, but Antonio had lost a lot of blood, He's very bad, barely hanging on. And he's asking for you, Ana. Whenever he drifts into consciousness he keeps mumbling your name over and over. So...well...please, could you somehow forgive him enough to come with me, to see him?"

Her frazzled emotions wanted to shout, So there! It was just what he deserved! Her muddled mind chose to be calmly logical: "It would probably be too late by the time we got there, anyway! And besides..." But her grieving heart won, as she ran into the bedroom, threw on her worn sandals and, snuffing the lamp, commanded, "Let's go, Geraldo! I look a mess, but who cares? Let's hurry!"

As the two young people stumbled down the dark, uneven dirt streets, Geraldo filled her in on some of the details. It had happened around one o'clock on that Sunday afternoon, when the cowboys and farmhands were sitting around after dinner. Geraldo himself had gone to spend the weekend with his buddy, so he too was in the informal circle. He had been having an animated conversation with Antonio about a horse the latter wanted to buy, when suddenly there was a loud bang, and Antonio was on the ground, bright red blotches appearing on his white shirt.

The boss and his family were saying it had been an accident, a stray bullet that had gone off when one of the cowboys had been "cleaning his gun." But Geraldo said he and a few others knew better.

It was on purpose, no doubt about it. On that Saturday pay day, a guy named Chico had been furious when he watched the boss pay Antonio, a brand new hand on the ranch, the same salary as he himself had received. And Chico had been working for Dr. César for ten years!

The double "coincidence" was too incredible: that it was Chico who was holding the gun which "accidentally" went off, and that it was Antonio, sitting directly across from him, who "happened" to be hit. Well, none of the guys who had heard Chico spout off to the boss doubted that the hot-headed veteran had intended to kill the brash young upstart.

"Is he going to die, Geraldo? Is my tall handsome *'Moreno'* going to die?" She heard no answer. She expected none. Her mind drifting backwards, Ana saw the bold chapter titles of her four storybook years as Antonio's *namorada* and *noiva* (girlfriend and fiancée), more vividly than the sparkling well-lit white walls of the hospital looming up straight ahead of her: Prince Charming Rides up on a

Bicycle...Dancing 'Til Three...Being Loved on a City Square Bench...Walking in the Rain...Our First *Carnaval*...Stopping for Early Mass on the Way to the Outdoor Market...Two-hour Bus Rides to and from Beach Holidays...Sunday Picnics in the Park...

"Ana? Are you listening? We're here, Ana! Are you ready to go in?" Startled back to reality, Ana shook, the weight of her mixed emotions too much to bear. It was as if someone had thrown her pink love, her gray depression, her red anger, and her khaki fear into a mixing bowl, started beating with all their might, and dared her to survive the resulting brown turbulence.

"No, Geraldo. I'm not really ready. You go see him and let me sit here. I need a little time." She sank into the nearest chair, from where she watched Geraldo's back grow smaller and smaller as he walked down the long hospital corridor, then simply stared at the empty space after he turned the corner. Suddenly overwhelmed with the hospital smells, Ana felt the need for air, and headed for the door.

Minutes seemed like hours. Staring at the apparently blank sky, she eventually became aware of a few stray stars flickering dimly, far away. Was God out there? Did He see her turmoil? Did he care about her anguish? Ana found herself praying: "Holy Mary, mother of God, pray for us sinners now and in the hour of our death." Over and over, she repeated the familiar words. Mechanically. Despairingly. Endlessly.

"Are you ready now, Ana?" Geraldo, back at her side, put a protective arm around her. Ana nodded, mumbling "I've got to do this" under her breath.

"Is he conscious? Is he better? Is he worse? What did the doctor say?" Geraldo, knowing she needed support more than information, just held her tightly as they moved along quickly, Ana staring down at the interminable dark red tiles.

Outside the closed door, Geraldo tried to prepare her. "He's white as his sheets, he's got lots of tubes, and well, he doesn't look very good, Ana. But you're strong. Be brave, okay?"

Bracing herself, Ana walked through the door Geraldo held open. Her blurred eyes quickly searched the row of beds, then turned back with a questioning look.

"He's over there in the corner, behind the folding screen," Geraldo assured her, as he gently guided her there.

"I'll wait here, so...well, so you can go in alone, Ana."

When she remained immobile, Geraldo awkwardly gave her a little push, whispering, "I'll be right here, girl, I guarantee. Now go on."

For a long time she stood by the bed, staring at the lifeless form. At that moment she knew with more certainty than ever before, that the words she had had engraved inside his golden engagement band were, indeed, still true: "Ana loves Antonio."

While her body stood frozen, her heart melted within her. Silently she loved him, stifling her sobs and longing to gather him up, tubes and all, just to hold him in her arms and be able to verbalize the words flying across the screen of her mind. For now, she must keep them to herself: "Antonio, Antonio. I love you, my *Moreno*. Please don't die!"

"Ana?" It was such a soft sound, Ana thought perhaps she had imagined it. But now as she focused on Antonio's lips, she saw them moving. Again Ana heard her name, barely audible. Looking into his just opened eyes, and carefully squeezing his free hand, she found herself unable to speak.

Slowly, however, Ana became joyfully aware that Antonio was squeezing her hand! Ready to burst into tears, she fiercely fought to control herself. But just when she was managing to return his attempt at a smile, Ana suddenly realized his beautiful dark eyes had closed again, and his hand lay limp in hers. Gone? So quickly?

Back at her front door, Ana fumbled for the key.

"It's here in my pocket, I know it is, Geraldo," she whimpered. "See? Here it is!"

"Okay, Ana. Are you going to be all right? Well...... are you sure you don't want me to stay with you a while longer?"

"Everything's fine, Geraldo. I just need to be alone. And—thanks for everything, hear?"

The next morning Ana awakened right where she had collapsed the previous night: on top of the clean clothes she had thrown on the bed when she'd hurriedly rescued them from the rain the previous afternoon. How long ago that was!

But now the clothes went unnoticed, as Ana hastened to wash her face, brush her teeth, put on a fresh dress, and dash out the door. She had to go to the hospital. She must know what had happened during the night. Her feet flew, covering the distance to the hospital in record time.

Charging past the reception desk, Ana raced down the corridor to that unforgettable door, and marched right into the men's ward. Panning all the other beds, she zoomed in on the bed behind the folding screen, daring her Antonio to still be lying on the bed. Alive.

He was. But soon the nurse confirmed what Ana's own inventory had suggested:

"Unfortunately he has slipped into a deeper coma. Are you a relative of his?" The pretty little nurse asked it in such a kind voice, Ana felt she could trust her.

"Well, not yet. But please let me stay? I'll be quiet. After all, I was going to be his 'legitimate wife,' so it's almost the same, right?"

The days melded into weeks. Yet each day, for as many hours as they would allow her, Ana sat by Antonio's bed. Sometimes despairing, sometimes hopeful, but always praying, she held his hand and determinedly tried to will him to live. The only time she left his side voluntarily was when the nurses invited her to the daily devotional hour held in the lobby. After the first time, she never missed a one.

There, the hymns they sang comforted her troubled soul. Then as the doctors and nurses took turns opening up that black book they reverently referred to as "God's Word," Ana heard them read and explain truths she had never even dreamed possible.

A loving God? A God actually interested in everyone, personally? A God really reaching out to her, Ana, in all of her human pain? At first it seemed too extraordinary to be possible, but slowly, the words from "God's Word" imprinted themselves on her mind, their truth penetrating her empty heart.

Several of the nurses befriended her and, as they came in and out, Ana felt free to ask questions, to express her doubts. Gradually she began to understand that this Jesus they all seemed to know and love was, indeed, God! Even more incredible, He loved her, Ana, and wanted to be a vital part of her life.

"I'm so sorry, Dona Ana. But he is gone," the doctor announced, having made a final check on Antonio's pulse and pupils. Standing beside her, Geraldo reached for Ana, bracing himself for her outburst of grief.

She, however, quietly went up to the body and kissed her former "reason for living." Ana then smiled at the doctor through her tears, and quietly explained to a puzzled Geraldo, "How can I be devastated? Thanks to God, this tragedy has a happy ending for me. You didn't know, Geraldo, but that night you went to get me, I had decided to kill myself, for without Antonio I had no reason to go on living.

"This month in the hospital has brought me to a lasting reason for living: Jesus! He is helping me to bear this pain, so I'm not alone. In Him I found the best exit possible from my old life, so that now I can start a new life!"

After being an integral but invisible part of the San Francisco Beat Scene, CYNTHIA NEWBY LUCE moved on to the University of Pennsylvania for a Masters in Experimental Psychology (Perception) and Anthropology. Back home in California, she worked for the Lowie Museum in Berkeley (UCB) then hopped on a Japanese freighter for Brazil in 1964. Brazil has been part of her life up to the present except for a nine year stint in an academic marriage, mostly spent in the US. She has lived permanently in a mountain village in the interior since 1975 writing fiction, non-fiction (some published) and doing archaeology.

Iraní

by Cynthia Newby Luce

It had taken some time to find the local tinsmith, maker of roof-gutters and drainpipes. He lived a good way out of the village, about six kilometers on the dirt road that followed the river through the lushly forested steep mountain valley, finally connecting with the asphalt that led to a bigger city. I'd known Sebastião and seen his wife Iraní in the village many times but had never been to their home. I wasn't sure exactly where they lived, however it was obvious I was getting close because I began to see various children in a wide range of ages playing, running and screaming in the road. They all looked remarkably like Sebastião and in some ineffable way, were a mini-mirror of his ways. Even though I would not call Brazil really third world, the scene I came to was classic: a house of mud and wattle walls, glass-less windows with only shutters of slats nailed together, bare earth with a slightly sour smell of urine; the sure signs of many people housed in a very small space.

I finished ordering the gutters and drainpipes from Sebastião, a dark, thin, little man whose quick movements and darting eyes reminded me of a spider-monkey. Then I digested the sight of his dumpy, once-more pregnant wife standing a little behind and to the side of him with a bunch of the smaller children loosely clustered around her.

She had a slightly smiling but sorrowful face and was mostly Indian in her looks—probably Puri—with other blood that seemed to have diluted the usual vitality and vigor of the pure unacculturated Indian. Her straight black hair hung lankly to her shoulders, her brown face furrowed in mysterious unvoiced pain; she was a woman not old but made old, exhausted. As I saw her discomfort, the dirty children flowing around her, noisy and demanding, I looked at her legs, misshapen with veins discolored and distended, covered with great lumps like huge marbles under the skin. I thought of how almost everyday one read about some joyous miracle involving a women and her mate who triumph over nature, overcoming infertility and producing, amid sanguine trumpeting of euphoric journalists, yet another one, two, or even four, five or six human beings.

Back in my car, relieved to have something between myself and the messes and smells, I was about to leave when the tinsmith, in a burst of friendliness, perhaps because he thought he had struck a good bargain, sought to prolong our contact. He leaned into the car with a conspiratorial air.

"Just think, soon there'll be another one," he said, gesturing proudly towards his wife. She shifted her weight on her feet as if in a slow motion dance away from pain. Realizing I must say something, I uttered the obvious and asked which this would be.

"Number thirteen," he answered, popping with satisfaction.

Some would say I did not have the right to speak further. But as a concerned citizen of this planet who has received an alarming statistic from a well-known and competent demographer who told me that if by the year 2015 AD nothing is done to curb the present rate of population growth, a person will have less than one square meter to stand on, I looked at Iraní's belly and couldn't keep quiet.

"Ah, Sr. Sebastião, perhaps now it is time to think of stopping," I ventured in the mildest of tones and smiled to blunt any effect from the full impact of what I'd said. For an instant I thought to myself that I hadn't been forceful enough, that he hadn't understood me. But a second later I was in for it.

"What do you mean stop?" he said loudly, straightening his body and puffing up with instant anger. "God said, 'Go forth and multiply,' and that is what I'm doing. Only God will decide when I'll stop having children."

"How does your wife feel about that?" I said before I thought, beginning to be irritated by the man. By then, though, he had given me a disdainful flick of his hand to dismiss me and gone off. Iraní and the children had also evaporated.

When the drains were done Sebastião installed them. He was dour and it seemed like he'd decided that there would be no more exchanges. And I, involved so intently in just living in this place—so different, so exotic—forgot about the man and his wife locked in their relentless fertility.

Then one very hot day I was driving on the dirt road going from the village to the nearby town. I saw a heavy swollen form propelled by the legs that had agonized me so to look at before with their purple blotches and marble-lumps. It was Sebastião's wife, Iraní. She was moving slowly through the heat and dust with the youngest one-and-a-half-year old in her arms, a toddler by the hand and another couple that must have been about four and five, trailing along behind. I couldn't take my eyes off her legs, and I stopped the car even though the children's faces showed the remains of something sticky which meant sticky hands, which meant everything would be sticky.

With a sigh and a furtive but grateful glance at me, Iraní and the children settled in the car and we moved off.

"Hot," I said, using the Portuguese word *calor,* which not only means a high temperature but the humid oppressive heat before a rain: a word often used to establish contact, a kind of commiseration and camaraderie. "It's not a day to go walking," I added inanely, knowing full well, of course, that she was only walking because she had to.

Iraní was on her way home after a visit to the hospital. Today, instead of being uncomfortable and passive, she was uncomfortable and agitated. The heat and my giving her a ride had interacted with her agitation, and she began to talk. I can't even remember the conversation that led into what became a great outpouring of her discontent.

Apparently, the old car I'd seen in the garage worked and Iraní's husband spent most of his money on gasoline for it. He liked to run around pottering and frittering away the hours. Gasoline was relatively expensive, so it was a kind of insanity to waste gasoline just cruising here and there.

Iraní had felt so weak that morning that she'd had to stop washing the laundry she took in to pay for food and medicine for herself and the children. Sebastião, however, had refused to take her to the hospital. She'd taken the early bus from town that passed her house in the morning heading for the village, but it only returned at 5:30 in the afternoon so she'd been obliged to walk home.

"They told me I shouldn't do washing but then I'd have no money at all. I've got to eat and I've got to see the doctor when I feel bad," she said, "even if I can't afford to buy medicine."

"Don't you have INPS?"--the medical insurance everyone had which cost at that time approximately seven or eight dollars per month--I asked, as the hospital gave out medicine free to the needy in those days. But of course she did not have it.

To me the only solution for this woman was to tie her tubes. However, after the intensely negative reaction of her husband to the idea of not having any more children, and realizing I had no right to meddle, I hesitated to mention the only sure way out that I could see that did not entail a drastic rearrangement of her life situation.

"Do you want any more children?" I ventured, ready for almost any response.

"My God, no," she said vehemently, sighed, and added in a voice devoid of energy, "I just do not know what to do."

Relieved, I told her that if she had a Caesarian section with this delivery she could ask to have her tubes tied. She seemed happy at the idea, not only because she didn't want any more children but also because it would mean less trouble with her veins. She asked me to help her talk to the doctor, which I agreed to do. We rode a bit in silence. For the first time I saw a half-smile on Iraní's face. Then she began to talk.

"Some years ago, I think it was two children before this, I went to the little hospital in São João to have a baby and the old doctor there was just messing around and nothing was happening. He thought the head was coming out but the nurse pointed between my legs and said, 'Oh, Doctor, what's coming out isn't the baby's head. It's her varicose veins!'

"When the doctor put the forceps under the baby it slipped up. The doctor said to me, 'Iraní, you can't have any more children. If you have any more, you are going to have internal bleeding from those veins. You could die.'"

Maybe if I'd been able to talk with the old doctor who knew Iraní so well, things would have gone more smoothly. It's a good thing I have a persistent streak in me because we now were obliged to deal with Dr. Rogerio, a young local fellow from one of the older families who had been born in the village. He had a practice that included working in the hospital in our village, and that seemed to infuse him with an ill-disguised and incomprehensible conceit. He was short and stocky of Italian peasant descent, with very curly blond hair and a pale complexion. In fact, everything about him was pale: his eyes, his near-white bushy eyebrows and near invisible eyelashes. All the time I was talking to him, although he'd occasionally smile in an appeasing and impersonal way, especially when refusing to give me clear-cut answers, he never looked at my face or in my eyes. I thought because I was dealing with a person of a higher level of education than 99% of the villagers, I could be direct, but I found it infinitely more complicated than I expected.

Dr. Rogerio knew of Iraní's case and had treated her several times and, if she were to be operated on, he would be the one to do it. I presented my case for a Caesarian section and tubal ligation at the time of her delivery but Dr. Rogerio wasn't going to give me any satisfaction and wasn't even going to discuss the matter with me in any reasonable way. He said he did not want to deal with the 'social factors', *i.e.* the husband, nor the cost or risk, and anyway, she was old; he had to wait and see and he wouldn't tell me anything one way or another.

"What will happen, will happen," he said.

Such a fatalistic attitude further deepened the channels of frustration. Of course there was a solution. I could see it, and Iraní, in her desperation and fear, could feel it. The maddeningly illogical obstructions the doctor conjured up, and the apparently insubstantial words that formed his illogical decisions, represented to me a whimsical will of iron. It was also clear to me, from this first talk with Dr. Rogerio, that it wasn't only his views of the social elements and the medical problems in Iraní's situation that were a problem, but there was a deeper current moving against me. I was a foreigner and also a woman who had perceived a situation in his domain with a sharper focus and different perspective, a foreigner and a woman who reached a solution he not only hadn't entertained but didn't want to be bothered with.

I was dismissed with a firm handshake and an impersonal smile with no eye contact which didn't allow for opportunities to try and discuss the matter further. The only concrete thing that did come out of it all was that I was expected to pay Iraní's medical insurance and medicine. Ironically, Dr. Rogerio had given me the faintest glimmer of hope that I could have what he thought I wanted (as if it were all for me) if I would assume payment of her medical insurance.

I wonder what Dr. Rogerio thought of my silent retreat down the street. I consciously tried to let go of the unvoiced anger by unknotting the tension in my chest as I had to save my energies figuring out what to do next.

To my dismay, before I could formulate another approach, Iraní went into labor prematurely. Because I was now paying her medical insurance she was taken to a better equipped hospital in a nearby town. The child was born naturally but dead. The tube-tying issue was conveniently forgotten. The only thing the dear Dr. Rogerio said was that she should rest and not have any more children!

Shortly after that I began hearing about Iraní from people like my friend Dora the dressmaker, who'd periodically helped Iraní out with bits of cloth and sometimes a little money over the amount she paid Iraní for doing laundry for her. One day Dora surprised me by asking how things were going with Iraní.

"The only way out for her is to tie her tubes," I said, as Dora was one of the few people to whom I could speak directly.

"Iraní's afraid, I suppose, of her husband," Dora answered.

"What do you mean? I know he's religious but she does-n't seem very worried about that."

"Several years ago she was really in bad shape from so many pregnancies. Everything was out of place and her hus-band had objected but they said she could not go on: they'd have to operate to put things right; she was in too much pain with things hanging out. They told the husband he'd have to leave her alone for at least a month. After the operation she stayed in the hospital five days and then went home. Her husband, who's an animal I'll tell you, was just determined to get at her. At night he'd pace up and down the dirt road in front of the house; he was like a bull pawing the earth."

As awful as it was, I had to smile at the image of that skinny little monkey-man pawing the earth in sexual frustration.

"Then, three days after Iraní was home, he jumped her from behind early one evening, and took her by force. It wasn't hard as she was so weak she could hardly stand. She had to go back to the hospital to be stitched up again. She was finally OK, but I don't think she's ever been 100% since."

I continued paying the medical insurance for Iraní and also the contraceptive pills which she took secretly. But her husband caught her taking them and kept railing away, saying it was a sin and threatening that if she continued to take the pills, he'd take it up with the church, and she'd fry in hell. But she took them anyway, she was so afraid of getting pregnant again. She also took tranquilizers as she developed what she called "attacks" from the birth-control pills.

But soon Iraní came to me saying Dr. Rogerio had told her she couldn't take the pills anymore because of her "nerves." She'd told him about her episodes of falling down and going blind. Reluctantly, I realized I had to try again. It seemed to me she was having something like epileptic attacks.

Everyone has had a dream at least once about running frantically, fleeing some impending disaster, but not being able to move, or running in place not nearly fast enough. My next conversation with Dr. Rogerio had that quality. There were all the facts, the most urgent one being that Iraní was a woman who had had so many pregnancies she was falling apart. She could not avoid sexual contact with her husband, and now, it seemed, could not take contraceptive pills without life-threatening consequences. Even though the only safe solution was obvious, Dr. Rogerio was as elusive as before and in another repeat, of what I call "treading water" conversations, I got nowhere and was forced, again, to retreat in silence.

I was living on a shoestring with a child to raise and did not have the money to take Iraní to Rio where I probably could arrange an operation more easily. (Besides, would her husband let her go?) As it was, it was sometimes a real sacrifice for me to pay her medical insurance and the expensive medicines every month.

But before I could formulate another idea to try and save Iraní I was suddenly called away to take care of my dying mother. It was five months before I could return and I was still rather numb from grieving when a short time after my return, a taxi deposited Iraní on my doorstep. She was obviously once again very heavy with child and more distraught than ever.

"Oh thank God Senhora has come back," she panted as I paid the taxi who then drove away smiling as he'd overcharged me and for once I'd not taken the time to argue.

Despite my having made an agreement with the butcher that he would offer assistance to Iraní in my absence and despite his telling me he'd give her money for medicine, she had, whether through fear of her husband finding out or some unpleasant hitch developing later, refused help and gotten pregnant. And now Iraní was scared. She was almost incoherent, and as she talked I found the whole thing made little sense. Plus the fact that we seemed right back to square one!

"After Senhora left, I really had trouble. My husband kept threatening to hit me; said I'd go to hell if I continued taking the pill. I got so bad it was hard to do the laundry in order to have enough to buy the pill; and my husband, you know, won't give us money for food and I had to feed the kids and all. My veins got so bad I could hardly stand and the doctor told me I couldn't take the pill anymore, that I could die taking the pill and I couldn't get pregnant anymore because that could kill me too. He gave me tranquilizers for my nerves but I got pregnant anyway. Now they say I shouldn't get pregnant and I have to have a Caesarian but I don't have INPS because Senhora went away and I can't work. If I have the child the normal way I could die."

I'd been walking Iraní into the house and towards the couch during this long outpouring and finally out of breath and at a gesture from me, she collapsed onto the couch, weeping.

She only calmed down when I assured her I'd get the medical insurance straightened out, which meant paying all the back months to reinstate her immediately. I also promised to talk to Dr. Rogerio again about tying her tubes. I must have sounded like God talking to her because she got herself together and even managed a smile and bestowed a sort a benediction.

"Senhora is a saint," she said and I grimaced inwardly at the new struggle I could see before me. St. Georgia slaying the dragon of....of what?....illogic, machismo, religious unreality, fatalism.

Could I do it?

It took some time to catch up with Dr. Rogerio. It was as if he'd gotten a whiff of my intentions and took pains to avoid me but finally I cornered him in the hospital and presented myself, putting in gear my well-rehearsed façade of calm, rational neutrality. As before, he put me off, smiling as if talking to a child, his glance with his pale eyes sliding away from any real contact in a way that was beginning to infuriate me beyond my ability to control my temper. I had to retreat again after being dismissed once more.

He'd dismissed me but the situation, like a noxious wad, sat in my mouth unchewed and unswallowed. Soon after my unsatisfying talk with Dr. Rogerio, one of Iraní's daughters arrived at my house one afternoon as I was enjoying that tranquil hour of the sunset and a comforting cup of tea on the verandah. That sensual glow that made things luminous in the reflection of the last smile of the sun had put me in such a mood of inner joy that it was a few moments before I could refocus on the agitation Iraní's daughter brought with her.

"Oh Dona Marta, please, you must do something. Mother is so bad, in so much pain, she fell down, and we're all so afraid. Is she going to die?" She was so upset I immediately took her into the house and got some sugar water into her, the standard remedy for a "nervous" reaction, especially for women. By the time I'd collected my thoughts, night had fallen abruptly.

"Where's your father?" I asked. "Why didn't he take her to the hospital?"

"Oh, you know Papa," she answered in disgust. "He disappeared with his car and hasn't come back."

Well, I couldn't put it off any longer. It was Dr. Rogerio time again.

And this time I found him at home. Seeing that the house was the very strong pink associated, the psychologists say, with dominant women, I knocked on the door feeling insecure indeed. My only hope was that I could I could assess the situation correctly and in the end, be effective. Up to now I'd just been spinning my wheels with this doctor.

It was Dr. Rogerio's wife, Magdalena, who opened the door and invited me in with a friendly manner. She was of a physical type so common in the village that she was to me indistinguishable from a dozen other women I saw all the time. Smooth pale skin, round dark eyes, small nose and neat mouth set in a roundish face and framed by short, straight, dark brown hair. For a moment I could not remember her name but she remembered mine.

Dr. Rogerio was sitting in one of the two brown overstuffed armchairs in the small living room. His wife returned to her seat on the matching sofa and motioned for me to sit on the remaining chair.

I thought I sensed a positive interest as Magdalena sat relaxed, with one foot tucked up under her. Dr. Rogerio seemed more tense but at least he looked at me as he turned in his seat to greet me.

"How are you?" he asked formally.

He hadn't gotten up; I suppose it was because they had both been watching TV which his wife had switched off before sitting down again. It was all so homey I hoped I would not be overwhelmed and defeated by the fact that I'd entered this cozy domestic scene and feel too inhibited to initiate a rupture in the pervasive mood. As my mind raced for just the right phrases to begin—polite but firm, it had to be—I wondered just how much of this was a game with Dr. Rogerio; how ego-involved he was. In the end I could think of nothing more diplomatic than to speak frankly and to the point without the usual preambles one was expected to use when being persuasive.

"I have to speak to you about Iraní because it's urgent," I began.

"Oh?" Dr. Rogerio replied quizzically, as if Iraní's case were not immediate, as if it were in the misty past or far-removed future.

"Her daughter came to my house just now and is waiting in the car. She's very upset because she says Iraní is in terrible pain. Dr. Rogerio, that woman has to stop having children. You know very well if she keeps on she'll die. And then who will take care of all those children? You just have to tie her tubes; there is no other way." I ended a bit breathlessly, afraid to say more as I could see by the way he was casting his eyes about that his impatience with me was mounting and I realized why; I'd presumed to tell him what he had to do.

"Look, Dona Marta, it's much too complicated to tie her tubes," he began. "You don't understand the situation."

"Tell me!" I demanded emphatically and tried to stare into his shielded eyes as if to drag out those elusive reasons hiding in the darkness of his mind and expose them to the light.

"Well, you know her husband's against any meddling and he could get angry. I'm not interested in tangling with him." That was his first thrust and I began to detect that hard male will building a solid impenetrable barrier behind his words.

"I think the situation has gone beyond his will," I countered. "The man is a selfish animal and I can prove it. Shall I call the daughter out of the car? She'll tell you how her father never buys food for the house, how he buys a little meat and demands they cook it for him and then he eats it all while his children watch in hunger. It's Iraní that passes out with pain washing clothes to feed those kids while Sebastião runs around in his car."

"Ah, I don't know," he began, I hopefully thought, wavering.

"I know, Dr. Rogerio," I started in again. I leaned forward bringing my face nearer. "Iraní doesn't want any more children, and it's her body, not his!"

"Yes," interjected Magdalena, "why not, if she doesn't want any more children."

"But she's almost into menopause, she's forty-three. Why go to all the trouble if she'll probably never get pregnant again?" he said to us both.

"How can you suppose that?" I said forcefully. "Has she shown any sign of menopause? On the contrary, she's the type that's fertile into her 50's, and every time she gets pregnant you think it's her last. She could have two or three more kids, and every time she's more likely to die."

"And if I operate and she dies? With those veins she might die, you know," he threw out, but it seemed to me he was on less firm ground.

"Dr. Rogerio, she has varicose veins all over inside, you know that. If you refuse to operate she is far more likely to die: It's as simple as that. Your refusal amounts to probably condemning her to death." I delivered this intensely, not daring to deflect my eyes to check if Magdalena was with me, but out of the corner of my eye, I caught her nodding in agreement.

Dr. Rogerio shifted again in his chair. "You say her daughter came to tell you she's in a bad way?" he asked.

The ploy was obvious but I realized I could do no more without creating what they would call a hysterical scene.

"We'd better take a look at her. Can you get her to the hospital? She isn't really due yet but there may be a problem."

Dr. Rogerio seemed strong again, in control. He could deal with the immediate present and didn't have to commit himself.

"Is her INPS paid up?" he asked me.

"Oh yes, all paid up," I assured him a little too eagerly and rose to go.

"Go bring her to the little hospital then; I'll meet you there," he directed as I went out.

Iraní's pain was due to pressure on her veins and not premature labor, so Dr. Rogerio medicated her and ordered her to rest.

I took her back home and gave her money for food as she couldn't do washing and was fretting about food; and I gave her more money for a car to take her to the hospital when it was time. She asked me about what Dr. Rogerio was going to do and I had to admit I wasn't sure. I told her to be adamant about wanting her tubes tied and not be afraid of demanding that it be done, because it was her right. Dr. Rogerio wouldn't tell Iraní or me just when he was planning the Caesarian. I think because he didn't want either Sebastião or me around.

The day finally came. Sebastião was out in his car and since I was on my monthly trip to Rio, I knew nothing about it.

A few days after I returned from Rio I was mulling over the miserable state of between-season vegetables at the greengrocer's when one of Iraní's older daughters, Flavia, ran up to me. For a moment I thought Iraní had died. But before apprehension could fully blossom, Flavia blurted out, "Momma had the baby. She's okay."

"What happened?" I wanted to know.

"I don't know, you'd better talk to her," she told me looking around to see which of the villagers was listening.

So I took Flavia home and went in to see Iraní and the baby, hoping Sebastião was away. But he was there, puttering around. His head deep into the motor of his car, he glanced at me slyly without raising his head, then pretended he didn't know I was there.

The house had the smell of black beans cooking, the usual urine, and now, fresh baby! Iraní lay on a narrow slat bed in the corner of the very small cramped room and was covered with a worn-out patchwork quilt, the baby at her side, a wizened, dark little thing, who seemed to be crying in anger. But Iraní smiled at me wide and clear.

"How was it?" I asked, "Are you in much pain?"

"Oh, it all hurts, and I don't have much milk, but thank God I'm alive," she said smiling again.

"Iraní! Did you really think something might happen? Did you think you might die?" I asked, peering out the open window trying to see if Sebastião were lurking about as she warned me he tended to do.

"If you want to know, I was terrified. I think the doctor waited too long. I think he couldn't make up his mind. I arrived at noon and walked and walked around until five in the morning, losing water.

"It was already morning and lots of my family and friends were already visiting me when Dr. Rogerio arrived and took me into the operating room and he said it wasn't going to be a normal birth. They did the Caesarian but the baby was stuck and they had to get a nurse and another girl and they pushed on top of my stomach to force the child out. They finally got him out and it was a big strong boy."

"And?" I asked, all of a sudden not wanting to ask directly about what interested me most. "Did they do it?"

Iraní shifted painfully, trying to see if her husband was around. Then she got rid of all the kids hanging about leaning against the door jambs, sitting on the edge of the bed and even peering in the window.

"Go on, let me talk to Dona Marta; go finish making dinner," she said as forcefully as she could. "The boys are the worst, they tell their father everything," she said, beckoning me closer and patting the bed for me to sit.

I perched carefully on the very edge of the bed and leaned forward.

"My husband doesn't know," she said in a loud whisper. "No one knows, and Dr. Rogerio made me promise I wouldn't tell anyone, but he did it."

"Oh, Iraní, that's wonderful; now you don't have to worry," I said and reached out to pat her arm.

"Dr. Rogerio also said I had to come back when the baby was weaned so he could do something about the veins. He said he'd better get that done before you came after him again because you're so '*brava'*—fierce." Iraní started to laugh but stopped because of her stitches.

The children were already creeping back and I heard Sebastião slam down the hood of his beloved car so I took my leave, promising to come back soon.

I passed out of the house with its intense compressed smells into the cool fragrant air freshened by the vapors of the passing river and the afternoon shadows invading the narrow valley. Everything, even Iraní, was calm. I should have felt harmonious and calm, too, but I found myself agitated. There were contentious voices yammering in my head at each other. One recriminating voice said I had no right to make waves, such violent waves. But just as intensely, another voice said that Iraní, as one human being to another, had asked my help and I'd done the best I knew how; even though, to Sebastião, I was some sort of she-devil who had led his wife into sin.

Driving home, I for once resisted being pleasured by the beauty of the land that so perpetually enchants my senses with primordial shapes and vivid colors of trees and flowers. The seduction of nature against the torments of culture. This time the torments won. I had never thought of myself as a prime-mover of anything but myself; had always refused to get involved. Now I realized that the best I could ever do was muddle through. What I didn't yet know, but was soon to learn, was that in this country there are always mysterious ironies lurking around the corner.

After her last child and operation Iraní was cheerful but looked very tired. Her husband, now that she wasn't producing any more children, brought even less money home and she still had small children to feed. She still fainted over her washing.

Then suddenly—may I be excused from smiling at anyone's misfortune—Sebastião, the old horny monkey-man, up and died!

"Oh," I thought as I remembered the years I'd paid the health insurance, "more relief for Iraní." The ironies, though, were cackling around the corner.

By some unthinkable, blind, dimwit bureaucratic mistake, Sebastião's death certificate was made out to be Sebastiana—a woman! It took us another two years of battling bureaucracy before Iraní could receive her widow's pension and rest her legs.

And though we laughed over the little error that cost so much time and energy to correct, both of us couldn't help but think that Sebastião had had, if not the last laugh, at least the last chuckle.

But wait, there is just one more thing.

It is now several years later and I saw Iraní the other day in the village. She looked much younger than her fifty-seven years and was smiling to herself and then even more broadly as she caught sight of me.

We exchanged warm greetings and then she eagerly confided to me what she was obviously bursting for me to know.

"Ah, Dona Marta, you know I think men are so funny. There is a young man coming around saying he wants to live with me. And every time I see the ex-mayor (newly widowed and eighty-five) he gives me a squeeze and says he wants to marry me!"

"Viva!" I thought, smiling at her, *"Viva,* Iraní, *Viva!"*

GEOFFREY THOMAS is British and came to Brazil over twenty years ago. Shortly after arriving, he found himself involved in farming as a partner of a farm in the interior of the state of São Paulo. He has been involved in some way with Brazilian agricultural ventures on a part time basis ever since.

Bauru Baseball

by Geoffrey Thomas

Tim looked across at the magnificent view. From where he sat, he could see the cattle which appeared as masses of white dots in the huge pastures. Further over, patches of darker green showed the areas where the crops were planted and were growing vigorously in the strong sunshine. Nearer the house, down to the left was the concrete work of what was obviously going to be the swimming pool and next to it was a small football pitch.

"I see you're quite a sportsman," he said.

"Oh, yes," said Otto. "You can see that's the football pitch. Just below that is where we play volleyball; up to the right is my ten hole golf course and..."

"Ten holes ?"

"A bit of one upmanship over the neighbours, I'm afraid."

"Yes..." Tim looked over to where a tractor was leveling off a large strip of land, "and what's that—the polo field?" he asked, smiling.

"Oh dear no. I don't like horses very much. That's the baseball area."

"I didn't know you played baseball." Tim had trouble imagining this round man with a glove on, chewing on a wad of tobacco and shouting encouragement from the infield.

"Oh, yes," said Otto. "All my Japanese neighbours are fanatics. I play with them."

He paused. "It's a bit of a long story..."

Tim sat down on the ground next to him.

"You know that I came here from Germany about forty years ago. I had had some small troubles with the authorities there, which I'll maybe tell you about some other time and, mainly because of this, I headed away from the big cities to settle here in the interior. Of course, at that time the town here was little more than a collection of houses with one paved road, and it was relatively easy to get hold of a small piece of land and start farming.

"My first trials were of two crops that I had actually never seen before, let alone had any technical idea of how they should be grown. But nature is kind, both pineapples and watermelons do well in this type of soil and I soon started doing very well and had masses of them which, in season, we shipped by the truckload into town.

"Of course, those were the good days, you know, before things got complicated by such things invoices or inspectors and taxes, and things like that. It was really very simple. Truckloads of fruit went out and truckloads of money came back. However, I soon noticed that the prices I was getting were always just a little below those in the market. At first I suspected the driver, but after a few inquiries which convinced me that he was as honest as the day is long, I just forgot about it and contented myself in getting the money, surviving and being able to invest a bit more.

"Then, one year, must have been about ten years ago now, we had one of those freak summers—a long cold spell followed by incredible high temperatures—making all the fruit in the region ripen at the same time and creating an enormous glut on the market. I was expecting low prices, but what happened was worse still; instead of a truckload of money, however small, the driver returned with a truckload of fruit, having been unable to sell it. I immediately turned the truck round and went back into town where I had my first brush with the Japanese Mafia."

He paused, picked up a bit of grass and sucked on it. "You may not know," he continued "but for some time now all the land around here has belonged to the Japanese. They are all third generation descendants of that first wave of immigrants who came to this country and made good by simple hard work. What I hadn't realised, was that all the fruit buyers in the market are also Japanese, in fact the whole organisation is rather like being in downtown Tokyo on a Saturday night. I was being treated as an outsider, a pretty sobering thing to discover in what I consider my country, too. Of course I complained, I smiled, I argued and I threatened, but all I got was the most polite treatment in all cases and the situation continued as before.

"Trying to resolve the situation by charm I invited all the neighbours and their friends and relatives to a huge barbecue here and laid on loads of meat, beer and even had some sake flown in, I was that desperate. The event was a total disaster. We all ate and drank ourselves silly, mainly because we didn't have anything else to do with our mouths; after all there's only so much you can talk about on the subject of pineapple and watermelon.

"After a certain time the conversation dried up, as it were. Everyone went home with drunken smiles all over their faces (nobody had touched the sake, by the way), but, over the next few months, the situation in the market didn't change.

"I was desperate at this point; I was, of course, surviving very well financially but the whole thing had become a challenge, a matter of honour. And that was when I discovered baseball."

Tim still didn't follow this, but kept quiet.

"Asking around, I found out that all the neighbours, the fruit merchants and, in fact, the whole Japanese community were baseball fanatics. Every Sunday they would all get together for the big game at which large amounts of beer were drunk, and heaps of betting money changed hands. It's rumoured that farms have been won and lost over infield doubles."

"So, the next Sunday, I sneaked over to my neighbour Fukuyama's farm and, sure enough, through the trees I got a glimpse of this great event taking place.

"I should explain that I didn't even know what baseball was at that time. Like most people in this country, if you throw a ball at me, I would never catch it, but rather let it hit me on the chest and drop to the ground in preparation for kicking. But, not being one to do things by halves, I sent away and within a few weeks, got all the books of rules, how to play the game, instructions, videos and a large variety of bats, balls and gloves. As a bonus, I got a do-it-yourself teaching aid called the 'Wham-O' which, when unpacked, proved to be a pole which one stuck in the ground and from which a plastic baseball hung down on the end of a piece of elastic.

"Having studied the books and videos and things, I took one of my bats and had a few preliminary hearty swings at various small bushes and the lower fruit on the mango trees in season—it's surprising what good targets mangoes make—and to my delight I got increasingly more accurate (and the bat more messy). The improvement was particularly fast when I made the amazing discovery that one did not have to wear the glove for batting, and I finally decided that I was ready for the 'Wham-O'.

"The ball on the end of the elastic tended to bounce up and down a bit which put it one degree of difficulty above your stationary mango, and it was some time and a considerable number of hearty swishes before I connected.

"The result was dramatic. The ball flew away towards the pasture, hung in the air for a second or two, and then came rocketing back at my head with equal, or even increased, speed. It was a close thing. I dived to the ground and fortunately had the good sense to stay there in my panic-stricken and shocked state for, if I hadn't, the darned thing would have got me slap in the back of the neck on the way back.

"For months I practiced with my 'Wham-O', watched videos, and generally did everything to become a potted expert in the game. At last I was ready for the testing time and, dressed casually rather as I am now, I appeared at Fukuyama's farm round about game time. The local inhabitants were, of course, very polite and slightly surprised, and invited me to stay and watch the game. It was very instructional, although not at all on the level of the only games I had watched on videos up till then; such things as 'Play-Offs' and 'World Series' played between various teams with names of birds, animals, articles of clothing and occupations. However, I learned a lot about how the game was played in the lower levels of amateurs and some things about the local rules (first bounce into the pineapples, for example, was a ground rule safety double because people tended to get badly mauled trying to get the ball out of there in a hurry)."

He paused, savouring the story, although he must have told it many times before.

"It took me three Sundays of patient watching before I was invited to play in order to make up the numbers (Shinohara's daughter was ill as I remember it) and, having avoided disgracing myself in the field, it was with considerable trepidation that I stepped up to the plate when my turn came at bat.

"Months of time and a lot of expense had gone into this moment, and I think I would have traded all next year's watermelons just to connect with the ball. Fukuyama himself was pitching and I tried to block out all the noisy Japanese chatter and concentrate on the ball as if it were coming to me on the end of a piece of elastic. I think Fukuyama took pity on me as I was obviously a beginner because, when the ball finally came, it looped gently down right in the line of the plate.

"I still remember that moment in slow motion as it were. You know like in the movies when they slow the action down for full effect; the big punch that Rocky lands in round fifteen to win the championship, or Chuck Norris launching himself across the room with a slow and silent 'Nooooooo..' on his lips as some nasty character is about to shoot his girl friend. With one almighty swing, which gets more perfect every time I think about it, I dispatched the ball not first bounce, not even in, but way over the pineapples."

Otto paused for effect as once again he remembered that moment.

"The one thing I always remember is the complete silence which greeted this almighty blow. Perhaps I can best describe it as 'awed' but it only lasted a short time before being followed by 'oohs' and 'aahs' and general excited Japanese noises and finally cheers and backslapping as I trotted round the bases. I was warmly congratulated until I finally left, although I was unfortunately not able to repeat the performance (or come close to it) that day. I can still remember looking back across the field as I left and seeing hordes of Japanese re-enacting my hit with exaggerated arm movements like Indians telling how many moons must pass before white man can get back into fort. The memory of that ball disappearing over the pineapples was one I knew I'd never forget. I felt sure that I had now solved my problems with integration into the Japanese Mafia. I was wrong.

"It happened to be harvest time, and the next week my produce went to market and was sold at a price which I discovered, after some research, to be no different from the previous times. It seemed that, after all the effort, my brave attempt at baseball philosophy had failed. There was nothing left but to pack up my videos, hang up my 'Wham-O' and give-up. However, I had a big investment in baseball and the truth was that, even without the memory of that over the pineapples home run, I had become hooked on the game. Mafia or not, I continued to play every Sunday until, quite unexpectedly, and in a very strange way, came the turning point.

"I can remember it as if it were yesterday. A bright sunny day and the game, a very close thing which had gone to the eleventh inning. The scores were tied and we had runners on second and third when my turn came to bat. By chance, Fukuyama was pitching again. He now treated me with the full respect of an established batter and had long since given up any charitable thoughts; with the game in the state it was he glared down at me in what might be described as a highly competitive way. If ever the 'watch the ball as if it were on the end of a piece of elastic' technique was needed it was now. Against the background of chatter, I concentrated hard and, when the ball came, met it with a long meaty swing. My timing was, however, just a bit off, and the ball rose mightily, but vertically, into the sun.

"As I had been trained to do, I threw the bat away (practically decapitating Suzuki's son), and headed off for first base. However, running is one thing and curiosity another and, as I pounded down the strip (perhaps "pounding" is not the right word considering my age, size and physical condition), I just couldn't control the urge to look back like Lot's wife and see what had happened to the ball...

"My last memory that day was that of seeing the ball coming down out of the sun with three Japanese waiting underneath; all were shielding their eyes with one hand while waving the others off with the other. I say 'last memory' because, traveling a bit faster than I had imagined, at this point I tripped over the base, colliding head on with Ozaki, the first baseman, whose eyes had also been on the ball and not on me.

"The result was disastrous. Ozaki was as fast as a rabbit in the field but stood only about five foot one in his baseball shoes and was as thin as a match-stick. In accordance with all the laws of physics and what Newton had to say on the subject of momentum, I shot straight through him, turned two somersaults, broke my left arm and my right leg, and woke up in hospital where I spent the next month in plaster and a neck brace.

"This, of course, put an end to my baseball career for a time and apparently cut off all the connections of my plan to get myself integrated into the Japanese Mafia. However, I must have passed the acid test, because they all came to visit me in hospital bringing me all sorts of little gifts and sadistic questions about how far I could move my neck. The next batch of watermelons came in at a marvelous price and, when I think of it, I believe it was the fact that I had suffered which finally broke down the barriers between us. Anyone who can go through such a painful experience in the name of baseball obviously must make the grade.

"Anyway, we're still playing a mean and competitive game of baseball every Sunday, but they're talking of expanding the kiwi plantations over the original baseball diamond so I decided that we'd better have some reserve playing area capacity just in case. As you can see there are no pineapples planted within hitting distance. Maybe if we practice hard enough that dream we all have of going to Japan for some friendly games may come true."

He got up slowly, looking off into the distance as he did so, and started to walk back up the hill.

"I've never been to Japan," he said. "Always wanted to, but never actually got the opportunity. Trouble is neither have any of my neighbours, and they've all forgotten how to speak the language. So someone's going to have to interpret. Maybe if I get some books, videos and a karate 'Wham-O' I can...."

And his voice was lost as he passed over the top of the hill.

HENRY STOREY and his wife, Zoe, have devoted more than 40 years to introducing and conducting Dale Carnegie Leadership and Communication Programs in the West Indies and South America. Henry, now retired, continues his life-long interest in the natural development of rich-soil and clean-water conservation for farm lands. On these subjects he still speaks and writes.

It's Not Fair

by Henry Storey

Old Fernando Costa was way out of character as he and his neighbor, the Judge, sat playing their daily game of checkers and drinking Brazilian beer. Fernando usually displayed a sunny disposition and good humor. This grouchiness and grumbling just wasn't like him.

When the Judge remarked, "That was a stupid move, Fernando, my friend," Fernando blew up.

"Oh, hell, I'm just in a bad temper today."

The Judge laughed and said, "That's pretty obvious. But why?"

"It's that boy of mine."

This surprised his friend. He knew that Fernando doted on the boy. He also knew that Fernando's son gave his parents every reason to be proud of him. Also, it is widely believed that fathers tend to lavish great fondness on their daughters, and Fernando had a very attractive girl just a year or two younger than the boy. Neither of the children had given their parents any worries over their health, habits, morals or the many other irritating things with which most parents have to deal.

Now, his son was becoming a quite competent musician with a high level of proficiency in playing the piano. Although neither Fernando nor his wife had any talent for music, they at least had an appreciation and were proud of Freddy's progress in that field. And since their large farm in Mato Grosso had prospered, they could comfortably indulge their son's ambition for fame and fortune in the world of music. Knowing all this, the Judge was astonished by Fernando's displeasure with Freddy, who was the apple of his father's eye.

In answer to the puzzled expression on his friend's face, Fernando said, "You are a man of wide experience and, in my opinion, great wisdom. I'm going to tell you why I'm upset and perhaps you can tell me what to do. Several months ago, Freddy received an invitation from the prestigious Arturo Toscanini College of Music in Rio. According to my wife, it was so named in honor of the famous Italian conductor who also got his start on the road to fame at an early age in Rio. This invitation was for my son to participate in a piano playing contest in Rio de Janeiro. This was a surprise because, although the boy had won a medal in Campo Grande last year in a competition for young artists, this invitation was for something quite different. This was an open contest, including professionals of all ages."

He paused for a moment before continuing once again. "One day I hope to sit in Carnegie Hall in New York or Albert Hall in London and listen to Freddy play for a distinguished audience, but I feel he is far too young for such a challenge as this one in Rio. I discussed the idea with his music teachers and, to my surprise, they said it would be good experience for him to watch and hear some of the really great pianists in Brazil and match his skill against theirs. They admitted he probably wouldn't carry off any of the top prizes but it would be good seasoning for him. And also he might just win one of the lesser awards which would be a big boost for his morale."

Fernando absently fiddled with one of the checkers. "I still was reluctant to give my permission. When I talked it over with my wife, I was very surprised that she thought it was a good idea, in spite of the fact that she knew I was opposed to it."

He paused again and the Judge prompted,

"And?"

"In a conversation with the Director of the boy's school, a musician who had been a former star performer in Europe, I told him I thought my son was not ready to face this excellent professional talent, that it would be intimidating rather than otherwise. Also, as he was only sixteen years old, I considered it unwise for him to spend several weeks in Rio alone. Perhaps if I could accompany him I might reconsider, but it was impossible for me to get away at that time. The director very graciously said he was going to attend the affair and would be glad to keep an eye on the boy."

Fernando slumped forward over the checker board, placing both hands on his knees.

"But I was unyielding. Then I told my wife that, when Freddy heard my decision, he would respect and obey it without question. My wife agreed but added that he would also probably think me quite silly to deprive him of this great opportunity. That did it! I could no longer defend my position in the face of that kind of opposition. So I announced my willingness to let the boy go. The night before Freddy left for Rio I gave him a generous amount of money for his expenses and said, 'There are three things I want you to remember while you are in Rio. Stay away from alcohol and drugs, have nothing to do with women and sex and be careful with your money. Don't gamble or lend it to anyone.'"

"Well," queried the Judge, "how did the boy get along?"

"He did quite well in the contest. You know he is not shy. Stage fright didn't bother him. Consequently, as he was well prepared by weeks of hard practice, he won a medal for his fingering technique."

"Sounds like a great success to me," commented the Judge.

"Ummmm. He'd finished his piano playing earlier than he expected and decided to see some of the famous sights of Rio: Sugar Loaf, the Corcovado, Maracana Stadium....some other places. He told me that he thought Rio had to be the most beautiful, the most fabulous city in all the world. So he joined a tour and on the top of Sugar Loaf a young lady sidled up to him and said, 'You are a pianist, aren't you?' Flattered that this very pretty girl had recognized him, he replied graciously that he was and for the rest of the tour these two remained together, chatting about who they were and where they came from. She had attended the session when he had won his prize and complimented him on his success. Later, when they were standing in front of the Copacabana Palace Hotel where the tour had started and finished, the girl mentioned that she was thirsty and he immediately invited her to have a drink with him."

"Ah," murmured the Judge knowingly.

"Yes," Fernando straightened and nodded his head. "It wasn't Coca-Cola she was thirsty for. She suggested they go into the Copa Bar which would be cool and quiet after the hot sun on the tour. She seemed right at home in the very attractive bar and he figured that she was perhaps two or three years older than he. Freddy is a good six feet tall and the two would easily appear to be the same age."

Staring intently at his friend, the Judge leaned forward.

"She ordered a gin and tonic, saying it was very refreshing in hot weather and, not wanting to emphasize his rural upbringing, he took one, too. And it was refreshing. They chatted while they were cooling off with another of these refreshing drinks. When the sun moved behind the hotel, they decided to stroll along in the shade of the tall buildings on Atlantica Avenue. As is true of all girls, Angela, which turned out to be her name, was fascinated by the elegant women's wear displayed in the smart shops they passed. When they reached the end of the beach and were about to turn toward Ipanema she squealed with delight. 'Just look at that lovely cashmere sweater. Let's go in and see it.' After carefully feeling the soft quality of the material and holding it up in front of her as Freddy had seen his sister and mother do many times, Angela exclaimed, 'How I wish I'd brought my check book. I'd buy it.'"

Clicking his tongue against his teeth in disapproval, the Judge scowled deeply.

"Freddy had to do some fast thinking. He'd already disregarded two of his father's warnings. Here was another strong but pleasant temptation he was on the verge of disregarding. Then he rationalized, thinking that he hadn't promised or committed himself to take his father's advice. He had lived quite frugally in Rio, so far, and he had plenty of his father's generous allowance left. And, after all, he was sure she would pay him back. The good will he felt and the euphoria engendered by those two gin and tonics tipped the scale."

Lifting his eyebrows, the Judge leaned back, his lips clamped together in disapproval.

"The look of gratitude at his offer to provide the money denied her refusal to accept his offer. They both walked happily out of the shop together, she with her beautiful sweater and he remembering her effusive and pretty expressions of thanks. There was no question in Freddy's mind that Angela could do a lot for a sweater like that. The walk back to the hotel didn't seem so long, although Angela said they needed a drink anyway and she insisted on paying for it."

Straightening, Fernando's eyes met those of his friend.

"Angela had learned that Freddy was staying at the Copa Palace since most of his piano performance had been scheduled for the auditorium there. She told him she was registered next door at the Excelsior and also said that her father was a real estate speculator and part owner of the Excelsior as well as part owner in a chain of hotels in São Paulo, Belo Horizonte and Curitiba plus some office buildings and apartments in São Paulo. He found out that her cousin had been invited to participate in the same contest as Freddy but had been eliminated in the first round and had returned to his home in Curitiba. After awhile, she looked at the clock and said, 'Freddy, I'm getting hungry and I have an idea. Let's have a private *despedida* (farewell party) for just you and me because it might be a long time before we meet again.

I'll go next door to my hotel to shower and change. You do the same here. Put on that beautiful blue suit you wore in your final performance and we'll go to a lovely little restaurant just two blocks from here and have our party.' It sounded great to Freddy."

The Judge nodded sagely. "I'm sure it did."

"When Angela met him in the lobby of her hotel she looked like an angel to Freddy and it wasn't that third gin and tonic influencing his judgment either. She really was a very lovely creature. He handed her a single white rose, bowing and saying, 'This is for an angel.' She smiled and answered, 'For those pretty words and this gorgeous rose you deserve a kiss,' and quickly planted one on his lips."

"Oh-oh," commented the Judge.

"The Swiss Chalet, where she took him, was everything she had claimed it to be. The fondue bourguinon, the well chilled Chablis, the soft lights and music all added up to an unforgettable evening. No one would ever have taken them for strangers who had met only a few hours before. And once more it was Angela who looked at the time and exclaimed, 'I must go as I have an early plane to catch in the morning.' Reluctantly, Freddy left the restaurant with a memory he would always recall with great pleasure."

Fernando paused again, then resumed his tale. "At the door of her hotel, a lottery vendor pushed a ticket toward them and Angela drew in her breath sharply. 'What is it?' asked Freddy. Pointing toward the vendor, she answered. 'That's my lottery ticket. The one I've been playing for years. Why must my check book always be in my room when I need it, especially at a time like this?'"

The Judge closed his eyes, shading them with one hand and shaking his head slightly.

"'Never mind. I'll buy it for you,' offered Freddy. 'You can't do that,' Angela protested. 'Why not?' he asked. 'Because that would be bad luck. And you must take half the ticket. That's an old custom in my family. I insist you come up to my room so I can pay for my share.' 'Have you ever won the lottery that way?' Freddy asked. 'No, but if I ever do it will be because I followed our rule.' So Freddy accompanied her, unwilling to end such a beautiful and short acquaintance. Of course Angela had another idea. The minute the door of her room closed behind them, she was in his arms, kissing him as he had never been kissed before."

Fernando sighed deeply.

"Some time later, after one last long kiss, she was up and dressed. In a twinkling she scribbled a note which she put on the dresser, blew him a farewell kiss and was out the door. When Freddy read the note, her message was, 'It's been wonderful.' And on top of the note was her check for half of the lottery ticket."

The Judge's hand dropped to his lap and his eyes popped open.

"Later, Freddy was browsing through the paper the waiter had brought with his breakfast. There was an announcement, in letters that seemed five feet tall, that their number had won first prize in the lottery. He had no idea how much they had won as the paper didn't say. Probably not much, he thought, but at least it was a good luck omen. As he was checking out of the hotel he asked the clerk how much the first prize in that day's lottery paid. The young man answered, 'Today is one of those special lotteries. A full ticket of ten pieces is worth fifty thousand dollars.' Freddy was stunned; he had five pieces."

After Freddy's return home, he told Fernando the entire story of his trip, leaving out none of the details. In relating the tale to the Judge, Fernando said that he was most infuriated by the smug and self satisfied expression on Freddy's face, as if to say that parental warnings didn't apply to him.

Looking squarely at the Judge, Fernando asked anxiously, "It was good advice I gave him, wasn't it?"

"None better."

"Then what should I do?" Fernando asked, still fuming at the memory of his son's exploits.

"Fernando, old friend, my advice is to do nothing. The boy is born under a lucky star, which in the long run is better than being born rich or clever."

LULA MAY REED was born and brought up in São Paulo where she attended the American graded School. Married with three grown children and three grandchildren, she is active in an "observer corps" at the São Paulo City Council, modeled after the League of Women Voters of the U.S.A. She enjoys reading, gardening, traveling and taking study courses. She has been published both in Portuguese and English.

The Legionarias

by Lu Reed

Evangelina shifted her weight from one foot to the other, anxiously patting her freshly washed, black hair as she glanced over one shoulder. She'd been in line for hours and now there was a mob behind her reaching well past the corner, all young women like herself waiting to compete for just forty places in the school. Dusting her hands nervously on her neatly ironed skirt, Evangelina stared straight ahead, making an effort to control her rapid breathing and agitated stomach. This was her chance, and her only one, to escape prostitution or work as a maid. Knotting her hands into fists she shut her eyes against the glare of the early morning sun. She could read and write, which many other girls her age could not do, and she was willing to work hard if she just had the opportunity.

A car crept past and parked not far away. Evangelina opened her eyes and watched the slender, well groomed woman lock her vehicle and enter a small house. She recognized Dona Cecilia, one of the founders of the school and, with a fresh surge of anxiety, she felt the line begin to move.

Inside the office, Cecilia touched her damp cheeks to other staff members. It was hot, even with all the windows open, and the perspiration on her face made her feel sticky.

"*Oi, tudo bem?*" she greeted the secretary.

"Yes, we've got more than two hundred fifty applicants today so we'd better get started."

Cecilia stepped to the door and smiled, motioning the girls inside and directing them to two adjoining classrooms. She watched as they moved to the desks on which forms and pens had been placed, her attention caught by one girl with proud carriage and a carefully laundered and patched skirt. The girl was nervous, but the brightest applicants were always tensely aware of the future opportunities available should they be accepted. This school, founded by a judge, Cecilia and four other women to combat the increasing numbers of ten and twelve years old girls involved in prostitution on the docks and in the brothels of Santos, offered instruction in basic office work, placement in jobs and guidance through work and school. For the girls living in *favelas* and *morros* it was a wonderful dream and worth their best efforts.

Cecilia stepped into the first room, her eyes roving over the seated girls, finding the one she had noticed entering the building. Moving to the front of the silent, hot room, she began to speak, her words almost automatic.

"Welcome. We're glad you are here and want to help if we can. We know you want to work so we must know how well you can read and write and also a few things about you. Just fill in the blank spaces on your papers and, if you need help, raise your hand. Take your time. Don't get nervous. The forms you have are not tricky, there is no right or wrong, no correct answer to guess. Just tell us about yourselves."

Obviously, some girls were confident while others looked at the forms despairingly and would have a hard time. From a corner of her eye she watched the girl with the proud bearing and patched skirt pick up her pen and diligently begin to write.

"Please leave the papers and pens on the desks when you have finished. We haven't space for everyone this time although we would like to have you all but you may come back again. We'll be in touch if you are accepted for this group. Be sure your address is clear."

Bending over the paper, Evangelina thought, "I can do this." She filled in her complete name and address, left father's name blank as she was the head of her family, gave information about her brothers and sisters and their school levels and then came the last question. What did she hope this course would do for her?

So many things and there were only four lines. She paused, thinking. She wanted a job that would pay decently, give her respect and the ability to live a decent life, feed her siblings, to be able to pay for all their school supplies...she began to write.

Evangelina finished and stood up. Dona Cecilia smiled at her from the doorway as she rose, hesitating a moment. Should she speak to the Dona, tell her about her wishes and ambitions, ask for help? Slipping past Cecilia she smoothed her patched skirt and stammered softly, "Thank you."

Cecilia glanced at her paper, noting the name, then watched the girl move down the cobblestone road, her head high, rubber thongs beating rhythmically against the ground. Turning back to the classroom, Cecilia saw that one of the girls had begun to cry. Quickly she moved to the youngster, encircling her with a comforting arm.

"What's the matter?"

"I can't do this."

"Can I help you?"

The thin shoulders quivered convulsively.

"No, I just can't do it."

"Maybe next time," Cecilia murmured.

She knew the girl couldn't read or write well enough to fill in this form or any other. She was one that would fall through the cracks, that would not be able to begin or complete this course or get an office job, that would certainly become a maid or a prostitute. Her heart tightened. Giving the girl a paper tissue, she said again,

"Maybe next time."

The girl left and Cecilia felt a rise of hopeless frustration. How many girls would they be able to help? A small token, a tiny number in the overwhelming crowd. She swallowed and turned toward the secretary.

"Let's bring the next group in. We have a lot to go."

****

That evening she met her close friend Sandra at her club.

"Hi, there. When are you going to start helping us with the Legionarias?"

"You look bushed. If that's the result of your day, I'll stay away."

"Come on, Sandra, you'd be great. We could do the things together and it would be fun."

Fun, Sandra thought dubiously. Well it might be. New and different, anyway. And she had nothing to do on Thursdays.

"What would we do?"

"A lot. You know we're responsible for the girls we accept, so we really stay in touch. If they are absent from work or school we step in and try to solve the problem, and they're required to attend weekly Saturday morning meetings so they feel connected."

In spite of herself, Sandra felt a stir of interest.

"How do you pick the girls?"

"It's hard. Each one fills out a form, then we separate the ones that have a chance by giving points. If a girl is head of her family, that's ten points, if she can read well enough to understand the questions and write legibly and coherently that's so many more. If she shows special need that's more and so on. About half of the applicants pass the first screening. Then we go out and visit all of them."

Sandra was dismayed.

"You go into the *favelas* and up the *morros*? Isn't that dangerous?"

"No, it's not dangerous and yes, we go everywhere and anywhere the girls live to see their homes and family. The cellars downtown are the worst with no light or air. We go in pairs, one does the talking and one observes and takes notes. Come on, Sandra. Try it."

"But what would I have to do?"

"Whatever you want, in your own time. We divide up the work and take it from there. Without pay. We're getting together at our headquarters, a *Compania de Docas* house, on Tuesday. Why don't you come along meet the team and see how things work?"

Sandra hesitated. Cecilia didn't usually talk about her work and had never been insistent before. It would be a whole new experience, of that there was no doubt. Maybe.

****

Two weeks later, Sandra and Cecilia climbed the narrow dirt steps of the *morro*, taking care not to slip into the stream of raw sewage that tumbled down the hill beside the path. As a small boy, followed by several friends, rushed past, the women pressed against wooden shacks lining the walkway. There was a slight movement of excitement on the *morro* like the swell of a wave as Cecilia paused to ask directions of a gnarled old woman.

Evangelina was cleaning her tidy but tiny two room home when her youngest brother and his friends burst through the doorway.

"Guess what? Two women, strangers, are coming up the *morro*. What do you think they want?"

Catching her breath, Evangelina crossed her fingers and whispered a prayer.

"I hope they're looking for me."

Propping the broom in one corner, she filled a battered pan with water and lit the burner, just in case. When Sandra and Cecilia arrived a few minutes later, fresh coffee was ready and Evangelina greeted them with a natural dignity.

"*Boa tarde*. Please come in."

Cecilia sat on the single chair and Sandra on a crate, an open notebook in her lap. With a look, Evangelina hushed the children who crowded curiously at the window and doorway. Sipping her coffee, Cecilia spoke.

"Would you be able to attend the preparatory course three afternoons a week for three or four months, Evangelina?"

"Oh, yes. I go to school in the mornings."

"The thing is, Evangelina, we believe it's important for you to continue your studies. If you were to work during the day, would you be willing to go to night school? The minor's court judge will give you a special letter so that you can transfer to evening classes. But it won't be easy. You will really have to want to do this very much."

"Oh, I do. I want to be able to get a real job, a good job. More than anything." Please, please, she cried silently. Give me a chance.

She shrugged when asked about her father and was vague about her mother who worked and brought money irregularly but whom she rarely saw. Her brothers and sisters, she explained, would continue to go to their primary school and then hang around with neighbors, and she would be home with them before going to night school. Evangelina began to feel a growing mixture of determination and excitement. She glanced at the children who were listening to every word. This was her chance and she felt she could, and would, fulfill the expectations of these women and her own dreams. The three of them smiled at one another.

"We'll come back and advise you if you are accepted into this group," Cecilia said, "I think you'll make it. And thanks for the coffee."

Retracing their steps to the street far below, Sandra and Cecilia spoke in hushed tones.

"Aren't we playing God?" Sandra asked. "How can we decide who to choose when the points are sometimes so close?"

"We try and pick those who have a good chance of succeeding. It is a big responsibility because we try to change the lives of the girls we deal with. Evangelina was a shoo-in, with her ability to read and write, nice smile and cleanliness. She'll probably do the course with ease and enthusiasm and it will be simple to find her a job. Without this change, her whole life and her family's future would be grim. This gives her the possibility of not only helping herself and her brothers and sisters but also of being an example to all the girls who know her or live nearby."

"What happens to the girls who aren't chosen?"

"I don't know. They just continue on their present paths. My heart goes out to them. Some are in tears and it's so hard to accept the fact that we cannot help them all. Perhaps if there were some other group that taught manual skills.....", her voice faded, then picked up again, "but we have all we can handle even with our limited aim and possibilities. We try to give our forty students a chance to get into the mainstream with jobs and pay. We try to boost their self-esteem. And that's better than nothing."

They reached the paved street and began to walk toward Cecilia's car, knowing that they were watched by dozens, perhaps hundreds, of hidden hillside dwellers.

"It's a lot of work for just forty girls."

"More than you realize. We have to have uniforms custom made for every one and we need monitors for the courses who will show personal interest in each girl. You'd be good at that, Sandra."

Her friend was silent and, after a quick glance, Cecilia continued.

"We also have to persuade people and companies to hire them. Graduation is a big and happy event at the City Forum and the diploma is a paper with the name and address of their first job."

Cecilia unlocked her car and the women slipped inside.

"Besides the follow up, we start preparing for the next group. It's great having you as a team mate for the visits. I just hope you'll decide to get involved with the whole program."

Sandra looked out the window, back up at the *morro*.

****

Three months later, Evangelina tried on the uniform in which she would work. It made her look like an airline stewardess and gave her a sense of belonging. She had been the outstanding student in her group, a natural leader, and had been carefully observed and encouraged.

Her brothers and sisters had all attended the graduation, dressed in their very best like other families, clapping loudly when her name was called to receive her diploma. She was thrilled to find she had been assigned work at City Bank. A bank sounded so important and serious. She was determined to do her best and, in three years, when she became eighteen, she might be hired on a permanent basis. She was literally glowing, as a whole new world opened up before her.

Emotions ran high, the girls and their families were carried away by flowers and speeches. Pictures were taken of each graduate and every family group so they could remember the occasion forever. Cecilia and Sandra hugged everyone, including Evangelina and all her family.

"Thank you so much, Dona Sandra," Evangelina said with tears in her eyes. "I could have never gotten through the course without you."

"Oh, that's nonsense. I just helped you see your best points."

Cecilia turned to her friend and gave her a hug.

"And I thank you, too, Sandra," she said. You've been great."

"Don't thank me. You were right. It has been fun and now we'll start on the next group. See you on Saturday."

NOTE: The Legionarias was founded in Santos in 1966 by a Minors Court Judge and five women and has operated continuously since that time.

PATRICIA LEE PATRICK was born in Brazil of British parents, grew up in Argentina, and was schooled in England. In 1984 Pat and her husband, an American auto executive, moved to the U.S. and then to Asia in 1986. In 1990 they returned to live in Ann Arbor, Michigan, where Pat is developing her new love of writing.

Her story is a true one which in the early 80's was still rare enough to cause a stir in the São Paulo community. Pat wrote about it for the first time in a Creative Writing course at the University of Michigan. In addition to writing, Pat has an active career as a Wellness and Fitness Instructor. She is studying toward a degree in this field while still keeping up with her three children, two stepchildren and two grandchildren.

Fear in my Court

by Patricia Patrick

It was 1:30 in the afternoon. It had been a busy, active morning. Our regular foursome had played three sets of exciting tennis—all very close games—deuce, advantage server; deuce, advantage receiver. We played each point determined to make it the winning point. Twice a week our foursome would rendezvous at this beautiful spot where there was a tennis court nestled amongst the eucalyptus trees on a private four-acre estate. What more could we ask for? The weather was in the upper 80's, sunny, warm, with clear blue skies. We played four hours of tennis after which we retired to the cool shade of a pergola bathed in bougainvillea. There we sat sipping lemonade and feasting on the delicious delicacies made that morning by Maria, our hostess' cook. We parted with promises to meet again the following week and we went our separate ways.

For me it was supermarket day and time to stock up the pantry for the upcoming week-end. This was a good time of day to do this; there were not too many people around. Everyone was either eating lunch, or taking his siesta before returning to work. I did my shopping; filled two carts full of groceries and a carry out boy helped me to my car. He loaded everything into the trunk whilst I rummaged around in my purse for small change to tip him. He closed the trunk, took his tip and went back to the store. I climbed into my spanking new, fiery red Escort GT which my husband had brought home for me the night before. I sat in my car for a while rearranging everything in my purse after delving into it for the tip, and checked the list for my next errand. I was totally oblivious to anything going on outside the car when suddenly I was startled by a voice in my left ear telling me to stay calm, not to utter a sound and to move over to the passenger seat. As I lifted my head, there out of the corner of my eye I could see a gun pointing at my neck.

To this day I don't know what went through my mind at that moment. All I know is I calmly moved over to the passenger seat, trying to get my long legs over the gear shift while clutching my purse to my chest. I sat there, frozen with fear, wondering what was going to happen next. My assailant jumped into the driver's seat—I never turned my head to look at him; I just saw this person out of the corner of my eye. The only thing on my mind at that moment was, How am I going to get out of this car alive? I followed his every move straining my eyes to look sideways at him waiting for that split second I could catch him off guard and grab the gun away from him.

Suddenly my moment came. He started the engine and in order to put the car into first gear, he had to lay the gun down on the gear box. In that split second I lunged for the gun with my left hand, clasped my purse with my right hand, pressed myself against the door to try and push the handle to open it. My ill begotten fellow passenger promptly grabbed the gun with his right hand and tried to pull it away from me. We wrestled back and forth—goodness knows where my strength came from—but at that moment nothing was going to make me give that gun up. After what seemed like an eternity I managed to secure the gun. I curled up into a ball hugging the gun and my purse to my chest, opened the car door and rolled out onto the pavement. All I wanted to do was get up and run, but the nightmare was not over.

My concern now was to stop the assailant from driving my car away. Not only was I about to lose a trunk full of groceries but more importantly, my tennis racquet was lying on the back seat and I did not want to lose it. It is interesting to note the degree of importance a human being will attach to possessions at a moment like this. In Brazil at that time a good brand name tennis racquet had to be imported into the country and cost four times what one would have to pay in the US. They were not as yet manufactured in the country. I was going to fight to make sure I did not let that racquet get away!

I stood up quickly and with trembling hands aimed the gun at my assailant. I pulled the trigger waiting for that ominous shot. It never did go off. The gun was not loaded. My shining new car drove off with my groceries and my tennis racquet. I stood there in a state of shock with the gun still pointing forward. What a threatening sight I must have been. Just as soon as I gathered my composure, I screamed for help. I shouted at the top of my lungs and everyone just walked away. I guess I, too, would have kept my distance if I had seen this shrieking madwoman pointing a gun into mid-air!

I lowered the gun and started walking toward the supermarket building, trembling from head to toe. Shock was taking over and the thought that I could have been lying there bleeding to death with a bullet in my head made me shake uncontrollably. The police eventually came. I was taken into a back room of the supermarket and questioned. The hardest thing of all was to convince the police that the gun was not mine; that it was I, a woman, who had single-handedly extracted it from the assailant! We are in Latin America, remember, where male chauvinism is supreme. How could a female weakling accomplish a feat like this?

No one would take the gun from me until I was taken to the police station. There under military guard, I was asked to fill out numerous forms, the majority of which pertained to the gun, its ownership, how it came to be in my hands and so forth. Two hours later I was free to leave the police station. A friend picked me up and took me home. My husband was out of town, of course. Don't these things always happen when the man of the house is on a business trip?

It was very difficult to walk into my home and cheerfully greet my children, who were wondering what had kept me. I tried to hide my feelings and act as though nothing had happened. It is at moments like this that one is grateful to be alive, unharmed and together with loved ones. Nothing material matters. All those petty things we worry about seem so totally insignificant when one has the vision of losing one's life flash before one's eyes.

The car was eventually found, with the front badly beaten up. The radio/tape player had been forcefully ripped out; the tires were flat; the groceries had disappeared but miracle of all miracles, my tennis racquet was found lying on the back seat as I had left it. Am I a lucky person? Yes, I do believe I am.

Born in Georgia, raised in Hanover, New Hampshire, and educated at Smith and Stanford, VIRGINIA ANN GEDDES' varied career includes social work assignments in Venezuelan, Brazilian and Peruvian urban slums as well as work as a teacher, businesswoman and painter. Currently writing short stories and a novel, Ms. Geddes lives with her three children in Brazil where she has resided since 1966.

The View from the Hammock

by Virginia A. Geddes

Suffused with contentment, Laura Rollins swung herself in the hammock, fingertips pushing on the upswing against the cool terrace tiles, and gazed across the summer lawn into the open game room where her lanky son David bent over the snooker table and Allison's son Henry chalked his cue stick. Five other shirtless young men lounged on bar stools, muscles gleaming with suntan oil as they waved cigarettes and beer cans, joking and challenging one another. Laura smiled at them with proprietary fondness. She'd known the boys since kindergarten.

Renting this beach house at Juqueí on the coast between São Paulo's port of Santos and Rio de Janeiro two weeks before the boys scattered to their different universities in the U.S. had been Laura's inspiration, and everything had worked out just right, even to her finishing the last painting promised for the March exhibit with Brazilian artist João Alvares. She pushed with extra force against the floor to distance her suspicions that the rush had sapped vitality from that canvas.

No, she thought, enjoying the way her body molded to the swaying hammock, she couldn't complain a bit. Her life was proceeding in perfect order, thanks to the routines she had set up over the years to guarantee the time and tranquillity she needed to paint. That steadiness of purpose had perhaps dulled her relationship with her husband Donald, but the woman in her had long ago ceded to the artist, whose needs reached exquisite fulfillment when she coaxed the intricately-balanced shapes from her mind onto canvas. Allison was forever warning her about sacrificing life to art, but Laura told her that she couldn't change even if she wanted to, which she didn't. Artists were their art.

This day of swimming and walking on the beach in easy conversation with her friend had filled her with a profound sense of well-being. Even though the tones of the sand, Prussian blue ocean and deep-turquoise sky seemed raw by contrast, something about the scene had triggered memories of a more harmonious, antique beach where her much younger, wilder self had responded to the joyful sensuality of the dark-favored Italian men. Recalling now that moment of surprise on the beach heated her loins with the force of the midday sun penetrating bare skin. Laura closed her eyes and waited for her breathing to slow again. Those turbulent emotions of youth had given way to the superior pleasures of having a tried and true friend, a talented son and, yes, a devoted husband. And on top of that to be a successful artist. Well, life was full. Life was complete.

Donald and Allison's husband would not arrive for the weekend until tomorrow, and the only task now awaiting the two women was preparation of the spaghetti dinner. Laura flicked through the cooking steps, savouring in advance the iced *caipirinha* made from cane alcohol, limes and sugar that would accompany her labor. If only Henry's Brazilian college friend would arrive before dinner.

Henry's inclusion of this newcomer in their beach party had left Laura with the vague impression that the boy was somehow needy, though Gil Mendes de Sá's family owned not only coffee plantations but also extensive orange groves in the state of São Paulo and was one of those extensive families that gathered hundreds of members for weddings, baptisms and funerals. David had added, with obvious admiration and envy, that while in high school Gil had gained quite a reputation as a successful disc jockey. Out all night, he had sniffed coke to make school the next morning. Gil didn't touch the stuff now, of course. Great!

A flow of jabber across the lawn in the direction of the front of the house suggested that Gil had indeed arrived. Eyes closed, Laura listened to the animated group approach her from behind, and then, before she could rise from the hammock, Henry was introducing her.

A brilliant smile and widely-spaced green eyes so heavily lashed they appeared kohl-lined filled Laura's vision as if she had been snatched up and placed in front of an enormous drive-in movie screen. Her body plummeted through some inner trap door. The voices around her silenced, and she registered neither what Gil Mendes de Sá said to her nor what she said to him. Then he was gone with the others.

She shook her head and swung her feet onto the cool floor. Laughing to herself about the utter craziness of her reaction to the young man, she composed headlines in her mind as she started towards the kitchen: Middle-aged woman bewitched by green-eyed Brazilian! Stunned artist meets her muse in the flesh on tropical beach at Juqueí! Mother of Wesleyan sophomore confesses, "I never knew true love until I met Gil."

Allison was already chopping salad ingredients. Laura minced garlic and onions and tried to hold up her end of the conversation while the green-eyed presence insinuated itself inside. As she stirred the hamburger meat into the frying garlic and onions, Laura struggled for lucidity. Her feelings were entirely inappropriate. Gil was less than half her age. Despite her sensation that they had connected with some fierce, natural force, he was, except for his passion for music, an unknown. That must be it! Her attraction to him would be that of artist to artist.

"You're no fun! I'm going to watch the news." Allison stored the salad in the refrigerator, waved her *caipirinha* and disappeared into the living room.

Chastened, Laura concentrated on opening the can of tomato extract and spooning it onto the meat. As she performed these motions, she experienced again the impact of the young man, and her grip on the hard facts she had just reviewed began slipping like a glass from soapy hands. Unopposed, her artist's inner eye reconstructed the almond shapes of emerald green with their deep, watchful expression.

Laura added salt and pepper, bay leaves, oregano and basil to the sauce while the fascinating, eyes and smile, endowed by her creative spirit with fresh mystery, transfixed her inner mind. Her skin tingled in anticipation of seeing Gil at dinner. She floated through the motions of setting places at the long picnic table on the front porch, pausing only once as she was struck by the drama of the waves curling and rolling to their destiny. A sense of inevitability seized her when the last seat available at dinner happened to be next to Gil. Her heart jumped behind her smile of greeting as she slid onto the bench beside him.

His presence at her side wrapped Laura in intense sensation. Her consciousness of his body heat was like suddenly realizing that someone had appeared unseen at one's back. Through her peripheral vision Laura followed Gil's every move. Though he didn't address her, he occasionally graced her with a shy, fleeting smile. Heart pounding, Laura finally spoke to him.

"So what are you going to major in, Gil?"

She had to grip the table edge with her free hand as the glowing gaze ravaged her.

"Writing, I guess. Maybe script writing. At least, that's what I enjoyed most this first year."

His voice was quiet, modest.

"What script did you write? What was it about?"

"It's about two lovers—two Colombians living illegally in the U.S. They have to be secretive and are afraid. It's a struggle to find even menial work, and, of course, they are exploited. Their relationship begins to fall apart."

"What happens to them?"

He smiled apologetically. "I don't know. I haven't finished yet."

Laura quivered with excitement at this revelation of artistic temperament. Some writers developed characters and situations and then sat back to see what would happen.

"So your characters are going to choose their own fates."

"I guess so."

"Do you think they will discover that their problem lies within themselves or in their relationship?"

"Oh, no. They are perfect together. The problem is just the difficulty of their lives as foreigners."

Gil sounded as if he were defending some past involvement of his own. What kind of girl had he chosen? Another artist?

Henry called Gil's attention, and when he turned away Laura only just checked a powerful urge to reach out and rotate his face back to her. The hairs rose on her arms. She had almost done something public.

"Hey," Allison called to her, "are you on the moon?"

Laura composed her external self and conversed. All the while, the presence at her side disturbed, prodded and dragged at her. When Gil left with the others, it was like a tugging leash gone slack. A cool draft blew through the space where he had been.

That night, caressed by soft waves of air spread by the overhead fan, Laura lay on her bed and reviewed the astounding emotions that had gripped her since Gil's arrival. It wasn't too difficult to identify her wild feelings with the giddiness of falling passionately in love. Her reaction was basically sexual, she decided, though she sensed the danger of these new emotions. She should ruthlessly stifle these feelings. She had had her thrill, and now she ought to return to reality.

Yet contemplation of the following day developing as yesterday, pre-Gil, when she thought herself so content, created in her a strong resistance. It now seemed impossible to give up this sense of expectancy that made her feel live again, vibrant and young. What harm would it do to let herself continue to enjoy these feelings while they lasted, as long as she kept them to herself? Gil hadn't noticed anything, and in any case, he would only be here for another few days. Couldn't she just indulge herself for once?

Brilliant sealight woke Laura the next morning, and her mind instantly filled with the luminous green eyes and smile. A rush of gladness bounced her out of bed. As she pulled on her bathing suit, she laughed at her relief that Gil wouldn't see her in it. She had heard the boys return in the wee hours and knew they would sleep until lunch. Nonetheless, her mirror image didn't totally displease her. Though her breasts and butt weren't as high and saucy as twenty years ago, she looked pretty good for a gal of forty-five.

Laura pulled on the Wesleyan T-shirt that David had given her and padded on bare feet through the silent house to the kitchen. She measured the coffee powder into the top of the coffeemaker and imagined Gil appearing now. What would he say? What would he do? Would his seagreen eyes hold hers in a moment of naked recognition? Uh-oh. This wasn't part of her deal.

At the sound of beach thongs slapping on tiles Laura turned towards the kitchen door, and with a start she recognized the form that filled its frame. Her eyes stuck like dry ice on skin to the puffy green ones.

Gil broke away. "May I please have a glass of water?" His voice scratched the morning silence.

"Of course. There's a pitcher in the refrigerator."

As they both moved forward, Laura's limbs locked into a magnetic field that propelled her towards him.

"That's okay. I'll get it," he said, not looking at her.

Laura halted and, weak-kneed, leaned against the sink. Was he avoiding her eyes? Had he understood and rejected her? Had she embarrassed him? Her skin chilled.

Gil picked up a glass from the drain, brushing her arm and again sending up her hairs. A hot flush told her that she had been fooling herself about the force of the chemistry involved.

Gil retrieved the pitcher from inside the refrigerator, poured water into the glass and headed for the door.

"Thanks," he said with a nod in her direction.

Laura carried her mug of coffee to the kitchen table, sank onto a chair and, cradling the mug in trembling hands, strove to recall each moment of their encounter. Oh, he was elusive, intriguing. And she was a foolish old woman who was getting in over her head. An old woman who was feeling young again. Was this the fountain of youth—passion?

Throughout breakfast with Allison and their morning walk on the beach Laura allowed silences to accumulate. Allison shot her several quizzical looks but made no comment. At lunch Gil was seated at the opposite end of the table from Laura. Was it on purpose? She noted Gil's quietness with approval. He was an observer, as befitted a writer. Could he be aware of her watching him?

Suddenly, her eyes locked with familiar brown ones. Had he seen her? Oh God, let it not be. She smiled tremulously at her son. After he looked away, Laura shut her eyes a moment against the fear and panic. She had been lucky this time, but sooner or later she would be caught. It wasn't worth it, she told herself, registering her inner turmoil.

After lunch the boys played snooker while Laura and Allison worked on a 3,000 piece puzzle of a Bavarian castle rising from a heavy, black forest. Laura's fingers reached for just the right pieces and fitted them in with amazing speed while at the back of her mind hung the heavy knowledge of the source of this increased sensitivity.

When Donald and Peter arrived in the late afternoon, Laura was startled at how old her husband looked. His jowls seemed to have sagged in the few days she had been away. True, Donald would be tired from a long work week in São Paulo heat, but that wasn't it. He acted old, not just tired.

She couldn't think of anything to say to him, but he didn't seem to notice and retreated to their room for a nap before dinner. Left alone, Laura claimed the hammock to read but instead closed her eyes and with conscious guilt conjured up the image of Gil. She couldn't let go of him yet. She just couldn't. The pre-Gil Laura seemed as inert as Donald.

During dinner Laura eyed Gil with reckless frequency. She heard snatches of Gil's stories of surfing at nearby Maresias beach and in Hawaii with a sense of unreality, as if the words did not fit the speaker. Writers didn't surf...but maybe young writers did.

Donald's hawkish gaze fixed her. She had forgotten how attuned to her, how jealous he could be. Surely, he wouldn't imagine that she was interested in a college boy, and yet, the chemistry at work had to be emitting strong signals easily picked up by a partner of so many years. The exhilaration left her and was replaced by a defiant resentfulness as she cut Gil from her line of vision.

That night Laura roiled in her bed. At three o'clock she slipped on shorts and a shirt and crept down to her hammock where she rocked in frustration. She made a new deal with herself. If by some miracle Gil should appear now, she would follow her gut feelings and let whatever would happen, happen. If he didn't, she would excise him forever from every recess of her mind where he could lie waiting for her weakness to call him forth.

The flip-flop of beach thongs intruded upon the calm dark. It would be too coincidental if it were he again, she warned herself, but as she twisted her head towards the sounds, she knew she was hoping. She strained to individualize the solid figure that lowered into a nearby chair.

"You couldn't sleep, either?"

The voice was unmistakable, though without the greenness of his eyes and the wideness of his smile, it sounded flatter than Laura remembered.

"I felt restless, though I usually sleep like a log." She paused, unsettled by the lack of a strong sense of his presence. His grayness seemed to depersonalize him. "Do you miss your family a lot when you're in the U.S.?" she managed to ask.

"Yes, my family and my girlfriend. She's a senior in high school in São Paulo."

Laura received the words like as slap. So. A girlfriend. Of course, he would have a girlfriend. This was natural. He would miss her a lot, even desperately. He was, what?...19 or 20 years old.

All of a sudden it was proving difficult to associate this pining college boy with the electric person hidden by the dark. Laura stared at the grainy form.

"It must be hard to be so far away for so long." By next year he would probably have forgotten this girl and most certainly his friend's mother who rose early, woke in the night and could more often than not be found in a hammock.

In a panic Laura strove to recapture the mystery of the eyes and smile, but the dark solidity of the boy intervened. Scrunching her eyes shut and concentrating with total force, she was rewarded by the sudden emergence from the blank background under her lids of the glorious green eyes, and she called upon all of her willpower to hold this vision.

"I'm going to take a walk on the beach. Want to come?"

The eyeless, smileless voice tore at the vision, shredding it, and Laura's eyes flew open.

"No, thanks. I'm going back to bed. See you in the morning. Be careful of holes," said her mother-self, coming to her rescue.

"Right. Good night..."

The gray figure rose and merged into the darkness. Laura swung herself with her fingertips and again called up the magical eyes and smile, but the image refused to form. She realized with a start that underneath her disappointment coursed a contradictory feeling of relief. Then a profound gratitude welled up within as she understood that her new sense of aliveness had not flown with the image of the youth. At least that. How wonderful that.

Unbidden, the intriguing eyes and smile appeared for a second before the almond shapes multiplied, filled with a gamut of emotional greens and intercepted one another in free-floating patterns that finally settled like *Paineira* leaves onto a fresh, creamy canvas.

JOHN de MARMON MURRAY joined the Boyden organization as a Vice President in the São Paulo office in April, 1990. A graduate of Deerfield Academy and Yale University, he has also completed advanced courses in business at Brazil's prestigious Getulio Vargas Foundation.

Mr. Murray's business career includes 32 years in Brazil, with extensive experience in Commodities and finance. He initially transferred to Brazil in 1963 as a coffee buyer, and then for twenty years he held various management positions with Cargill Inc.'s Brazilian subsidiaries. He is active in civic affairs in Brazil as President of the Yale Club of Brazil, Director of the Canadian Chamber of Commerce and Chairman of its Economic Affairs Committee. He also serves as Chairman of the National Advisory Board of the Salvation Army.

Clouds of Revolution

by John Murray

I: Santos, 1963

It was only ten a.m., but the word was out that there was going to be trouble again. Bobby pulled down the metal shutters that covered the front entrance of his coffee brokerage. He looked up and down the narrow Rua XV de Novembro and couldn't help but feel the gloom of this gray September morning in Santos.

What a way to make a living, he thought. The port is in turmoil. There are over fifty vessels anchored on the bar. Agitators have the stevedores all worked up and general strikes in Santos are now almost daily occurrences. The Cubatão gangs are even worse. Trained leftists have whipped up strong anti-American sentiments in the industrial unions, so much so that expat Americans, especially those connected with USIS or other semi-official types, feared for their lives. Some with reason, as a hit list was circulating!

The Army was biding its time. Bobby was sure that eventually they would be obliged to intervene but the situation would have to get still worse before he could expect a revolution from the right. "Jango" and his brother-in-law,

Brizola, were bringing this beautiful country, Bobby's country, to the edge. The powers that moved Brazil, the coffee barons, the political elite, had got themselves into a real jam this time—played right into their hands. And now what do they have? Yeah, Bobby reflected, they have Jango, with his sexy wife, Maria Theresa, on the cover of *Time*, no less. There she was, dressed like a cat herself as she posed next to their pet jaguars, which they kept caged on their Delaware-sized *fazenda* in the Pantanal.

"Oh well, I'm young, and maybe I can help things move a little faster. Teddy wants to meet me this weekend—let's see what he wants. At least I know this port city as well as anyone."

Indeed, Bobby wanted to help. His father had been an American ship captain, killed at the end of War II. Bobby was born and raised in Santos by his Brazilian mother. He knew Santos inside out, from the clubs in Boqueirão, to the *chopp* houses in the commercial district, to the "*Chave de Ouro*" on the waterfront, where the hired ruffians were given their orders.

II: Guarujá

Bobby looked at his watch. It was Sunday morning, and the line-up to board the ferry boat was already becoming long. He pulled his steel blue Willys Rural into line behind the seemingly unending extension of red and white *Fuscas*.

Teddy is not normally late, he thought. Well, by the time we get to the ferry-boat he'll be here, and in the meantime I've got Rosie to keep me warm!

Everybody else had their radio turned on, and everyone seemed to be in a picnic, happy, kissing mood, so why shouldn't he? There was a patch of blue in the sky "big enough to cut out a pair of Dutchman's breeches", as Rosie would say. It promised to be a better than normal day for this dismal month of September.

"Maybe after we meet Ted, we can drive over to Perequê and do a job on the shrimp and *caipirinhas*?"

Rosie flashed her truly winning smile and nudged closer, nodding her approval.

"There he is! Damn, why does he have to look like that? I know it is colder in São Paulo, but that raincoat! He should put a sign on his back — 'Bond'. And we are supposed to be inconspicuous tourists on a Sunday excursion to Guarujá!"

"Damn it! Can't they ever line this ferry up so that you don't have to rip the bottom off your car every time you go on or off?" he said as he bumped aboard. Bobby was really pissed off but he was also alert as Teddy, who had walked aboard the ferry, stuck his head in the window.

"Hi buddy, hi Rosie, how are you lovers this delicious Sunday morning?" Teddy never seemed to be tired and was always relaxed and cheerful. God knows how many other "encounters" he would have this same day. He slipped into the back of the Rural and took out a yellow manila envelope. "The pictures are inside," he said as he passed it over to Bobby. "We got them from Rio. Your aristocratic coffee baron is into this up to his eyeballs, and not just intellectually. He is a violent one!"

How could it be? Bobby thought. Jairo is the son of one of the wealthiest coffee growers in Brasil. Like me, he grew up in Santos, even if under more privileged circumstances. His is a *Quatrocentão* family, one that I've always respected. No one could love Brazil more than Jairo's father. These are good people. How could he be selling his country and his family short? Maybe after two years at the Sorbonne he really believes this shit!

"Ah!" said Teddy, reading Bobby's thoughts. "A famous man once said, 'Knowledge he has gained... but not... understanding.' Don't worry about what makes Jairo tick".

"Okay, smart ass", said Bobby, "What do you want me to do about it?"

"Look, we have information that there will be a meeting tomorrow night. Jairo has invited a group of his new friends to dinner and has reserved a private room at the coffee exchange. Apparently there is a small but sophisticated arms shipment on one of the ships that is waiting on the bar. Jairo, using his father's influence, has devised a way to get the stuff ashore. We can stop them. The only trouble is that we do not know the name of the vessel. That is where you come in, laddy!"

"Shit!" Bobby thought out loud. "This is really a long shot. As a frequent user of the coffee exchange club, I could get myself in the vicinity but how am I going to listen in on their conversation? Maybe I could arrange a snooker game tomorrow. It might look a little suspicious, being Monday night but Jairo wouldn't know that... it might just work! And, those private dining rooms are right off the snooker room. It is worth a try!"

When the ferry arrived at the Guarujá side of the canal, Teddy stayed aboard and sitting on one of the wooden benches, took the return ride to Santos. Bobby and Rosie had other plans.

The thought of tomorrow's adventure exhilarated these temerarious young people. Reaching Enseada, Bobby drove the Rural unevenly onto the sand and down to the water's edge. He then merrily accelerated, racing down the long stretch of beach, splashing through the several rivulets until he reached Tortuga. There he and Rosie climbed the rocks to a place where they could observe the giant turtles playing in the currents below.

Someday I'd like to build a house on this spot—if I live so long, thought Bobby. But dreaming was not for this Sunday.

Back in the car, the two of them proceeded on past Pernambuco to the fishing village at Perequê. There were a half a dozen thatched roofed kiosks open for business. Seeing them coming, Heitor, their favorite "fisher-barman", smiled broadly, at the same time cleaning the wooden table and benches with an alcohol dampened cloth.

The sky's blue patches had broadened a bit now and it became an unexpectedly pleasant mid-day. Being Sunday, the patriotically colored chug-chug fishing vessels bobbed happily at anchor in front of them. The fried shrimp was plentiful and delicious but the temptation to wash the shrimp down with too many *caipirinhas* was more than Bobby could resist. Rosie, however, was used to this process and when it was time to start back, she took the wheel. Sighing to herself, and well aware that tomorrow the adrenaline would run high, she knew that there was no sense in trying to talk Bobby out of his commitment. Bobby seemed to think he owed something to his father; the roots were too deep. He would do what he thought he had to do and she would be waiting because she loved him.

By the time they reached the ferry landing, all romantic moods had vanished. An hour's wait provoked a discussion about the port authorities' plan to build a road to Guarujá . It might be convenient but just imagine all the Paulistas that would invade their island paradise.

III : The Bolsa

The next day was business as usual. No strikes. And no tanks on the streets of downtown Santos. Like everyone else, Bobby's small office staff had fallen behind and there was a lot of catch-up work to be done. He spoke to Londrina by radio early in the morning. The crop looked good and another frost was unlikely this year. He closed the door of the "soundproof" booth built into the corner of his office and cranked up the phone. Finally connecting to the international operator, he placed a call to New York. Screaming into the receiver, he then proceeded to place a larger than normal short position, at the same time thinking, This is going to be my day!

He had scheduled his snooker game for 8 o'clock. At 7:30 he crossed the street and entered the turn-of-the-century building that housed the "Bolsa", or coffee exchange. He called for the cubicle elevator that would rattle its way up to the third floor. His three friends arrived soon after and the foursome were already well into their game when Jairo swaggered down the hall and confidently slipped into the private dining room at the southeast end, hardly taking notice of these "boys" at the snooker table. Watching this rich man's son, however, Bobby could only think of one thing: the son of a bitch!

At ten o'clock Bobby knew he had to make his move. He had been drinking *chopp* all night so it wasn't necessary to fake his "roll" as he meandered to the door of the fateful room. He opened the door to the private dining room instead of the men's room next door. The faces around the chamber shot eyes at him that surely were meant to kill. Bobby let out a loud burp, absently apologized for the intrusion, and backed out into the corridor. It was all very quick, but it had been enough. Bobby's eyes focused on the name that was scribbled on the black board that had been set up at one end of their banquet table. "Lloyd Bolivia"—jackpot! As he closed the door, he heard the traitor tell the others, "Don't worry about that one. He is one of the local merchants that hang out at the English club. They all drink too much, find clerical jobs in coffee or shipping and never amount to anything."

Well, I don't know about that one, buddy, thought Bobby, but I'm about to cause you one hell of a lot of trouble!

****

Wednesday morning Bobby stood at the window of his twelfth floor apartment at Ponta da Praia. He listened to the last of the blasts, and he could clearly see the fire through his binoculars. Later in the day the Tribuna came out with a special edition, headlining the mysterious explosion that had destroyed one of the Lloyd's vessels.

Six months later, the Brazilian Army led the coup that put Castello Branco in place as Brazil's new leader. Jairo and many like him were exiled after being roughly held on a prison ship anchored at approximately the same location as the Lloyd Bolivia when she went down.

According to Teddy, Jairo went to Chile where he joined the Allende forces. Being the violent type, however, Jairo was soon fingered, captured and disappeared along with the other 10,000 or so Chileans who were never heard from again.

IV: New Year's Day 1995

Sr. Roberto celebrated his sixtieth birthday last November. Still known to his older friends as Bobby, he had built the home of his dreams overlooking the waters that once were a playground for the giant turtles. He left the coffee business while still a young man and built a successful career in a completely unrelated field. A headhunter at Boyden had once described him as "street smart, willing to take risks and a very good negotiator".

He eased his silver Versailles up the long asphalt driveway under the wooden sign he had strung out indicating the name of his retreat, "On the Rocks". He called to Rosie telling her that he had got a great deal on five kilos of the big shrimp. He then told his favorite grandson, Eduardo (sometimes called Ted) to prepare the boat; he would like to take a spin before sunset.

Uncapping a beer, he slouched into a chair and turned on the TV just to get a glimpse of Fernando Henrique's inauguration ceremony. "God, all this pomp and circumstance seems to be out of place—don't you think so, Rosie?" Bobby was about to turn it off in disgust, when he noticed a bald man lurking behind the new President. At first he wasn't sure, but when he saw the profile it was unmistakable.

The arrogance was still there. Jairo had not only survived Chile but he was still used to getting his way. Bobby, feeling old, sighed. There was still something he had to do.

Eduardo called, "Hey gramps, Granny Rosie wants to know if you have made your New Year's resolution. I've made mine. Do you want to know what it is?"

Taking a deep breath, Bobby said, "Tell Rosie I made mine less than a minute ago but don't tell me your thoughts, lad. New Year's resolutions are to be kept to oneself!"

photo by Mario Cravo Neto

VICKY SHORR, John Perkins and their baby, Sid, nearly missed the plane from New York to Brazil that bright day in April, 1982. But Pan Am had already loaded all eleven of their bags—so the plane was held, and they arrived in Brazil the next morning, to stay for a year.

Ten years later, they left in the rain. With two new children, a boatload of furniture, and an unbreakable bond to a land they now loved. These stories come from Don't Complain to the Maids, Vicky Shorr's portraits of some of the people in that place. She has recently completed The Education of Joan of Arc. She is a graduate of Wellesley College, and the founder of the Archer School for Girls in Los Angeles, where she currently lives.

Sergio

by Vicky Shorr

I picked him up at the *feira*, the fair, the street market, one day. He was one of those countless young men who travel around São Paulo with the markets to pull the ladies' carts for them. Real urchins, but charming, for the most part, and energetic, and I liked them, even the bad ones, the older ones, who "watch" the cars.

And slit the tires if one doesn't pay them—but who wouldn't pay? They charge pennies, and they smile so brightly when you say, "Yes, of course, please guard my car,"—from yourselves, you know and they know. And they bound over when you return, to take the flowers from your arms, and open your car door for you with all the chivalry in their strong, young, male souls.

And when they get too old? One couldn't help but wonder. When these darling boys and young men get just that little bit older, and the cooks and the ladies don't want them perhaps walking them home anymore? Then what?

He was just about there when I met him. I was passed over to him when my usual porter—whose skill at loading carts, combined with his dazzling, if toothless at sixteen, smile had made him a prize, a gem, a little bombom, as they spell it, for the ladies in whose pleasant neighborhood this somewhat expensive fair took place each Friday—was occupied. This new one was pale—his friends were all dark—and he didn't smile, but he seemed nice enough for me to bear for one hour. So off we went, down the narrow center, on our quest for pink mango, truly ripe papaya, tiny gold bananas if we were lucky, and the herbs and spices that made magic in the kitchen, when bought from that very old vendor who blessed them herself.

So he pulled and arranged and re-arranged as I bought more than could have fit in that cart, but for his labors. And I noticed that as he was given a banana here, a peeled orange there, a taste of coconut perhaps, he seemed glad enough to get it. So I paid him more than the twenty-five cents he asked for, and the next week, he was waiting for me.

This time he pulled my cart home, and the cook gave him a coffee and a piece of her manioc cake. She was a "caker," a true cake-maker, and she was so pleased by the respect and appreciation he manifested toward her and her *oeuvre* that she suggested we invite him to scrub down the front walk.

Which he actually managed to do, without the proper, basic material, due to a linguistic breakdown. He asked for a kind of heavy-duty steel wool, which I thought meant "soap powder", and sent the fifteen-year-old kitchen girl to the laundry room to get it. She was still too new, too shy, too awestruck to be earning the eighty-five dollars a month that, it turned out, was supporting her worn-out mother and the pack of little ones at home, that it was well beyond her to tell her foreign as-if-from-Mars patroness that what was required was not soapsuds, but that the boy be given a bit of money and sent to the market to buy steel wool...

Actually, she came from such backwoods simplicity that when her mother brought her to me, she was dressed in a skirt made from the fake fur of an old car seatcover that someone had ditched out there in the periphery where they squatted. She couldn't talk, just twisted her hands in front of her and rocked from foot to foot, smiling occasionally, another toothless smile. And I resented the mother at first, coming each tenth of the month and scooping up the girl's whole salary—but thank God I comprehended the direness of it all before too long, and helped where I could, before the mother died, aged thirty-eight, of old age.

Oh, God, the poor mother. "Her name is American," the mother told me that first day. American? "A-bi-ga-yoo," she said, triumphant. American?

"Que ?" I asked.

"A-bi-ga-yoo!" they repeated, big toothless smiles, together this time.

A-bi-ga-yoo? "From the Bible too," they assured me. Finally they scratched it out in big, shaky letters—A-B-I-G-A-I-L. Spoken Portuguese could do marvels with English spelling, as we learned, and learned again.

But our Abigayoo—Biga, for short—first had her teeth fixed nicely, then started appearing in old clothes from the household, and then her own clothes, nice clothes, always neat and clean, and never a hair out of place. Or a loss of dignity—never an inch. And it paid off, for the cook took an interest and got her married—to someone really nice, he seemed, though it's all such poverty down there, relentless, with such utter lack of opportunity, that one prays for her future rather than bets on it.

Anyway, Sergio, for that was the boy's name, got Biga that first day, and if he'd drawn the cook or the maid who'd been there longer, it would have gone easier for him. They would have come to me and gotten money for the steel wool. But Biga brought him soapsuds and a small bunch of rags, and he scrubbed the moss off the front walk with that, and his fingers were bloody by the end. But the whole household was most impressed, and he became a personal favorite of the cook.

He started coming regularly on Friday mornings, and they went to the fair early, without me. And then she put him to washing the windows with newspaper, "the way it ought to be done", and he balked at nothing. He was gentle and kind. He was given enormous plates of food on Fridays, and then he'd come Saturdays, to wash the car, and before long, we realized that we liked having him around.

The cook found an old white jacket in my costume box, and starched it for him. That's when I realized that the ragged clothes he wore were not an existential condition, they were not, like shoes in New York, a reflection of taste and style, almost of soul. No, Sergio's soul had nothing to do with the ill-fitting rags that one had 'till then called "his" clothes.

We gave him a few things, khaki pants, old Brooks Brothers shirts, and he changed. Took on a different aspect. Looked—collegiate, almost. He became a real person to me then.

He was eighteen. Well, driving lessons, I thought. Why not? Nothing was expensive those days in Brazil. Inflation, yes, worse each month, each day—but the dollar always danced above it. A straight trajectory up, like an arrow from the gods, and it was as easy as "sweet rice" to be bountiful.

So, driving lessons for Sergio. The driving school was at the bottom of the hill. He could walk down, get the prices, and walk back up. I would merely write the check.

Thirty-five dollars, I think it was. He worked around the house now all the time. Sometimes in the late afternoon, he'd sit and listen dreamily to the beautiful nursemaid, Carmelita, read to him from the Bible. "Believers," they called themselves, all the women in the house. Newly converted Baptists, Jehovah's Witnesses, Mormons—it didn't matter. All offered the same package: a brand new hand. A chance to change their whole lot in life.

The Catholic Church had offered them penance and redemption, but these poor, working people in Brazil mostly didn't sin. They were sinned against, mightily and without end, by the very people the Catholic Church kept forgiving and forgiving again.

But the Evangelicals had no truck with the rich whatsoever—at least, not in Brazil—and offered a full social life, starting day one. The cook went first, and took her whole family, and when the rest of her neighborhood saw her big sons trotting to prayer group on Wednesday and Saturday nights, dressed in cheap, new dazzling jackets and ties, and never once stopping anymore at the local pool hall, and no more smoking, no more drinking—they all followed, the whole neighborhood, into the light blue *Assembleia,* the store-front church, with rough benches and a huge mural of Christ visiting what appeared to be the interior of São Paulo State.

And the "pastors", no longer "fathers", preached long and loudly—about the subservience of women, the time I went. But the cooks and the maids and the heavy workers I went with, family wage-earners, strong, proud women all of them, didn't seem to be listening to that. They seemed to be just sitting in the satisfaction of their families, off the street, here together, alive and quite well, for the moment, maybe for always, now. Maybe this really was the change that was going to come.

So Carmelita, young and beautiful, no family left, mother died recently, in her thirties, of "sickness", brother just shot in unclear circumstances, younger sister unwilling to work as a maid, which meant prostitution, there being no alternative—Carmelita had joined whatever sect it was that was running through her neighborhood. And though at the time I suspected Sergio's attention to her Bible readings was perhaps motivated by earthly impulses, who knows that he wasn't beginning to see himself as one of the ones in the jackets and ties as well, as someone with a future, who was going somewhere.

He was so quiet, wasn't smiling unduly, or walking around like the cat who'd swallowed the canary, or anything. When he sat down every day to his meal of beans and rice, meat or chicken, pasta or potatoes, salad, oranges, bananas, cake and coffee, he gave no sign that this constituted to him a feast beyond wildest dreams. He comported himself with the same quiet dignity they all did, these young ragged gods with their smiles at the street market, who never let you know that what they live on is rotten fruit.

Well, Sergio worked and listened and ate and went to his driving lessons, and one day, asked to be allowed to live in the house.

"Where?" I asked him. The maids' rooms were filled with young ladies, the sofa in the playroom was uncomfortable, I thought, and what would he use for a bathroom?

"I could sleep in the laundry room," he said quietly.

The laundry room? There was nothing there but the ironing tables, the washing machine, the giant sinks. And the rough cement floor. It was cold, and the roof leaked. We couldn't put a bed there.

"No, no," he said, "I don't need a bed."

Well, any gods, forgive me. Americans, they say, are dangerous children. "Don't need a bed?" I said. "Of course you need a bed." Everyone needs a bed, I still thought. So, "Oh, dear," I said, "I don't see how we can do it just now," and he did not fall down and plead.

He simply went "home" at six p.m., when he was no longer needed, and he never told us that there was no such place. That every night required a creative solution—most of which made our laundry room seem like the Ritz.

And one night, as he sat in somebody's shack, where he was hoping to sleep for a couple of days, there was shouting, and then the garbage was on fire outside the door, and as they all ran out, coughing, choking, fighting the smoke, it was Sergio who was shot—by mistake. There was an ongoing dispute over "terrain" in that slum. Sergio hadn't even known. The guy who shot him was sorry.

One of the street-market boys rang our bell the next day to tell us. He ate Sergio's breakfast and offered to direct us out to his father. We got there in time to pay for the funeral, thank God, so Sergio had one. As we were leaving, bewildered, speechless, guilty, Sergio's father, a thin, wasted hillbilly whose tragedy—like all the rest of them in that vast new measureless slum where they were squatting—had been ever leaving home, ever once thinking that there was something better out there—this displaced countryman took our hands and looked into our eyes with great gratitude.

"Sergio died happy. He felt that his star had finally changed," the old man said. "He'd gotten lucky—with the driving lessons."

Dona Marthe

by Vicky Shorr

Did the photo actually survive? Did I see it, or was it that she described it so vividly that it was as if seen, as good as seen, better, perhaps? She was old when I knew her—the photo was when she was young, and were people even snapping photos then, in Vienna, say in 1920, when she was ten and playing "shop" with her brother?

"We loved to play," she reminisced one day, looking at my children's little attempt at "shop"—called, aptly, "bar" in Brazil—"my brother and I. And my father had a little shop made, with little tins and chocolates, and tiny scales that really worked. My brother was always the salesman and he forced always me to be the lady. There was a photo."

Did she actually find it one day and show it to us? At one of her "brunches"—very charming and very foreign in Brazil, there not even being a word for "breakfast" in Portuguese. "*Tomar cafe*", "to take a coffee", was what they said and did down here, though at Dona Marthe's house there were really proper eggs and various breads at her breakfasts, cinnamon rolls, smoked fishes, sausages of all description, beautiful fruit—and it would have been there that one either saw or almost saw the photo. Marthe Fransizka, aged ten, soft brown hair brushed back, with a ribbon, and her brother, weighing, measuring on his precocious scales, seriously—too seriously, no quarter given, no ounce escaping unweighed, or unpaid for.

And one wondered, considering or even imagining the photo, one wondered wildly, for one moment, is that why Hitler did it? The shopkeepeer thing? Is that what it was? The little Dona Marthe, her face too judicious, her brother too precise, two future shopkeepers too quick and clever for the German race to bear?

Dona Marthe—tall and stately now, European elegance personified. They had been well-off in Vienna—with enough to lose that they surely wouldn't have left in time. But then one day, in 1938, her husband came home—walked in the door, fell in the door, face down, speechless. Black, from head to foot, hat, hair, face, three-piece suit, covered with soot. Someone, "they," the new Nazis, had come to his office that morning, for no reason, and with no explanation—and in great high spirits dragged him to a cellar somewhere.

And there, amid much jesting on their part, he was forced to load coal onto trucks all day—in his suit. They made a point of that, it was part of the fun for them. All day. It had started early in the morning, and there was, as was to prove customary with the Nazis, no lunch and no break. There were others there, Jewish businessmen, in their suits. Former businessmen, because they emerged from that cellar *tabulae rasae*, wiped clean, naked and reborn. Naked in that all they had and were—age, name, past, and future—had been stripped from them. Reborn in that they had crawled out alive.

Most of them. Not all. Several former venerable and respected pillars of the Viennese mercantile and cultural community gave up the ghost in that cellar, so completely unaccustomed were they due to age and circumstance to loading coal onto their backs at the command of jeering, hearty young men with whips. Who, by the way, seemed themselves quite accustomed to, even adept at, beating their faltering elders to death.

And who, for some reason, hated the very guts of all these businessmen, whom, after all, they'd never seen before—unless it had been to haul coal for them, and receive a handsome tip, amidst the pleasant exchange of social niceties. The weather, the price of eggs, the next holiday—but now there were no more holidays. And the businessmen who made it out of that cellar had nothing left to lose in Austria—and funnily enough, that is what saved their lives.

Dona Marthe and her husband arranged to leave immediately. They were no longer constrained, as were many of their less experienced friends, by the impossibility of taking with them any real assets. They left gladly enough with their lives and landed first in England—"soup kitchens," Dona Marthe remembers, and illness, a cold winter. The reconstitution of the family as a charity case. Dona Marthe was nearly thirty. There were two children—a boy, six, and a girl, eight—and the husband, who never recovered from that day in the cellar.

It wasn't just the physical work—the nearly impossible lifting, dragging, loading, drudging, that naturally finished with his back forever. Still, what he died from prematurely was severe mental depression, not his back. He knew only too well from that day forward what lay precisely and directly beneath every single act of social intercourse that there was—every one. No matter how pleasant the surface, how cheerful the smile—he had seen it. Not through a glass darkly, he would laugh, his laugh now a bark, but face to face. He knew now, as he too had been known in that cellar—then the laugh would turn to the cough that he'd picked up in England, and by the time they landed in Brazil randomly. Some were sent to Chile, some to Argentina—he was no help at all.

If only it had been Chile or Argentina, Dona Marthe sometimes thought, there might have been a chance. There was a level of civilization there that might have helped, a cultured class, real libraries—though of course what he needed were neither libraries nor discussion groups nor all the Opera of La Scala, but for someone to have shot Hitler in 1935.

Well. Dona Marthe arrived in Brazil with three dependents, no useful language or relations, and no money left. She was not a nurse, nor could she here be a maid. She had been able to be a maid in England—a "couple", they were there, briefly, where their duties included bridge in the evening with the employers, while the scullery maids washed up.

But in Brazil maids were maids, and there were more than enough already, and nobody wanted a complicated one. The husband limped around trying for a while, and they lived, as happens, somewhere, and somehow put the children in school. A refugee community was forming, and those first fortunes were just starting to be made. Brazil was then at the beginning of a road these Europeans had already traveled. They knew what was coming, all the twists and turns and stops. Anyone among them who still cared—and it wasn't everyone—could be there waiting, with something their new countrymen were going to want or need.

So suddenly there were in Brazil brand new pharmaceutical lords, emperors of well-made tools, sidewalk-paving magnates, garbage-truck kings, most of them not even speaking Portuguese—any one of which Dona Marthe's husband could have been, but wouldn't, and then he died. And Dona Marthe was still tall and beautiful, but she didn't have the rent on her house.

Then she discovered, among her few papers from "before", some handwritten notes of her grandmother, telling how to make a true "Palffey Knudl"—an ancient, aristocratic knudl not for filling stomachs but for sheer pleasure. It had originated, this dish, in some specific castle on the Polish border that her grandmother knew. The name was the family's, or one of their knights, who had brought such plenty to the land that a dish might, once in a while then, thanks to him, be light. Be something to eat along with something else.

Dona Marthe's memory stirred. She invested in some of the good new pots and pans that the French refugees were now getting rich on in Brazil, and announced to her acquaintances that she would give cooking class. Some of the wives signed up, and some of the daughters and then sons, and word got out, and more wanted to join. These Dona Marthe had to put on a waiting list, where they stayed for quite a long time. Till someone died, or became ill, or moved away—for no one, once in, ever seemed to want to quit.

They would cook, in her tiny, cramped, highly organized kitchen, the aristocratic knudl, and cakes made of nuts ground so finely they became the richest flour in the world. Or the chocolate "salami"—her son's favorite—made by Hopplmeier, or some such, the most marvelous confectioner in Vienna, where you went on dark winter afternoons, after the theater—remember?—or the opera, or ballet. After "Tales of Hoffman," or the Zauberflaute—everything had a connection to a life and culture of the past. Gone it was, shattered like a mirror, but Dona Marthe, in cooking class, would hold up a piece, and look, you could see! It wasn't the whole mirror, true—but you could see!

Her life, slowly, became—a life, again. There was routine, some security, a bit of a garden. Among her grandmother's notes, there were recipes for skin cremes. She gathered some roses and made some—her own skin was fabulous, was famous. Her friends started fighting for the bits of creme she made. One of these friends whom she'd favored—both cooking classes and the skin creme—had a husband who was now rich again, and had an extra house, one that they had now moved on from. It almost wasn't worth selling, his wife pointed out. She brought Dona Marthe's case to his attention, and he decided to enter the grand world of philanthropy by giving Dona Marthe this modest but really very charming house for her own.

She was thrilled, the whole refugee community was thrilled—and impressed. He moved to the next level of invitations, his children were accepted into the British school, and Dona Marthe no longer had the rent thing to kill her every month.

And the kitchen was—relatively speaking, of course. Dona Marthe only rarely allowed herself bitter comparisons—marvellous! There was room, with some careful, though no longer fanatic, organization to put nearly everything out, and still breathe and move about. And the garden—Dona Marthe immediately put in rose bushes, just the kind she needed for her face cremes, and they were happy there and thrived. The rest of the house—well, there was a nice-sized living room, and bedrooms, one for the maid, now, too, and if the location wasn't the best, still there was a good wall around the place. It seemed safe. Dona Marthe increased the size of her cooking classes. She felt, as she had not planned to do again in this life, at home.

She began to cook a bit for pleasure—little dinners, the brunches. Her guest list was the history of Europe in the forties. The first guests, of course, were the first refugees, the Jews. But after '48, they were joined by the next round—the Poles, the Czechs, Hungarians, even East Germans. She might not have predicted in, say, 1941, that she would ever choose to have Germans at her table. But she couldn't have known then either that they would find themselves, these former cats and mice, transformed almost miraculously, as if by their flight, to birds of a feather down here, where compared to everyone else, they were exactly alike. So they flocked together, and eventually there was Mozart on Sunday afternoons, supported by the Jews and the Germans, and delicatessens where one discovered that what one had thought, in the States, was Jewish food was German food as well. Exactly and precisely. The same pickles, smoked fish, herring, rye breads—everything. The Jews and the Germans ate the same stuff.

And quite often they ate it together in Brazil, and Dona Marthe ended up feeling that perhaps that was the point. She allowed herself to enjoy the whole wide range of friendship offered by Brazil's easy immigration, which, if it let in Nazis, had let her in as well.

So one met the world in her little salon. There was the Hungarian Countess who now sold rugs and resembled nothing so much as a blond gypsy fortune teller at a party. She and her husband the Count had arrived in Rio in '48 with their jewels, and had been immediately befriended by a Brazilian whom they met at the bank. They had, these two, been through the War, and had also managed to give the slip to the Russians—but they still somehow allowed their new Brazilian friend to put their jewels into his bank box. Then of course he vanished, and all was lost.

"Well," as she would smile forty years later, "not all."

"What did you do?" I asked her aghast, dollars in my pocket, but not so many as to be incapable of imagining just how bad it could be without them. A refugee, then, not an ex-patriate.

She smiled again, a knowing smile. Earned, authentic—quite unlike the easy cynicism affected by, say, agents in L.A. "Life," she informed me, "carries you along."

Life had carried them all along, everyone in Dona Marthe's world. They had that lightness, they knew both how to float and that they would—though their children didn't. Their children were Brazilian communists, mostly, university types, and they weren't about to do any floating. They were masters of the waters. They would dam, tear down the old, build up the new! They hated the U.S. categorically, the way the old ones loved it, and they had their stories, too—repressions, beatings, tortures, exiles, but somehow one neither believed them, nor cared. This was Brazil. There were warm winds blowing.

And one could sail on, around the turbid young ones, to the Polish prince, who was regaling their mothers and grandmothers with tales of his new old manor in France—bought with his Brazilian Coca-Cola fortune. The peasant woman from a nearby farm there had brought him a rabbit and with much bowing and scraping, explained that her family had been accustomed, from time immemorial, to keeping their wine in the manor house cave. Could they, would he, possibly, in the grandeur of his noble, if foreign, heart, consent to continue the arrangement?

The prince, charmed, extended his largesse—and then the peasant woman called in her stolid son with his thermometer. He would be there, she informed the prince over her shoulder, three times a day for a week, to check the temperature. At the end of which time, she informed the prince that she would under no circumstances keep her wine in his cave.

And once I met the man who'd given Dona Marthe the house. He was a short, very red-faced Roumanian who'd escaped the gas chambers via the Russian front, and escaped the Russians somehow on skis, and landed in Brazil with no melancholia whatsoever, and proceeded to teach everyone to plant soybeans and make orange juice.

He was a great swimmer, barrel-chested, bright blue eyes, and had a big house at the beach, and two wives, it turned out. Dona Marthe was great friends with the first one, the official, European one—and she had reacted with shock and anger, rather more obviously than was her custom, but she was old now, when the Roumanian, clearly out of his head, had actually tried to bring the Brazilian one to one of Dona Marthe's brunches.

"She will be lost," Dona Marthe told him firmly at the door. "No one here will speak Portuguese," she said, not even seeing the woman for all the hair, the cleavage, the lipstick—cherry red. He understood, of course, and they left, but when he died, it turned out, through some impossible oversight, to the horror and astonishment of absolutely everyone, that he had mistakenly left Dona Marthe's house to the Brazilian "wife." Who deeded it directly to the gardener out of spite.

Now, if she'd kept it for herself, or given it to any one of her numerous children from previous alliances, anyone at all with somewhere else to go, Dona Marthe would have had a chance to fight it in court and stay on, at least for a while. But as it was, to give it to a poor person—someone virtually homeless, to whom it constituted true asylum—the outsider wife's revenge was perfect. This gardener would avenge every single party she didn't go to, and more, the few she did, where she was surrounded and cut off, unhorsed, by all of them, even the "husband", speaking German—this in her own country where they couldn't even speak the real language right, not at all, it was a joke to hear them trying—this gardener would not be turned aside at Dona Marthe's door. There could be some small temporizing, perhaps, but there would be no denying the poor gardener his house. This was one of the few places where Brazilian law was clear and unmitigated. The Brazilian wife enjoyed instructing the Europeans on this point.

And Dona Marthe, hair white and upswept, still tall, but with a bad arm now, more than eighty-five years old, was put to flight again. Not literally, you could tell her, but in her dreams, the wife and the gardener were Nazis, and though she knew it was simply a matter of renting another house, and she could afford it now, her children could afford it, she kept looking around at everything as if for the last time. The books she'd put together, the kitchen—of course her roses had to stay, but her children and grandchildren reassured her that everything else would accompany her. They had found her a new place, and she would be happy there.

But she somehow didn't seem to be listening to them, she kept standing in the middle of rooms, as if hearing something else, and then finally, when it was really happening, that violence to her living room, the boxes and the tearing apart, Dona Marthe sat down on her half-wrapped, threadworn sofa and started—for the first time in her life in front of her children—to cry.

It was a wild, voiceless sobbing that shook her and frightened them, and they couldn't make her stop, couldn't calm her. They tried awkwardly to stroke her arm, but she wrenched herself away from them, and they were forced to stand back in awe and watch her heaving back tell them the truth of all that had happened in Austria, all that had happened in Brazil.

They lay her down, finally, with cold cloths on her eyes. She was speaking a garbled German they could not understand, and they thought then that she was going to die, there, still in her own house—or worse, right away in the new place. But she sat up the next morning, shook herself and got on with it, and a week later, she was pouring her Viennese kaffe for them in her new kitchen that she liked, actually. She laughed suddenly and looked up.

"You know, it made me remember, when we were leaving Austria, they sent Storm Troopers over to make sure we didn't take anything. They marched in, the boots and the coats, their faces in that hard new way of looking at us. But there was some delay, I can't remember, and they stayed with us for a day or two.

"I gave them meals. They would forget—and then remember—to hold their faces stiff to us. On the last day, the youngest one came to me alone, in the library. He confessed that he'd only joined because he'd been promised the 'books on sex' that all Jews have. But they'd looked through our books and hadn't found them. Would I tell him where they were?"

She laughed. She looked younger. Life had carried her along.

"I was stunned," she said, "and then had to keep myself from laughing, can you imagine, even at that hour one can laugh? I gave him the only Freud we had—The Interpretation of Dreams. He was very disappointed. He shook his head sadly—he felt that the Nazis had deceived him, he said. And the worst of it was that he now saw that Jews were nice people. What was he going to do for the rest of the War?

"They shook our hands as we left. They wished us good luck, and hoped we'd find a place where we could live in peace forever." She looked around her. "It's funny—he came to me again, these days." A sigh. "He probably died in the War, and we lived. Ah, well, he should have come to Brazil."